Jordyn

Risqué Behavior

Qiana Rae

Princess of Erotica Books

ISBN: 978-0-9916187-2-9

Dedication

This novel is dedicated to Yvette (Nikki) Williams-Marshall.

Gone way too soon, but never forgotten.

May you and your loved ones rest in Heaven.

Love,
Kiki

TABLE OF CONTENTS

Acknowledgments

First off, giving thanks to my Lord and Savior Jesus Christ for without HIM I would be nothing. Secondly, I of course have to thank my husband, Devon, for allowing me the time to do what I love and for being there for me during my most frustrating moments. I want to also thank all of my loyal fans who have continued to follow me and patiently wait on another one of my fabulous novels to keep you entertained while you're on your lunch breaks, sitting under the dryer at the beauty salon, or just taking a nice, hot bath! Sorry it took so long, but perfection takes time! Thank you Jesus for giving me the drive and determination to step out and write under my own imprint of Princess of Erotica Books. It is truly a liberating feeling!

Thanks to each and every one of you for blessing me by showing your support with your encouraging words, kind gestures, and feedback. I promise to continue to work hard to keep you wanting more.

Love,
Qiana Rae,
The ONE AND ONLY Princess of Erotica

INSTAGRAM: iamqianarae
FACEBOOK: Author Qiana Rae
TWITTER: @authorqianarae

CHAPTER ONE

I stared closely at myself in my heart-shaped mirror as I sat at my vanity, carefully placing each of my individual eyelashes, one by one. They added mystery and sex appeal to my dark slanted eyes, which I used to tease my many prospects. Once my lashes were intact, I waxed my thick brows to a perfectly defined arch. I removed my curlers from my jet-black, newly sewn-in Brazilian hair, which brought out the beautiful bronze undertone of my golden, caramel complexion as it fell against my skin. My cherry-red lip-gloss caused the lights of the vanity to reflect off of my full, sexy lips that made all my men go crazy. I pulled my long, slender, legs through my black, lace thong, and put on my matching black corset. I then slipped on my garter belt and carefully unrolled my black fishnet thigh-highs, trying my best not to tear them with my long, stiletto manicured nails.

Once I had on all of my sexy undergarments, I admired myself in my full-length mirror, playfully throwing my hair from side to side, and making sure everything else was in place. I pushed up my voluptuous cleavage and put on my favorite satin black mini skirt, red leather jacket, and red patent-leather six-inch heels. My men loved a tall woman, so I always enhanced my already five-foot-eight-inch frame with the tallest heels I could find so they could have the enjoyment of climbing this tree.

My name is Jordyn and I considered myself the baddest chick in Manhattan. I didn't care what nobody else had to say because my opinion was the only one that counted. Anybody who couldn't see the beauty that I possessed had to have been either blind or crazy.

As I headed out, I took one final look at myself because I set out to satisfy and never disappoint. So far, I had achieved my goal. On my way to my nightly destination, I reminisced about my childhood, as I often did. These days, bitches always looked at me like everything was handed to me, unbeknownst to them, they would've never been able to walk a day in my shoes. I had experienced more in my twenty-five years of life than people experienced in their entire lifetime. Life was hard, but I didn't let it get me down. I continued to move and live the best life I possibly could, and I continue to do the same to this day.

My daddy was a heroine addict. He wasn't always like that though. Maybe I should say he died a heroine addict, but before he became a victim of his addictive behavior, he was the most loving father that any child would've loved to have, and the type of husband a woman would kill for. He would've done anything for me and my momma, but she obviously didn't appreciate a good man.

I was ten years old, and I had been begging my daddy for the past couple of years to take me to a place called Fun Factory, which was a place for kids that had video games, go-carts, laser-tag, and everything else a kid would love to do. My daddy would always tell me no because we didn't have the money. I could always tell he felt bad after seeing the disappointment on my face, so I always tried to act like it was no big deal. My daddy worked hard every day to support me and my momma, but he didn't have the best job in town, so his paychecks would all go to bills, and we were lucky enough to have a little left over for food until his next paycheck. My momma didn't work because my daddy was old school and he believed that the woman should stay home and take care of the cooking, cleaning, and kids. I was the only child, so she didn't have much to worry about there.

One Friday evening, when I was already in bed, my daddy came in my room from a long day of work, sat on the edge of my bed and asked, "You got plans tomorrow?"

I sat straight up in my bed and said, "No, why?"

He smiled at me and said, "I've been saving up since you first mentioned Fun Factory to me and I'm happy to say I finally have enough to take you. I know it took a while . . ."

Before my daddy could finish, I jumped from up under the quilt that was full of holes and gave my daddy the biggest hug I had ever given him. I was the happiest I had been in a long time, but when I released my daddy's neck and looked at him, he had tears rolling down his face.

"Daddy, what's wrong? We don't have to go if you don't want to," I said, feeling like crying right along with him.

"Jordyn, I'm just happy that I could make you happy. We're gonna have a good time so be ready!

My daddy gave me a kiss on the forehead and walked out of my room with his head held high. I was so excited that I couldn't sleep. I tossed and turned thinking about everything that I was going to do the next day. I could hear my momma and my daddy through the thin walls, talking and laughing. I hadn't heard them sound so happy in months. They were always arguing and my momma always seemed like she was angry at the world, but tonight was different. I was thinking that maybe God had finally heard my prayers. I prayed and prayed that things would be how they used to be, when my parents were happy and I never heard them argue. I also prayed that one day I would be able to go to Fun Factory. If God didn't do anything else for me, what he had done in that one night was enough for a lifetime.

The next day, I got up bright and early, to prepare for my fun-filled day with my momma and daddy. The house was quiet, so I crept downstairs to the living room, where my daddy had been recently sleeping on the couch. The couch was empty, which made me nervous. I thought maybe my daddy forgot about me and left, so I ran upstairs, sounding like a herd of wild horses and started banging on the door to the bedroom that my momma and daddy once shared, crying out to my momma. She came to the door in her long floral gown rubbing her eyes and said, "Jordyn! What's the matter with you?"

"Daddy! He left me!" I said, still crying and breathing heavily, barely able to get my words out.

My momma pushed the door wide open and there I saw my daddy in the bed, under the cover where he used to sleep. My momma folded her arms and sternly looked at me, telling me to go back to bed. I wiped the tears from my eyes, lowered my head, and slowly walked back to my room. I was upset about the way my momma had yelled at me, but at the same time, happy that my daddy was sleeping in the same bed as her again. So much was changing so quickly, but I wasn't complaining.

Later that afternoon, my momma greased my cornrows so I could look halfway decent for our undoubtedly once in a lifetime outing. I threw on my one and only pair of beat up gym shoes and stood at the door waiting for my new parents. I heard my daddy talking to my momma as he walked down the hardwood stairs, but my momma wasn't behind him.

"Is she almost ready?" I asked.

"She's not gonna join us today. She has stuff to do around the house, but I'm sure she'll come next time," he said, as he smoothed his dark bushy eyebrows with his thumb."

My daddy looked just as disappointed as I did. Everything was perfect and she just had to fuck it up like she always did. He had worked so hard trying to save up the money for us to do something nice together, and she chose to stay at home to clean the house. It didn't make sense to me, but I just tried to not think about it and enjoy my day with the one person in the world I knew loved me unconditionally.

Our day was more exciting than I had ever imagined. My dream had finally come true. There were kids of all ages everywhere. I had never even seen Fun Factory because we lived in the Bronx in New York, and Fun Factory was in New York City. We didn't go to those parts often because it was overly congested and expensive. The building was three stories high, and when we pulled into the parking lot, my heart began beating out of my chest at the sight of all the go-carts speeding through the racetrack. My daddy looked at me through his rearview mirror, and I could only see the upper part of his face, but could tell he was smiling by the creases around his eyes. We did everything there was to do, including go-carts, paintball, laser tag, miniature golf, and video games until every penny of what he had saved up for just that day was gone.

On the way home, my adrenaline was still pumping from all of the excitement, and all the sugar I had didn't help either. I sat in the back seat, still cheesing from ear to ear, talking my daddy's ear off, telling him how much fun I had just in case he hadn't noticed. The city's lights were shining brightly in the evening's darkness and I was amazed at all of the people outside walking in the dark. I looked around in curiosity, wondering where the kid's parents were that were walking around in groups along the sidewalks. We came to a stoplight and I heard a loud noise beside our car. I looked over and it was a Harley Davidson motorcycle. I only knew what kind it was because my daddy had Harley magazines all over the house because he always wanted one, but could never, and sadly, would never be able to afford one. Before my eyes could make it to the front of the bike where the driver was seated, my eyes met the eyes of my momma's. She had her arms wrapped around a man who looked to be at least ten years younger than her. Her long hair was pulled up into a little schoolgirl ponytail, which I had never seen her wear, and it blew in the wind. Her head was lying on the unfamiliar man's back so comfortably that I knew that she had to have known him very well.

I could never forget the feeling that I had seeing my momma with another man. When she saw me, she had no remorse in her eyes. In fact, she grinned at me and turned her head to face the other direction and I literally felt like her ponytail slapped me across my face. I wanted to tell my daddy, but I sat there with my mouth wide open, waiting on my momma to look back at me and explain to me what she was doing on the back of that Harley. Right before the longest red light of my life turned green, the young handsome man riding my momma around the city cranked the throttle a few times and my daddy looked over at the bike in excitement. As he stared, he didn't notice that the light had turned green. That was until the bike started pulling off. At that moment, my momma turned her face back towards me, but this time my daddy was looking, too. I don't know if my daddy's foot went numb due to what he had just witnessed, but as he stared at the love of his life on the back of that Harley, with her arms tightly wrapped around another man, he slammed on the gas and we flew through the crowded streets almost running over several pedestrians until he regained consciousness and slammed on the brakes. Shaken up, I looked out the front windshield from the back seat, watching the burgundy Harley continue on its way darting in and out of traffic, and my momma looking back at us as we sat motionless.

After remembering just a piece of my childhood, I had made it to my destination. The place I went to make ends meet; the strip that belonged to me and four other women, trying to make a living for ourselves.

CHAPTER TWO

The evening weather was still hot and humid, which was the way it always was in the middle of July. I parked my silver Volkswagen Jetta in the dark parking lot of an old burnt down factory that was near my corner. It was my usual spot, which was a few parking spaces down from Dré. Dré was my pimp who looked out for his girls. As long as we could look across the street and see Dré sitting in his black sixty-four Chevy Impala, we knew that there would be no bullshit going down. If one of our prospects stopped and talked too long without asking one of us to join him, that was a problem for Dré. In his words, "You either gon' take it or leave it." There was nothing to discuss. In this field, time was money, and with the economy the way it was, time was too precious to waste.

I got out my car, looked over at Dré, and waited for his nod, which was my approval that my appearance was up to his standards. His driver's side window was cracked just enough for me to see and smell the scent of his blunt floating through the air. He would normally give me the nod right away, but today was different. His window began to come all the way down and I could see Dré sitting up in his seat just enough to stick his head out the window. He held out his blunt to shake the ashes and said, "Come here girl. You look like you need some of this."

Dré's eyes were low and I could smell Absolute on his breath, so I already knew what he was on. I walked over to his car and knelt down to his level, acting naïve about what he really wanted.

"What's up, baby?" I asked, grabbing the blunt out of his hand and taking a puff, inhaling deeply. Before I could exhale, Dré grabbed me by my neck and pulled me close until our lips met. I pressed my lips up against his and opened my mouth as Dré sucked in my high.

Dré exhaled, patted his passenger's seat, and said, "Come on ova here and get in for a minute."

I stood up, and as I walked around the front of the car, I watched him through his windshield. He rubbed his hand down his smooth jet-black goatee and grabbed his braided beard as he watched me closely. He reached over and pushed the door open. When I sat down, he squeezed my thigh and said, "You lookin' good tonight. I keep sayin' I need to get you off my payroll and save you for myself."

I blushed and fluttered my fake lashes as I always did when he ran the same game on me over and over. I knew it was just to get what he wanted, but I didn't care. He made me feel good, so I always reciprocated. His golden skin glistened from the thin layer of sweat forming on his forehead. I gently wiped it and proceeded by rubbing my long nails down his long, neatly braided cornrows that were tied at the end with a rubber band.

"Gone and do what you need to do so you can get on out there. I can't be actin' like I'm playin' favorites."

I unbuckled Dré's belt, then unbuttoned and unzipped his jeans as he continued to puff away. He lifted up just enough for me to pull down his pants so I could get to what I needed to and go to work. I pulled out his rock-hard solid dick and rubbed my hand up and down its shaft. Dré leaned over and rubbed his fingers through my hair and tried to be slick by putting pressure on the back of my head, easing it down toward his long, thick blessing that I wished one day I would be able to feel inside of me. Without struggle, I got into position and licked the tip of his dick, tickling it with my tongue ring. I gripped it tight as I prepared to indulge in the rest of my feast. I slid it all the way in my mouth until I could feel it move past my uvula and finally feeling the gagging sensation that I got off on. My throat squeezed his dick tightly, and I held it for a while, released it, and started over. My throat, jaws, and lips were like suctions that no man could resist. I called them my "triple threat".

"Jay, stop girl! Why you playin'!" Dré pleaded as he moaned, but I knew he didn't mean it. He never did. I never quit a job in the middle of it getting good. Not even with my pimp.

"You don't want me to stop. I want you to say my name, baby," I said as I continued to lick his head.

"Jay!"

"No. Say my real name. I love the way you say it," I said right before I started sucking harder and faster. I always knew what that did to him.

"Fuck Jordyn!" he exclaimed, as I felt his dick begin to pulsate.

"Yeah, baby! That's what I want you to do. Fuck me."

I felt his dick pulsating faster as I gripped it even tighter and within seconds I could feel all of Dré's liquid pearls running down my chin. Swallowing the rest, I put my hand under my chin, trying to make sure I didn't get anything on my work clothes. I opened the glove compartment and grabbed some tissue, gently patting my skin, careful not to disturb my make-up.

Dré leaned back in his seat and said, "Now that you den had your warm-up, gone out there and make me some money.

Every time Dré and I were intimate, I felt good during the moment, but afterwards, I always felt like shit. I knew he probably never had any intentions on being any more to me than my pimp, and sometimes my lover, but I would still dream about us actually making love. I used to think that maybe if I kept satisfying him whenever and however he needed me to, he would make me his woman. He had now been my pimp going on two years, and six different corners, and it was the same-ole dick suckin' routine each and every time. I should've known by now that nothing was ever gonna change, but I was the typical naïve woman who had hope.

Regretting my actions for the millionth time, I slammed the car door, walked over to my car, popped the trunk and grabbed my overnight bag and a bottled water. I swished the water around my mouth, and grabbed my toothbrush and toothpaste out of my overnight bag. I brushed away all the traces of Dré out of my mouth, cut my eyes at him to let him know I wasn't happy, and walked towards my corner. Before I could get there, I saw the other four women staring in my direction as they paced back and forth waiting for someone to stop who would pay their rent for the month.

"What the hell were you over there talking to Dré about?" Dena asked, wrinkling up her face and poking out her full, bright red lips.

Dena watched everything that went on. If she felt she wasn't being treated fairly, she made sure everybody knew about it. None of the girls were very fond of me because I got the most attention of all of them. They knew what was going on between me and Dré, but none of them had the balls to actually say anything to him about it. They would throw jabs at me here and there, but it didn't bother me none. They didn't have to like me, but whether they liked it or not, they had to share the same corner with me. They probably wouldn't have been so worried about it if they didn't feel as though I was a threat, but they obviously did.

"Um, sweetheart, I don't think that's any of your business. I don't ask you what's going on in your world, so don't you ask me."

"Bitch, I will whoop your ass right here in front of Dré's punk ass!" Dena said, walking towards me, pointing her finger.

Lexi, the skinniest one of us all tried to hold Dena's big ass back. She wasn't huge, but she was a lot thicker than the rest of us, which made her think we were all intimidated by her. What she failed to realize was that I had been through way too much to be scared of another woman. She began acting like a wild animal trying to pull away from Lexi. I had to give it to her, to be so small, Lexi was taming the hell out of that wildebeest. The other two girls, Peaches and Stasia, continued to walk the corner as if nothing was happening, which was smart on their part because they knew Dré would be over any minute to cuss our asses out. After throwing her head all over the place trying to get at me, Dena's natural styled, honey-blonde hair was standing on top of her head. Her high-yellow skin was red from anger. Suddenly, she became calm and Lexi let her go. Lexi's shirt was partially ripped, exposing her tattoo on her shoulder, which was the Capricorn zodiac sign. She was way into the stars and religiously read her daily horoscope. She would even keep me updated on what mine said, even though I really didn't believe in that stuff. I turned my head and saw Dré heading our way.

"Oh shit," I said under my breath, hardly in the mood to hear any of his bullshit. I folded my arms and twisted my body around in his direction, rolling my eyes.

"What the fuck y'all think y'all doin' disrespectin' my corner. I allow y'all to stand here! Remember that! Now is there a muthafuckin' problem?"

I pushed up my cleavage and walked in the opposite direction. Dena's ass started crying like a goddamn baby.

"What's wrong with you, hoe?" Dré said without any shame.

"I'm just sick of this shit. You act like you don't appreciate what we do for you! The only person you show any appreciation to is that bitch!" she said pointing at me.

I couldn't believe what she had just said to Dré and how she said it. One thing for sure was I knew she would regret it. Lexi stood there in shock, shaking her head and running her fingers through her straight, shoulder-length black hair. Dena didn't know Dré like the rest of us knew him. She hadn't been around as long as we had. We knew what we could and couldn't get away with when it came to him, and talking to him like he was a bitch was not something he was too fond of.

Dré grinned while running his fingers down his beard and said, "Come with me, baby girl."

Dena's entire expression changed. Smiling, she ran her fingers through her wild, kinky hair and followed behind Dré. She turned around, glaring at me and flicked me off. I felt sorry for her dumb ass. She actually thought Dré was thinking about her ass when he had something totally different in store for her. That crying shit didn't get to him. He could've cared less. I had to learn that the hard way.

When I first met Dré, I was twenty-three, working at one of the local McDonalds. I was trying to pay my way through school and save for some other things that I desired. I was tired as hell from working the midnight shift and going straight to school from work. I had been praying for a miracle. Sad to say, my miracle was a pimp who was looking for a hoe.

Dré walked into McDonald's at around two o'clock one morning. We were all half asleep, but when his fine ass walked in, all us women woke up. Dré was Puerto Rican, but in my eyes he was all nigga. Only a black man could be strapped like he was. I was always attracted to a man with long beautiful hair. At that time, he wore it slicked back in a ponytail. I was working the register, and the first thing I remembered him doing before saying a word was licked his beautiful lips.

"Welcome to McDonald's. How can I help you, Sir?"

Dré grinned and in a low voice said, "You can help me by telling me why a beautiful woman like yourself is spendin' her nights flippin' burgers and droppin' fries when you could be somewhere cuddled up with your man."

That was the first time Dré ever made me blush and he knew exactly what he was doing.

"Well, if I had a man, then I probably wouldn't be working at McDonald's because any man that was worthy of being my man would know how to treat his woman and wouldn't allow her to work in a place like this."

Dré laughed, showing off his sexy dimples. "There probably ain't too many men who know how to handle a woman like you. Your beauty probably intimidates most. I could show you some things that all that beauty could get you, so you don't let it all go to waste. I'll show you how to work it so you'll never have to step foot in another McDonald's. Not even to eat. You'll be eating at much finer places when I'm done with you. You just have no idea."

And there you have it. Dré had won me over that easily. Dré and I exchanged phone numbers after I took his order, and that was my last night working at McDonald's. He molded and trained me into the hoe he wanted and needed me to be. I put more money in his pockets than any of the other hoes on the strip because I obviously possessed something they didn't have and they could never figure out what it was. They always tried to compete, but never could. The first thing I bought with the money I had earned was breast implants, which was one of the things I had been saving for the entire four years I had been working at McDonalds. I was tired of being a fine-ass flat chested woman. Dré was very proud of what he had created and even though we didn't always get along, I appreciated him for giving me the confidence I needed to succeed in this business.

An hour had passed and Dena still hadn't returned. I looked over towards the parking lot, and Dré's car was still there, so I knew they had to have been in the car. It was a slow night. Normally, I would've been picked up by now. Dré was good at picking corners. He would first stake them out to see what types of cars rolled through, which gave him a good indication how profitable it would be. He also carefully observed the number of laws that swarmed through the area, if any. So far, none of us had ever been arrested, besides Dré.

A few minutes later, I noticed a clean, white Lamborghini slowing down. It pulled up next to the curb right in front of where I was standing. I had seen this car driving along our strip on plenty of other occasions, but never once did it ever come close to even slowing down, let alone stop. As it came to a complete stop, the other three girls, Stasia, Lexi, and Peaches tried to ease their asses over in my direction, hoping they had a chance.

The passenger window slowly began to come down, and the man inside was finally in clear view. He was a dark-skinned brother. He wasn't just any ordinary dark chocolate. He was the sexy Morris Chestnut type of dark chocolate. He smiled and his white teeth sparkled like he belonged on a Colgate Commercial. He had a low haircut with the perfect razor lining and no facial hair. He was the sexiest man I had ever seen and I hadn't felt that way since I had met Dré.

I leaned over, resting my forearms on the inside of the window. I didn't feel as comfortable greeting this prospect as I normally did. Even before we said a word to each other the vibe just wasn't right and I became nervous. As soon as I started to speak, my heel slipped off the edge of the curb, and I stumbled, almost falling headfirst all the way inside of his car. I was already embarrassed and it didn't make it any better to hear the girls in the back of me snickering.

"I am so sorry! I guess I should practice walking the runway a little bit more, huh?" I said, trying to break the ice, even though I think it had already been broken.

Mr. Sexy Chocolate smiled, trying to keep from laughing, and I was sure he was calling me a klutz to himself. "You ok?" he asked, still with a slight smile on his face.

"Well, if I wasn't, you got your laugh for the night, right? Now what can I do for you Mr. . . . ."

"Chance. My name is Chance, and yours?" he asked with a deep, sensual voice

"Jay," I replied

"Jay, I know a gorgeous woman like you has to have a beautiful name, too. What's your real name, love? That is, if you don't mind me asking?"

I normally didn't tell clients, or potential clients my real name, but again, this just felt different, so I did.

"My name is Jordyn."

"I knew it. Gorgeous! Nice to meet you, Jordyn," Chance said, as he did the strangest thing I had ever seen since I had been in the business. He reached out his hand for me to shake. I reached my hand through the window and placed it in his. As he held on to it he said, "You know, I see you out here every night and you look like you have so much more potential to do something a lot bigger than stand out here on this corner and let men disrespect you."

I snatched my hand back and said, "What the fuck! Are you a fuckin' stalker? You been watchin' me, huh? Get the fuck out of here! And where do you get off telling me what type of potential I have? Nigga, you don't know me! I've heard every line in the book and no matter who says it, it's all the same!"

Chance started getting out the car, and I looked over in Dré's direction because he didn't play that shit. I was surprised he hadn't already come to my rescue, especially as long as Chance had been sitting there talking to me.

"I think you should get back in your car!" I said as I fumbled through my purse looking for my pepper spray."

"Jordyn, I didn't mean it like that. Just listen to me. I was trying to give you a compliment," he said as he got closer and closer. I was still digging for my pepper spray, but couldn't focus on that, due to the fact I was now able to see the body in which that gorgeous face belonged to.

"Hey nigga!" I heard in the distance.

Chance and I both looked over and saw Dré without a shirt on, zipping up his pants. His six-pack glistened like someone had rubbed baby oil him, but that didn't distract me from realizing what was really going on.

"Muthafucka!" I shouted.

"I'm sorry!" Chance said, apologizing again.

"Not you!" I said as I rushed right into the traffic with horns honking at me as I tried to get to Dré's foul ass. "What the fuck are you doing? Now you fuckin' Dena?" I asked, as I got as close to him as possible, pointing my finger in his face.

After slapping the shit out of me, Dré said, "Bitch, I'm comin' to help yo ass, or should I say protect my investment? Don't you ever question what the hell I'm doin'!"

"Hey man! Keep your hands to yourself!" Chance shouted from the other side of the street, waiting on the traffic to pass.

I held my cheek as I looked behind Dré and saw Dena getting out of his car, straightening her clothes. She looked at me and grinned maliciously. I was so hurt that I turned back around to head back to my spot without even paying attention to what was coming towards me. Suddenly, I heard a loud horn that sounded like it was only inches from me. I looked up and saw a huge semi trying its best to stop and I felt like I was stuck in pause. The next thing I knew, I was laying on the ground. I couldn't tell whether or not I was still in the street or on the sidewalk, but I could hear voices asking me if I was ok, and I struggled to open my eyes.

"Call an ambulance! She hit her head!" I heard Chance say, and at the sound of his voice, I tried even harder to open my eyes.

I then heard Dré say, "Nigga, you don't know her. She ok. Take yo ass home."

"I'm not going anywhere until I make sure she gets to a hospital."

"I called an ambulance. It should be here any minute," Peaches said."

"Bitch, did I tell you to call anybody! All y'all get the hell outta here! We all gon' be locked up!" Dré shouted.

After that, I must've passed out because I couldn't remember anything else from that evening. I was hoping it all had been a dream.

CHAPTER THREE

After seeing my momma on the back of the Harley, my daddy and I didn't say a word the entire rest of the way home. I didn't know what was gonna happen once we got there, but I had a nervous feeling in my stomach. I felt like crying for both me and my daddy. I was young, but very mature for my age. I knew a lot more than other kids my age knew, including things I had no business knowing about. One thing I realized after seeing my momma on the back of that Harley was why she didn't need my daddy to sleep in the same bed as her. She was giving up the pussy to another nigga', and my daddy probably already had a feeling it was going on, but was hoping he was wrong. That day, the shit stared him right in the face and he couldn't do nothin' but admit his wife that he loved so dearly and would've done anything for was a hoe.

We pulled up in front of our home, which was the smallest on the block, and there wasn't one light on in the entire house. Not even the porch light. My daddy cut the car off and sat there quietly, gazing out the window. I didn't interrupt his moment. I knew he needed it. A few minutes later, he snapped out of it and told me to come on. When we walked in the house, my momma was nowhere in sight. She didn't even have the decency to come home after getting caught up, to at least try and explain herself, but I guess there was really nothing to explain. She was either scared to come home or just didn't give a fuck. The way she looked at me on the back of that bike, I went with the "she just didn't a fuck" theory.

By the time I finished my bath and got ready for bed, my momma still hadn't returned. I went to my momma's room to tell my daddy goodnight, and he wasn't there. I went down the stairs and saw him sitting in his favorite reclining chair, staring at the wall. Obviously, he didn't hear me coming because when I tapped him on the shoulder he jumped.

"Hey, Jordyn. What's wrong?" he asked, still being a good daddy, trying to console me, when he was the one who needed to be consoled.

"I'm sorry," I said with tears in my eyes.

"Sorry for what?" he asked, looking confused.

"Sorry for begging you to take me to Fun Factory. If we wouldn't have gone, then momma wouldn't have left with that other man."

My daddy put his hands on both of my shoulders and said, "Listen to me. None of this is your fault. Your momma and I are both adults and know right from wrong. We all make mistakes. As a matter of fact, I've made plenty of them. I haven't been the best husband or daddy I could've been," he said with sorrow in his eyes. "I'm sure your momma has a good explanation for what we saw, but even if she doesn't, sometimes adults make bad decisions, but I promise you everything is gonna be ok."

I wanted so badly to believe him when he said everything would be ok, but deep down I knew it wouldn't be. I knew if my momma had a good explanation, she would've jumped off of that Harley and come with us, but she didn't. She was content where she was and didn't feel like she owed us shit. I couldn't believe my daddy had allowed the words to leave his mouth that he hadn't been the best daddy or husband. I could only speak for what I saw when it came to how my daddy treated my momma, and he always put her on a pedestal and treated her like a queen. Regarding me, as far as my daddy was concerned, I could do no wrong, and he did everything in his power to make sure I had everything I needed and some of the things I wanted. I gave my daddy a big hug as the tears I was holding back ran down my face, and I went to bed.

Later that night, I heard a crashing sound. I sat straight up in my bed and looked at my alarm clock. It was almost 3am and I knew there was way too much noise in the house for it to be that time of morning. I jumped up out of my bed and crept out of my room through the hallway. I heard my daddy downstairs shouting. I had never heard him sound so angry. My momma was shouting right back. I stood at the top of the staircase and continued to painfully listen to my parents sound like two people that wanted totally different things, when they had once been completely in sync with one another.

"How could you just not care about your family?" he asked, with hurt in his voice.

"I do care about my family! I cared enough about you to let you stay when you messed up! We used to have fun together and now we don't. The love that was once between us just isn't there anymore and I'm tired of pretending!"

"Who was the guy you were with?"

"He's my man!" my momma said without any shame.

My daddy hesitated and then asked, "Do you love him?"

My momma, only five feet tall and ninety-five pounds, stood in front of my daddy, who was 6'3", two hundred fifty pounds, looked up at him and said, "Yes, I love him and refuse to live without him!"

My daddy raised his hand with his fist balled up, and as soon as he was about to send my momma flying through the nearest wall, I ran down the stairs, screaming, "Daddy!"

I stood in the middle of the two of them and my daddy looked down at me with shame in his eyes. I couldn't blame him for feeling like beating the shit out of my momma, but I wasn't about to let that happen. My daddy plopped down in his chair, rubbing his big hands over his face. My momma stood there, realizing she had just dodged the worst beat down in history. She rubbed her hand over my braids, and without saying a word, went upstairs to her room and slammed the door. From that point on, everything got worse with every day that passed.

My momma began spending more and more time away. She treated my daddy like he was a stranger, but he still tried to remain the same good husband he always was, buying her gifts with any extra money he had, and still tried to be affectionate towards her. She would push him away every time he tried to hug or kiss her. It hurt me to watch my daddy try so hard, when the sweet woman we both once knew had become so cruel and nasty. She barely even spoke to me. She had become so bold that she had the nerve to let "her man" pick her up from our house. My daddy, the man that he was, let that shit go on for a couple of years. I was waiting for the day that my daddy would get fed up of being disrespected and run outside and beat the shit out of that disrespectful nigga', and that day had finally arrived.

I heard the familiar sound of the loud motorcycle that I had begun to hear on a daily basis, and then heard my momma walking briskly down the hall towards the stairs. I opened the door to my bedroom and could smell her sweet smelling perfume that she only wore when she was going with him. Before she could get to the bottom of the stairs, my daddy was headed out the door. She ran out after him, and I flew down the stairs and stood in the doorway, anxious to see what I had been waiting on for way too long, which was for my daddy to beat the shit out of the man who stole my real momma and sent home a bitch.

My daddy snatched that loser off of his bike, and threw him to the ground. My momma tried to stop him, but with her small frame, all he had to do was gently push her and she fell back. The "other man", who I learned name was Marcus, Jumped back up in a stance, looking like he was ready to fight. He was a few inches shorter than my daddy, and a lot smaller than him.

"This bitch don't want you! Why won't you accept it, old man?" Marcus said, still with his guards up.

That really pissed my daddy off, and he snatched Marcus' ass up by the collar of his leather jacket, and said, "You bet not call my wife not one more bitch! She might be a bitch for wanting your scrawny ass, but you won't be the one to call her one!"

One thing I could say about Marcus was that he had a lot of balls.

"I'm sorry. Let me change my wording. Why the fuck do you wanna fight over this hoe?" Marcus asked.

My momma must've known what was about to happen. Still on the ground from my daddy pushing her, she tried to quickly get up, as she shouted, "Please, no! He didn't mean it! Just leave him alone!"

At that moment, I felt like my momma was the dumbest woman alive. This Negro had just called her a bitch and a hoe, and she was still trying to take up for him!

Next thing I knew, my daddy slammed Marcus down to the ground, straddled him, and punched him repeatedly in the face until there was blood everywhere and Marcus was unconscious. When he was done, he watched my momma as she ran to Marcus' side, crying. He then walked towards me with no look of remorse on his face, moved me out of the way from in front of the doorway, and went and sat in his favorite chair. I stood back in the doorway, watching my pathetic momma as she screamed and shouted. The neighbors looked out trying to see what was going on and my momma told them to call an ambulance. It was so amazing to me how much it seemed like she cared about this other man. It was like nothing else in the world mattered to her at that moment except for him.

Right behind the ambulance, two police cars pulled up. I continued watching as the paramedics began checking Marcus' vitals, put him on a stretcher, and into the back of the ambulance. As they pulled off, the police approached my cryin' ass momma, asking her what happened. Before she could open her mouth, I flew outside, shouting, "He tried to kill my daddy!"

"Is this your child?" One of the officers asked my momma.

She gave me the nastiest look before hesitantly saying, "Yes."

The officer looked at his partner and nodded, telling him to take me in the house. When we got inside, my daddy was nowhere in sight. The officer asked me what happened, and everything I told him was exactly how it happened. All I did was add that Marcus threatened my daddy's life. My daddy was all I had left and there was no way I was letting him go to jail over something that was my momma's fault.

After listening to my side of the story, the officer asked me where my daddy was. I didn't know, but I figured he must've been upstairs, so I went to look for him. The first place I checked was my momma's bedroom and he wasn't there. I then heard a loud noise come from the bathroom. I ran to the end of the hall where the bathroom was, and the first thing I noticed when I walked in was the shattered vanity mirror on the wall. My daddy was standing right in front of it, with blood dripping from his head.

"Daddy! Are you ok?" I asked grabbing his hand. "The police wanna talk to you. Momma tryin' to send you to jail, but I told them that Marcus tried to kill you. Now you have proof!"

While my daddy cleaned the blood from his head, he said, "It's not right to lie, Jordyn. If I do that, then I would be considered a hypocrite, and I'm sure you probably don't know what that is, so just know that it's wrong."

"I know what a hypocrite is, and I know lying is wrong, but it's not wrong when it's for a good reason. You're all I got, Daddy! You can't leave me!"

My daddy sadly looked at me, held a towel up to his head to stop the bleeding and walked out the bathroom, down the hall towards the staircase. I followed behind.

"Hello officer. How can I help you?"

"Well, I see that some violent acts took place today, and because of it a man had to be transported by ambulance to the hospital. I also see that you have some injuries as well. I need to know what happened," the officer said, as he pulled out his pen and pad to take notes.

I looked up at my daddy hoping he cared about me more than my momma did and would do what was best for me.

"Well officer, my wife and I have been having some disagreements and this man shows up at my home unannounced. I had no idea who he was. My wife went outside and I followed her so we could talk. As soon as I walked out, he began screaming vulgarities at me and attacked me. All I did was defend myself."

The officer looked up from writing, making sure my daddy was done talking. I took a deep breath and exhaled. He then put his pen and pad back in his uniform pocket and said, "Ok sir. That's all the info I need. Your wife is outside with my partner. We'll contact you if there's anything else we need from you."

I looked out the door as I watched the officer walk towards his partner and my momma. She looked liked she had calmed down and was no longer crying. As the officer that my daddy and I had just finished talking to began telling my momma the story we had told him, she began shaking her head in disagreement. She wasn't happy about whatever else the officers said to her either. As soon as they got in their cars and pulled off, she briskly walked towards the door and stormed in. I jumped back out of the way as she ran up on my daddy. He opened his mouth to say something, but before he could, she shouted in the angriest voice I had ever heard her use, "I hate you!" After that day, my daddy was never the same.

The police stopped back by, asking my daddy if he wanted to press charges against Marcus, because of course they chose to believe the story of a child and father, instead of believing my momma, who they probably just looked at as a cheating whore. My daddy refused since he knew the truth. My momma continued to see Marcus, but knew better than to flaunt it in my daddy's face again. I didn't understand then why she didn't just leave, but as I got older I began to understand. My daddy supported her for so long that she didn't have any job experience and knew she wouldn't have been able to support herself. I guess she didn't trust Marcus enough to take care of her, but still loved his dirty draws.

My daddy became extremely depressed knowing he had lost the love of his life. Anyone who knew them from the time they first met would've never thought their relationship

would've ever gone down that road. They were the most
beautiful, envied couple around. They both would've done
anything for each other, but something turned my momma
completely against my poor daddy.

My home life was so fucked up, I preferred to be at school
than at home. I hated each day when that final bell rang at
school dismissing us for the day. I didn't want to go home if my
old parents weren't gonna be there. I prayed everyday on the
way home that when I got home and opened my front door, my
daddy would be sitting in his favorite chair smiling, and my
momma would be sitting on his lap with her arms wrapped
around him. That day never came.

I began coming home to emptiness. She began seeing other
men, besides Marcus, so she would be gone most of the time
when I got home, and I had no idea where my daddy was half
the time. I thought maybe he had gotten a girlfriend, but I just
couldn't envision him with another woman. No matter how
badly my momma had treated him, he would always be in love
with her and no other woman would've ever been able to take
her place. The sad part about that was my momma knew it.

I started seeing my daddy less and less. The less I saw him,
the more my momma was at home. I started to believe that she
just hated being in his presence. She only talked to me when it
was necessary, and treated me like shit. At first she wouldn't
talk badly about my daddy to me, but that all changed when he
disappeared for five days. She even called his job and they said
he hadn't been there either. I think the only reason she
pretended to be concerned about him was because he wasn't
there to give her the money she needed to buy stuff for the
house, and on top of that, she didn't like feeling solely
responsible for me. I felt like she hated me, just like she hated
my daddy and I couldn't wait for him to come back home.

The night he finally came back, he was unshaven, dirty, and
had on the same clothes he had on when he left five days prior.
That made me know for a fact that he didn't have a girlfriend.
His speech was slurred and he stumbled as he walked, which
made me believe he had been out on a drinking binge. My

momma looked at him with her arms folded and shook her head without saying a word.

That night after he showered, and I was already in bed, he came into my room and apologized for leaving me. He told me he just had a lot on his mind, but he thought of me the whole time and told me it would never happen again. My daddy always kept his promises, so I had no reason to believe this time would be any different, but it was. Over the next couple of years, his disappearing acts happened again, and again, and again. I became used to being alone and doing everything on my own. The days I didn't have anyone at home with me, I cooked for myself, ironed my clothes for school, and got myself to school everyday. Everything was a mess and I wondered what I did so wrong to deserve that.

One night when I was home alone, I sat at the end of my bed listening to complete silence, wishing to hear anything, even if it had been my parents arguing. I got up and walked in my momma's room and laid down in the middle of the bed with my eyes closed, remembering when I was younger how I would crawl in that same bed in the middle of the night and cuddle up in between my momma and my daddy. They would both wrap their arms around me, making me feel safe and secure. I opened my eyes and let the tears run out.

I needed something, anything to help me feel close to them. I felt abandoned and didn't know how to cope. I got up and slid open the sliding glass closet door and admired all of my momma's beautiful clothing. I grabbed one of her colorful spring blouses off of a hanger and put it up to my nose just so I could smell her and remember how she used to be; so nurturing and caring. I then grabbed a pair of her jeans and some flats and decided I would wear that to school the next day.

I went to school the next morning wearing my momma's clothes. All the kids laughed at me, and the teachers looked at me strangely, but I didn't care. In my eyes I looked good and felt good because that day was the first time in a long time that I felt close to my momma and no one could take that away from me.

When I got home from school that day, surprisingly, my momma was home. When I walked through the door, she looked at me and as she laughed uncontrollably, said, "Jordyn, what in the hell do you have on?"

"Wearing your clothes is the only way I can feel close to you. You don't love or care about me, so what else am I supposed to do?" I said, right before running up the stairs.

She came upstairs after me and at first just stared at me as I sat on my bed crying. She seemed like she had completely forgotten how to be a mother. Finally, she decided to come over, grab me and hug me tight. I couldn't believe this was really happening, so I pinched myself. *Maybe God sent my momma back!* I thought to myself. I was hoping that he'd send my daddy back too because I had been living with complete strangers.

"I know it has been a mess around here and I'm sorry. I haven't been the greatest mother lately."

You think? I thought to myself. I was so happy to hear her admitting her faults and making me feel like she cared again, until she said, "But you have to understand that your momma does have a life and I have needs. Your daddy isn't able to fulfill my needs anymore, so that's why I have other men in my life . . . To help take care of us." I almost threw up when she tugged on her blouse that I was wearing and said, "They're the only way we're surviving right now and how I'm able to buy these nice clothes you like to wear. I have to do me. These men love me and will do anything for me, so just sit back and enjoy the ride." She smiled, gave me a kiss on the forehead, and walked out.

Right then, I didn't know whether I should've been happy because she had a conversation with me, or if I should've been pissed for her to really think she could make me believe that my daddy wasn't supporting us. I knew better than that. She had me fucked up. I fell asleep thinking about that dumb ass talk my momma had given me. She really didn't know how to be a mother anymore. How in the hell does someone lose that?

The next morning, I woke up and went into my momma's room to find something to wear. To my surprise, she was in her bed asleep. That was the first time in a long time she had actually slept at home. I thought I'd try my luck and go downstairs to see if my daddy was home. I got to the bottom of the stairs and saw my daddy sitting in his chair. I got so excited and thanked God for answering my prayers. I ran over to him to make a gruesome discovery that I would live with as a part of my memory for the rest of my life.

I felt like someone was snatching all of the air out of my lungs. I dry heaved a few times then vomited on the floor next to the chair that held my daddy's lifeless body. I tried to scream for my momma to come help, but nothing would come out. I stood there staring at my daddy with his eyes open, looking straight up at me. He was wearing the same gray t-shirt and black jeans that he had on the last time I had seen him. He had a red tourniquet tied around the upper part of his arm. On that same arm were needle tracks where he had been shooting up like crazy. His hand hung over the arm of the chair, and right below on the floor was the needle that once contained the heroine that killed him. I knew for a fact that my life would be changed forever. There was no more hope of my daddy coming back. He was gone forever and at only thirteen years old, I was stuck trying to deal with my crazy ass momma on my own.

CHAPTER FOUR

I woke up in a cold sweat, looking around trying to figure out where the hell I was. I saw that I was hooked up to a few machines and my head was wrapped in a few bandages. I had figured out that I was in the hospital, but for the life of me, couldn't figure out why. The curtains were closed, but I could see the sun peaking between the small space where the two baby blue curtains met. I also noticed a beautiful plant with three "get well soon" balloons attached, sitting on the ledge in front of the window. I laid there looking around for about a half hour, until a nurse came into the room pushing a cart in front of her with all of the equipment to apparently check my vitals.

She was an older white woman who had to have been in her fifties. She was humming a tune of something that wasn't familiar to me at all, still not noticing that I was awake. When she finally finished setting up her equipment, she turned towards me and jumped like she had seen a ghost.

"Oh my goodness! I am so sorry Miss . . . "

The nurse quickly grabbed her paperwork off of her cart, looking embarrassed because she didn't know my name. She looked down at the paperwork with a confused expression on her face, and then looked up at me with a slight grin.

I put her out of her misery and said, "Don't worry about it. Just call me Jordyn." I then winked and gave her a friendly grin.

"Thank you, Jordyn. I am so sorry. I didn't realize you were back with us. My name is Debbie and I'm your nurse."

I sat up in the bed and said, "Back with you? What do you mean? What happened to me?"

"Well, from what I hear you were almost run over by a semi last night, but a handsome young man who was here to see you earlier pushed you out of the way. As a matter of fact, he brought you that beautiful plant over there," Debbie said as she pointed towards the window. "There's even a card attached. Would you like to read it?"

I still could not remember anything that happened the night before and assumed that the man who Debbie was talking about was Dré, but couldn't imagine him leaving a card. I looked at Debbie and said, "Sure, but wait. First, you still haven't answered why in the hell my head is all bandaged up."

"Oh, that," Debbie said as she giggled. "Don't you worry. It looks way more serious than what it is. In the process of your knight in shining armor protecting you, you hit your head on the ground and suffered a pretty severe concussion and a few minor cuts. Nothing some antibiotic cream and Tylenol can't handle. We already did some tests and everything seems fine, but we have to hold you for observation until the doctor feels comfortable with letting you go home."

I was thinking to myself about how much this damn hospital bill would be, but I couldn't let that worry me. I just needed to get out of here and get back on my corner where I belonged. Debbie walked over to the plant and snatched up the card that was sitting next to it. She then walked over and handed it to me with a big smile on her face. I sat the card on my lap while Debbie took my temp and blood pressure.

"Well, Jordyn, everything still seems to be fine, so I'll let you get some rest and the doctor should be here a little later."

"Thank you, Debbie."

"You're quite welcome, hun."

As soon as Nurse Debbie left, pushing her cart out of the room, I opened the envelope that I was so curious about, wondering what in the world had gotten into Dré to make him leave me a card, and hoping whatever it said jogged my memory of what had happened to me.

Jordyn,

> **I know I don't know you very well, but I feel like I do. It scared me to death when I saw that semi just a few feet away from you. I've never felt as passionate about something as I did when I jumped in front of it to save your life. I hope you can return the favor just by giving me a call so I can see you again. . . while you're not working next time! My card with my contact numbers is enclosed. Don't hesitate to use them. I hope you like the plant and balloons.**

> **~Chance**

After reading the card, I felt my eyes get big and I said, "Chance! I remember!" How could I have possibly forgotten a fine ass man like him? Then I remembered how he tried to judge me, and tell me what I shouldn't be doing! That completely changed my attitude. He may have saved my life, but I didn't ask him to. He may have been sexy as hell, but I knew there were plenty of other sexy men in the world who would accept me for me. Chance don't get no other chance! I put the card back inside of the envelope and tossed it on the table next to the bed. I laid my head down, staring up at the ceiling and drifted off into a deep sleep.

I didn't know how much time had passed when I was awakened to a quick knock and the door. As I opened my eyes, I saw the door opening.

What's the point in knocking if you're just gonna walk in? I thought.

A Chinese man walked through the door, who I figured had to have been my doctor.

"Hello, Jordyn. My name is Dr. Hong. How are you feeling?" he asked while standing over me with his arms folded.

The first thing I thought was, *No accent?* He was no doubt Chinese, but spoke better English than I did. I sat up in the bed and said, "I'm feeling ok. I just can't remember much from last night."

Dr. Hong took his bright light out of his pocket and stretched each of my eyes wide open, beaming it into both as he continued to talk to me. He then slowly unwrapped my head as if something was going to fall out if he moved too fast.

"Well, you did hit your head pretty hard. Temporary memory loss is a normal symptom of a concussion, but it will gradually come back to you within the next couple of days. I'll prescribe you some Ibuprofen, but you have to make sure you get lots of rest. I just need to finish up your discharge papers and you'll be free to go home. The nurse will let you know when it's ready. Any questions?"

"No, doctor. Thank you."

"Have a good evening, Jordyn."

After Dr. Hong left, I was so happy to be able to get out of there, I jumped up with the quickness to put my clothes on. I didn't realize how much pain I was in until I got up. My head started pounding, and the room was spinning. I was wondering why Dr. Hong said he was prescribing me pain medicine when I wasn't even in pain. Now it was quite evident!

While sitting on the end of the bed, waiting on my pain to pass, I realized I didn't even make arrangements for anyone to come pick me up. I had no family, and no one I really considered a friend. Those hoes on the corner certainly weren't friends. The only person I could think of who I could halfway consider family, even though I sucked his dick from time to time was Dré, so that's who I called. The phone rang a few times, and just when I thought his voicemail was gonna pick up, he answered.

"Who is this?" Dré answered loudly in his grimy voice, causing my head to pound even more than it already was

"Hey Dré. It's me, Jay. Can you please lower your voice? My head is pounding, and I can't remember shit with this concussion that I got."

"What you mean you don't remember nothin'?"

I can't remember anything that happened last night that put me in this hospital. The nurse had to tell me what she knew, which was only that I almost got hit by a semi. Were you there?"

"Naw, I wasn't! Now you know I would've been there for you if I knew that. I had to leave the strip a little early last night, but everything was cool when I left."

"I'm calling cuz I need a ride home and you know you're the only person I can count on," I said in my baby voice.

"You know I got you. What hospital are you at?"

"North General."

"Aight. I'll be there in about a half hour."

One thing I could say about Dré was that he was always reliable. Whenever I was in any type of trouble, he was there. Before I was making the kind of money to be able to make ends meet every month, he would loan me the money to make sure I got by. Of course my mouth would have to work extra hard for it.

After hanging up from with Dré, I went in the bathroom to take a quick shower. I took off that ugly ass hospital gown they had put me in. I knew I had to have been unconscious when they brought me in because if I had been conscious, they would've never gotten me into that ugly shit. Before I stepped in, I glanced in the mirror at the huge knot on the side of my head. Then I looked down at my body, admiring my voluptuous breasts and the rest of my body. Men went crazy over me now. I just wondered how they would react once I saved up enough money to get the rest of the work done on my body that I desired. All I knew was that nobody would be able to tell me nothing, and women would be scared to even have their men around me!

After I jumped in the shower and threw on my clothes from the night before, I looked around the room to make sure I had everything. As I was grabbing my plant and balloons that that asshole Chance bought me, Nurse Debbie walked in the room. I had forgotten all about the discharge papers.

"Looks like I caught you right in time! Looks likes you were about to leave," she said.

"I sure was. I forgot I had to sign out!" I said as I laughed.

Nurse Debbie handed me a pen and the paper to sign. As I glanced over the information and signed my name, I could feel her staring at me. When I looked up, she was still staring and smiling.

"Is there something you wanna say to me, Nurse Debbie?"

"I'm sorry for staring, but I can't believe how beautiful you are. It's amazing! I've never seen one of you so naturally beautiful."

"Really??? I asked sarcastically."

"Oh, did I offend you? I meant it as a compliment."

I giggled, rolled my eyes, and shook my head as I walked out the room, leaving Nurse Debbie standing there looking as stupid as she was. I had never known a nurse with such bad manners. Some stuff you just don't say out loud.

When I finally made it outside, I saw Dré's fine ass sitting right in front in his black Impala waiting on his bitch. Before I got in, I heard someone calling my name from behind.

"Jordyn!"

I looked back, and this bitch, Debbie, was scurrying through the parking lot. When she finally reached me, she was out of breath.

"I'm glad I caught you! You left this sitting on the table in your room." As her nosey ass looked into Dré's car window to see who I was riding with, she deviously said, "I'm sure you wouldn't have wanted to lose this. He seems like such a nice man!"

Debbie was holding the envelope that had Chance's card with his contact info on it. I hadn't decided what I wanted to do with it yet, so I told Debbie thank you and threw it in my purse. I would decide what to do with it later.

I got in the car and Dré immediately asked me what that was all about.

"Nothing. That was the nurse bringing me my prescription from the doctor. I guess I forgot it."

He stared me up and down and licked his lips. He always knew what the hell to do! Then he reached over and gently rubbed the knot on my head.

"Damn girl."

"I know. It looks bad, doesn't it?"

"Yeah Jay, it's pretty bad. It'll be cool though. So, you don't remember anything from last night?" Dré asked inquisitively.

"Nothing much, and I hate feeling like this. Like I said on the phone, the only thing I know is what the nurse told me, which was that I almost got hit by a semi and a guy that came by the strip last night saved me. He even sent me this plant." I said, as I looked down at the beautiful peace lily and attached balloons Chance had sent. Even though he had been an asshole, sending a plant had been a very nice gesture. Dré look over at the plant for a hot second, and quickly turned away, looking straight ahead. He began stroking beard, which he did when something was on his mind.

"Is something wrong?" I asked with a smirk on my face. I sensed a little jealousy, and Dré definitely wasn't the jealous type, so that just stroked my ego.

Dré looked over at me and said, "Ain't nothin' wrong with me. I'm just hopin' you already know, bump on your head or not, you will be out there tonight."

I exhaled at the thought of how apathetic Dré was. I was beginning to realize the only thing he cared about was money, and would probably replace one of his hoes without thinking twice if we made him mad enough.

"What the fuck you huffin' and puffin' about? This is business. It's the profession you chose, baby, so deal with it! Next time be more careful crossin' the street," Dré said as he laughed as if the whole ordeal was funny.

I turned sideways in my seat to look at Dré head on, and folded my arms. "What the fuck are you laughing at? I could have been killed, and where were you when you should've been looking after your hoes? That's your job, right?" Before Dré had the chance to answer, I kept going, and if felt good to release some anger. "And what I wanna know is how the hell did I end up in the street when a semi was close enough to almost hit me? Did one of those bitches push me out there? Let me find out you're covering for them!"

Dré stopped the car and threw it into park. If I hadn't have had on my seatbelt, I would've gone straight through the windshield.

"Shit Dré! You trying to give me whiplash along with my concussion?"

Dré lifted up from his seat and hovered over me, putting his finger in my face.

"Bitch, if you question my integrity again, somebody gon' need to cover up your murder for me! What the fuck I need to cover for somebody for? If yo ass wasn't jealous and shit trying to snap while on the job . . ."

Dré's expression suddenly changed and he slowly eased back down in his seat. He then put the car in drive and turned the radio up loud enough so that if I did have something to say, he wouldn't have been able to hear me. Just then, the last thing Dré said hit me. I then remembered why I was in the street in the first place. I looked over at Dré and screamed louder than the radio was playing, "You muthafucka!"

Dré turned down the radio and said, "What now, bitch?"

"You left me, didn't you? I remember now. My memory is coming back faster than what the doctor said it would!"

"Girl, I don't know what you talkin' about. Obviously that concussion got you hallucinating," Dré said nonchalantly.

"Oh, you know exactly what I'm talking about, and you should also know I won't be out on the corner tonight."

"You betta think twice about that one." Dré stopped the car once again and said, "Get yo dumb ass out my car with yo fucked up face!"

I looked out the window and we were in the middle of nowhere.

"Dré . . ."

"Get the fuck out bitch!" Dré shouted as he reached over me to unlock the door.

I pulled the door handle and looked back at Dré as the door started to open. I guess I wasn't moving fast enough because Dré pushed me out. As I was falling, my plant slipped out of my arms and hit the ground right after I did.

"And I better see yo ass on that corner tonight," Dré said as he threw my purse out of the car and pulled the door shut.

I sat in the street staring at nothing but road in front of me. I had no idea where I was. Dré had taken some back road that I wasn't familiar with. I didn't know what to do. I had no friends, no family, and I had way too much damn pride to call one of those bitches from the corner. All they were gonna do was pump me for information and try to see how the hell I ended up in the middle of nowhere, and personally, I didn't feel like lying. I stood up, dusted myself off, bent down to pick up my plant and other belongings, and began my journey to find my way home.

The longer I walked, the more lost I felt. I could've called a cab, but I didn't know my current location, so I continued to walk until I came up on a street sign, which wasn't for almost three miles. I finally came to a four-way dirt road intersection where I saw two dull green street signs, which were both hanging halfway off of their posts. I pulled my cell phone out of my purse and pulled up my contact list where I had stored the numbers for a few different cab companies. That was a necessity in my line of business. You just never knew where you would end up.

"Classy cab service. What is your pick-up location?" The voice of a young, very flamboyant white man said.

"Um, I'm at the intersection of 119th and Tumbleweed Drive.

"Ma'am, I'm sorry, where exactly is that?"

"Hell, I don't know! I've walked three miles in this blazin' heat, holding a big ass plant, might I add. I'm sure y'all make enough money on a daily basis to invest in navigation systems in your vehicles!" I replied in the most sarcastic, irritated voice I had.

"I do apologize ma'am. It's just that I've never heard of a Tumbleweed Drive, that's all, but rest assured I will have someone there as quickly as possible."

I felt bad about the way I had just took my frustration out on the polite young man who was on the other end of the phone.

"I'm sorry about snapping on you. None of this is your fault. It's my fault for putting too much trust in a no good man who has done absolutely nothing except used me from day one."

Oops. There I go again thinking out loud. I thought.

"I'm sorry, love. Forget everything I just said, besides I'm sorry. I'll be here waiting."

The young man hesitated, probably not knowing if I was gonna continue or not and said, "No problem ma'am. We'll see you soon."

After ending my call, I found a spot on the side of the dirt road, sat my plant down, which looked like it was dying of thirst, and I sat down right next to it. As I sat there, waiting on my ride, I became angrier and angrier as I thought about all the things Dré had said to me. I actually thought his ass cared about me. How wrong was I? I guess he cared enough to leave me laying on the side of the road like a stray cat. A complete stranger cared enough to stay with me and make sure I was taken care of. That one fact alone caused me to be extra curious about that mysterious, sexy hunk of Hershey's chocolate. My mood completely changed, and I felt a feeling of tranquility come over me as I thought about Chance; a man I didn't even know. I realized then that I would have to get to know more about this man.

CHAPTER FIVE

By the time the cab driver found me, it was a whole hour later. He didn't even try to get out and help me with my things, but I couldn't even blame him. He was so overweight, it looked liked he was a permanent fixture inside of the cab. He was sweaty and his blonde hair was so greasy, It looked like he had styled it with that thick ass Crisco out of the can that my momma used to use to fry chicken. Things got even worse when I got in the backseat of the cab. The smell was unbearable! I didn't know if he had the windows down because he didn't have AC or because he couldn't stand his own odor. The whole way home I held my shirt up over my nose and only spoke to the driver to give him my address. My shirt wasn't enough. I tried to hold my breath to the point of feeling like I was gonna pass out. I felt like the cab company needed to pay me for enduring such a traumatic experience!

Before he could even park in front of my apartment building, I sat forward and threw a twenty in the front passenger seat. I grabbed my things and jumped out before the car made a complete stop. The cab driver hung his head out the window trying to tell me to wait for my change. I turned around, told him to keep it, and walked as fast as I could to the steps of my front door. Even once I got inside of my apartment, I could still smell the cab driver and his stinky ass cab!

The first thing I did was sat my pathetic looking plant down in front of my picture window so that it could get some natural light. The once big, shiny, healthy leaves were now dull and drooping. I knew it had to have been dehydrated after being out in the heat for so long so I went in the kitchen and pulled out my watering pot so I could bring the poor thing back to life. I then curled up on my tan leather sofa that felt nice and cool to my warm, damp skin.

The phone rang loudly in my ear and I jumped up with my heart beating out of my chest. I must've fallen asleep.

I cleared my throat before answering, and said, "Hello."

The person on the other end didn't respond, but I heard something that sounded like cars driving down the street in the background, so I tried again. "Hello? Is anyone there?"

"I'm sorry. I have the wrong number," the man with a deep, very sexy voice on the other end of the phone said. Then I realized that voice was not only sexy, but also very familiar.

"Who is this? Do I know you?"

"No, I'm truly sorry. I dialed the wrong number."

"Chance?" I said.

"Jordyn?"

"Chance!" I said, this time with anger in my voice. "How in the hell did you get my phone number? You really are stalking me, aren't you?" I jumped up off the sofa and looked out the window to see if he was lurking somewhere outside of my apartment.

"I'm sorry. I shouldn't have called," Chance said, sounding remorseful. I just had to talk to you. I have been thinking about you since I left you at the hospital.

"That's very nice of you and all, but I don't know you from Adam, and you still haven't told me how you got my number!"

"I overheard the nurse say that your last name was Parker at the hospital and I looked you up. It seemed like calling you would be a good idea until I actually did it and heard your voice."

I tried my best to be mean to Chance, and it was easy at first, but he seemed so sincere, and like an all around nice guy, so I decided to cool down my tone. "It's ok. I've thought about you a few times, too."

"Really?" Chance asked. I could hear the smile in his voice.

"Yes, really. I was just curious about what type of guy you really are."

"Well, basically what you see is what you get, but if you'd like to learn more, I can definitely make that happen."

I hesitated for a moment because I didn't want to seem thirsty, even though I actually was. So thirsty that as I talked to Chance, I had one hand underneath my shirt, fondling one of my rock hard nipples.

"Jordyn, are you still there?"

"Yes, I'm here."

"Well . . . Can I maybe stop by and see you? That is, if you don't have other plans. I wouldn't want to impose on you."

As I opened my mouth to accept Chance's offer, there was a loud interference in the phone that prohibited me from hearing anything else.

"Chance?" I yelled. I couldn't hear a thing and the sound became louder and louder.

The next thing I knew, I was laying on my couch with my hand up to my ear, but no phone. I looked down and my other hand was underneath my shirt, and my loud ass alarm clock was going off letting me know it was time for me to get ready to go to work. I was pissed. Not because it was time to work, but because that entire occurrence was a dream. Chance was working my mind overtime and I didn't know a thing about him. There had to be something special about him. Maybe he was the one, and if he was, I definitely couldn't let him get away. Or maybe all of this was just a side-effect from my concussion.

I needed a plan, but in the meantime, I had a decision to make about whether or not I was going to step on that corner. Dré told me I better be there, but the way he did me, gave me even more reason to want to rebel against his ass. Dré didn't play when it came to his money though. I knew if I didn't get out there, I might not have been allowed to step on his corner ever again. I looked around at my apartment and all the nice things I had. Being able to work that specific corner was a privilege. That's where all the ballers were and I definitely didn't need that taken away from me. I was accustomed to living a certain way and I definitely wasn't about to regress.

As I got dressed, I didn't feel the excitement that I normally felt about going to the corner. I was never really excited about going to fuck a bunch of desperate men. I was normally aroused at the thought that I would be seeing Dré. Not tonight though. I planned on ignoring Dré to the point that he would feel the need to apologize. If he didn't apologize, I would then know exactly how he really felt about me.

I straightened my hair and wore a part down the middle. Dré always loved when I wore my hair like that. He said it made me look like an Egyptian queen. I beat my face with my shimmering purple eye shadow and mauve lipstick. After I was done with my face, no one could ever tell that I had almost been killed the night before and laid up in a hospital bed all night.

To match my make-up, I wore my purple bustier, black satin booty shorts, fishnet stockings, of course, and purple pumps. There was no way that nigga Dré would be able to resist all this. Before walking out the door, I once again thought about not going, and what the repercussions would be. They were too severe for me to even think about. I came from nothing and had accomplished so much. To be honest, I knew if it wasn't for Dré, I wouldn't be shit. I walked out the door without looking back.

I was later than normal getting to the corner, which was intentional. I wanted Dré to think I wasn't coming. Even if was only for a half hour. When I drove down our strip, I saw the other four girls strutting their stuff like they were on a real runway. I pulled into the parking lot right on the side of Dré. At first I couldn't see him, but then he sat his seat up and looked out the window. He was holding an unlit blunt in one hand and holding his phone up to his ear with the other. He stared out of his window and watched me the whole time as I did my normal routine of checking my makeup, then putting my purse and other valuables in my trunk. As I was closing my trunk, I heard him still talking on the phone. I began walking towards the corner and heard Dré say to whoever he was on the phone with, "Hey, let me holla at you in a minute. I got some business to handle."

I knew what that meant, but I continued to walk, throwing my juicy ass from side to side in my satin shorts, getting off on the fact that I knew he was watching.

"Aye. I know you ain't gon' just walk past me without saying shit. What the hell wrong with you? I thought I taught you better manners than that."

I stopped in my tracks without turning around and said, "What in the world do you think I possibly have to say to you, Dré?"

"Bitch, turn around while I'm trying to talk to you."

I took a deep breath, exhaled, and slowly turned around with my hand on my hip. I flipped my hair over my shoulder and said, "Now what?"

Dré smiled, put his blunt in his mouth and lit it. He then took a couple of puffs, still staring at me, as I stood there looking dumbfounded."

"I finally said, "Can I please get to work now? I do have a hospital bill I'm gonna need to pay for."

"You go when I tell you to go. I don't know where you all of a sudden got this smart mouth from, but I can put something in it for you to shut yo ass up. Maybe that's what you want."

I took my hand off my hip and folded my arms."

"Is that what you want, Jay? You want daddy's dick in yo mouth?" Dré said and laughed.

"That's the last thing I need right now, love. I'm over you. This is all business."

"That's how you feel, huh?" Dré asked, as he took another puff of his blunt. "You shole look good as fuck tonight. What's the special occasion?"

"No special occasion. I'm just feeling myself more than usual tonight, and I'm feeling really good about it."

"Is that right?"

"Yep."

"Girl, get yo ass over here and show me how good you feel."

"Dré, I'm really not in the mood tonight.

Dré opened his car door and slowly stepped out. He already had his pants unzipped and his dick had forced its way through the opening.

"Jay, do I look like I got time to be playin' with you?"

Trying to hold back, I grinned slightly. It made me feel good to know that Dré desired me, but I still wanted to play hard. I had a proposition for him. I began walking towards Dré and when we stood face to face, I kissed him, smearing my lipstick onto his luscious lips. He dropped his blunt and put it out with his shoe, put both arms around me and kissed me vigorously.

"Come on, baby. Let's get in the car," he said, breathing heavily.

I pushed him back and said, "I'm not getting in that car to just suck your dick. I deserve more than that. I've been around longer and made more money for you than any of those hoes."

Anxiously, Dré said, "Ok, ok."

"You say ok, but do we have a deal?"

"I said ok, didn't I?"

I walked over to the passenger side of the car. Dré had already opened the door from the inside. I looked over towards the corner. It looked like all the girls had gotten picked up except for Dena. She was standing there with her arms folded, looking directly at me. Evidently she had been watching the whole time. *Good for her ass!* I thought. I was tired of getting the short end of the stick and it was about to end right here, right now.

I sat down and Dré had already pulled his pants all the way down to his ankles, and was ready for me. I gently stroked his dick as I gazed at him and smiled. I couldn't believe what was about to happen. After almost two years I was finally gonna get a piece of Dré and I was nervous as hell. Keeping my eyes on Dré, I lowered my head and navigated my tongue around the tip of his dick, which already had pre-cum at the tip, that I always loved the taste of. I knew exactly what to do to make Dré feel good. He gently pulled my hair up into his hands as I bobbed my head up and down, suctioning my lips and jaws to the walls of his shaft.

I knew Dré like the back of my hand when it came to sucking his dick, so when I knew he was about to cum, I stopped, sat up and began kissing him. He tried to push my head back down, but I knew better than that. I was determined to make sure he upheld his part of the deal no matter what.

"Keep on goin'. What you stop for?" he asked, sounding frustrated.

I looked at him and shook my head. I turned my body towards the passenger side door and removed my shorts and fishnets. I got in doggy-style position. I could feel Dré getting closer to me, and then I felt him unzip my bustier. It fell onto the seat underneath me, and Dré fondled my titties from behind. I grabbed his dick, which was still wet from the job I had just did on it, and I slowly slid Dré inside of me. I moaned softly, as he did the same. With every stroke, he squeezed my titties tighter and tighter.

"Oooh, Jordyn . . ."

"Yes, baby?"

"You feel so damn good. I didn't know this was what I been missing."

I moaned even more and it felt even better after Dré spoke those words to me. I was ecstatic about what was happening, but there was one strange thing about the whole ordeal. Every time I closed my eyes as we fucked, I envisioned I was with Chance. I didn't know what that was all about, but it seemed to make the moment even more worthwhile. Dré started shaking just as he would when I would give him head, so I knew what time it was. It felt like Dré had an eruption and everything he had inside of him, he released inside of me. Afterwards, he kept his arms wrapped around me and kissed me on the back of my neck. I rested the side of my head on the window, feeling like I was in Heaven.

I finally felt Dré move after a few minutes. I still didn't move. I heard him pulling up his clothes, and he got out of the car without saying a word. That worried me. I quickly grabbed my clothes off of the floor and got dressed. I got out the car, putting my shoes on, and looked out towards the strip. It was empty. All the girls were gone to make that money except for me, and Lord knows I needed it.

I walked around to the other side of the car where Dré was standing, smoking another blunt. He was just staring out towards the strip. I stood directly in front of him and he wouldn't say a word. I looked towards the strip to see if I could see whatever the hell he was looking at. There was nothing but the city's lights.

"Dré, you ok?"

He looked at me and handed me his blunt. I took a puff and handed it back.

"Bitch, why didn't you tell me?

"Tell you what?" I asked curiously.

"How good you are. I would've hit that a long time ago. Or maybe I wouldn't have. Shit, I don't know. Yo ass got a nigga' trippin'. That's some dangerous pussy right there girl. How you keep that shit so tight?"

I smiled modestly, and said, "Kegels."

"Well, you keep on doin' that shit. No wonder you keep your customers so damn happy!" He took a few more puffs of his blunt and just stared at me shaking his head.

"I guess I'll go ahead and freshen up so I can get to work."

I started walking towards my car to get my overnight bag with my supplies out of my trunk.

"Nah," Dré said.

I turned around and said, "What?"

"Not tonight. Gone home and get some rest."

"Dré, I need this money."

"What I say!"

"I have bills! I just can't take a night off. What all of a sudden changed?

"Don't you got a concussion?"

"Yeah, and you knew that when you picked me up from the hospital earlier! I remember you telling me that I better be out on the corner tonight!"

"Yeah. My bad. I don't know what I was thinkin. Go home. I'll pay yo ass for tonight."

"Dré, you are not gonna pay me for sex! You are not a client."

Dré grinned and said, "How about we just say it was a gift?"

He stuck his hand in his pocket and pulled out a bundle of money. He counted some of it out and held it out in front of me. I stood there staring at him, refusing to accept it.

"Girl, take this shit."

I continued to stand there.

"Don't piss me off, Jay."

I snatched the money from Dré and turned around to walk to my car.

As I got a few feet from my car door, Dré said, "Jay."

I turned around.

"Goodnight," Dré said.

"Goodnight, love."

I got in the car and drove off, not sure how I felt about what had just happened. Dré was kinda hard to read. It seemed like he had enjoyed what had just happened, but why in the world would he send me away? I had so many thoughts going through my head. I guess I'd just have to take it day by day to see what was going to come of this.

The first thing I did when I got home was counted how much was in the bundle of money Dré had given me. When I finished counting I shook my head. He had given me three-thousand dollars. That was way more than I would've made in one night, especially after Dré got his cut, and he knew it. Why he had given me so much, I don't know.

I took a shower and laid in bed daydreaming. I wasn't able to sleep because I wasn't used to sleeping at night, and if I was used to sleeping at night, I don't think I would've been able to because my mind was going a thousand miles a minute. I wondered if Dré and I would ever have sex again, and what he meant when he said I have a "dangerous pussy". I didn't know if that was a good thing or bad thing. Maybe the whole thing scared him. I had never seen Dré act the way he was acting. He actually had put down his guard a little bit, but he wasn't fooling me. After I had seen him snap earlier, I wouldn't put anything past him.

I still wanted to get to know Chance, even though from what I saw, he seemed to be in a totally different league from myself. I already knew any man driving a Lamborghini was out of my league, but I still wanted to know what his intentions were because he obviously had some, and I believed he had been preparing for a meeting with me for a long time. I jumped up out of the bed and grabbed my purse. I found the envelope with Chance's business card inside amongst the clutter and actually really looked at it this time. Chance's last name was Robinson, and he was the president of Robinson Property Investment Firm, Inc. That gave me a little more insight as to who he was and what he did for a living. I knew he had to do something big for him to own the car that he did, but I also knew some niggas did a lot of stunting and for all I knew, that car could've been a rental. Chance's cell and office numbers were on the business card. His office hours and address were also listed. Now that I knew a little bit about who I was dealing with, I decided that the next morning I would be on a mission; a mission that I was determined to fulfill even if it ended up leaving me disappointed.

CHAPTER SIX

I woke up bright and early the next morning. So early, I was able to see the sun rise. On any other normal day, I would've just been getting in from work. I got up, threw on my robe, and went to the kitchen to turn on the coffeemaker. As I waited for my coffee to get ready, I rummaged through the clothes in my closet, looking for something that wasn't too obscene for my visit to see Chance. My body was very impressive, so I definitely didn't want to cover my bountiful assets with too much material, so I would need to find a happy medium.

After drinking two cups of black coffee, as I did every day, I showered and put on the outfit that I had chosen out of the dozens I had to choose from. Not knowing what to expect from this visit, I made sure I had on the sexiest undergarments that I owned. I knew I shouldn't have been going into this expecting anything sexual to happen, but that way of thinking was embedded in my head. I wore a pair of Aztec print leggings to accentuate my voluptuous ass, and a matching tangerine low-cut crop top that showed just enough cleavage. I put on my black, Red Bottom stilettos to elongate my already long, shapely legs even more.

I couldn't leave my face out. I beat it like always, but today, with subtle earth tones, and flat-ironed a few strands of hair that were out of place from the night before. I looked in my full-length mirror before heading out, turning around looking at my ass, and blew a kiss to myself because this bitch was ice cold!

Chance's office was about twenty minutes outside of Manhattan in New York City. There seemed to be something trying to stop me from making it to my destination, but I wasn't gonna let that happen. I got held up by two trains, so then when I decided to get on the expressway, traffic was backed up from a bad car accident involving a car and semi. I got off the expressway, thinking I was better off driving through the city. That's when I found myself at a stop sign waiting on a long ass funeral processional to pass. Whoever died must've been important because after waiting for at least five minutes, cars were still coming.

The whole thing made me think of my daddy's pathetic funeral. My mother and I must've looked like the most dysfunctional family anyone had probably ever seen. My daddy had a small three thousand dollar life insurance policy through his job, which didn't help much, so as much as my momma hated it, she had to let go of her pride and reach out to family and friends that she had previously disowned, and raise enough money to have my daddy a decent funeral.

One night, while I was walking past my momma's room to go to the bathroom, I overheard my momma talking to one of her boyfriends that she had over. Now that my daddy was dead, she had started bringing men over to the house before we could even get the man in the ground.

As I stood on the other side of the wall to my momma's bedroom, I heard my momma say, "I should just cremate the muthafuckin' crackhead!"

Her man friend laughed and said, "Woman you crazy as hell."

"But I'm serious! It's not like he'll know any difference, now will he?" My momma said, cracking up. "He put me in this position by going out doing some stupid shit! He was not the man that I married."

I could no longer listen to the bullshit my momma was saying about my daddy, so I politely knocked on the door. I heard my momma whisper something, then heard her feet as they hit the floor.

"What?" she said as if I was bothering her when she opened the door.

I peeked around her to find, of course, another man who looked to be at least ten years younger than her laying in the bed underneath the cover, exposing nothing but his six-pack. He looked liked my momma had just finished oiling him up with baby oil.

My momma repeated herself. "What do your little nosey ass want?"

I took a deep breath and exhaled, and before I knew it something took over my body, and I couldn't control my words.

"I just wanted to say . . . Bitch, you're the reason why all this is happening. Daddy was the best man you'll ever have in life! No one else will ever put up with your unappreciative ass! You made your bed now lay in it!"

My momma began laughing hysterically, turned to her friend and said, "Lenzo, did you hear what this child just said to me? I swear kids just have no respect for their parents anymore."

My momma's friend, who I had just learned, name was Lenzo, laid there smiling, curiously watching to see what was going to happen next.

My momma then looked back at me and said, "Child, I hope you got everything you needed to off of your chest. You talk about me, but your daddy was a crackhead! What kind of role model was he for you? You better learn real fast who's taking care of you and putting a roof over your head. You better be glad that I even claim you as my child! Look at you!"

Tears streamed down my face as my momma told me how she really felt about me.

"Now you wanna cry? Really? Get out of my face before I knock your teeth out of your mouth!" My momma said as she slammed the door in my face. I stood there for about five minutes without moving. I was numb. I could hear my momma laughing, acting as if nothing had just happened. When I finally came to, and was able to move, I looked down and saw that I had pissed on myself.

My daddy's funeral was a few days later. As big of a bitch as my momma was, I didn't know how she pulled it off, but obviously she was able to get some people to feel sorry for her and loan her some money. Knowing her, she probably used my name to persuade people to help. However she did it, I was content that my daddy would be getting a proper burial somewhere where I would be able to visit him, and not just have his remains sitting in an urn on the coffee table.

The funeral wasn't extravagant. I wouldn't even say it was mediocre. There was no church, no limousines, preacher, soloist, and no flowers, besides the few that a few friends and relatives had sent. My momma didn't even have any obituaries made. All we basically had was a funeral home and a hearse.

When my momma and I walked into the funeral home, there were about twenty people there. None of which I recognized. My momma and daddy never really had many friends or family that they communicated with, so I never got to know any of my family on either side. I didn't know specifics on what had gone down. What I did know is that my momma and daddy's side didn't get along, and definitely didn't want my momma and daddy to get married, but they did anyway, which caused a wedge between them and their families. They loved each other that much during that time that they didn't even care.

A few people came over to my momma expressing their condolences.

One woman looked at me and said to my momma, "I didn't know you had another child."

"I didn't," my momma replied. "This is Jordyn. Jordyn, this is your Aunt Sandy. She's your daddy's sister."

Sandy looked at my momma and said, "I guess it's truly been a while. A lot has changed." She then looked back at me and gave me a tight hug and whispered in my ear, "Let me know if you need anything. I'm not far." She then walked away and took a seat in the front of the chapel.

My momma introduced me to several other people, introducing them as aunts, uncles, and cousins. From the back of the funeral home, I could see my daddy's body laying lifeless in a cheap-looking casket. Something I would've never chosen for him. I left my momma's side as she continued to be fake, smiling in everyone's face, and slowly walked down the middle aisle of the chapel until I made it to my daddy.

I breathed hard, and shook harder. Tears began flowing down my caramel skin. I leaned over the casket hoping my daddy could hear me. My voice quivered.

"Daddy, I miss you so much. Why did you have to leave me? What am I supposed to do now?"

I kissed him on the forehead for the last time and began to cry harder and louder. I felt someone come up behind me and wrap their arms around me. I actually thought it was my momma until I heard the voice.

"It's gonna be ok. Your daddy is in a better place and you'll see him again some day."

I turned around and it was my Aunt Sandy. I wrapped my arms around her and cried on her shoulder. She held me as she walked me over to her seat and we sat together. I just couldn't understand why I had never known her. She seemed like a very nice woman, and she and my momma didn't seem to have a problem with each other. Then again, it was a funeral, and I guess being cordial was the right thing to do during a time like that.

I watched as people walked up to my daddy's casket, one by one, paying their last respects. I didn't see my momma for a while, so I looked back to see if I could find her in the back, within the small crowd of people who were talking. It didn't take very long for me to pinpoint her. She was sitting a few rows behind Aunt Sandy and me, instead of in the front, where the wife should've been sitting. Lenzo was right beside her.

They were smiling and giggling in each other's faces like everything was perfect. My Aunt Sandy looked back to see what I was looking at. She twisted up her mouth and cut her eyes at my momma, and that's when I saw the resentment between the two. My momma rolled her eyes and continued focusing on what mattered most to her.

I left out of the funeral home before my momma so that we could head to the cemetery. As I stood at the car waiting on my momma to come unlock the doors, I saw her heading towards me with Lenzo by her side.

"Lenzo is riding with us, so you need to get in the back," my momma said sternly.

I wanted to ask her why that nigga wasn't riding in his own car, and why was he even there at all, but I had finally realized that arguing with my momma made her treat me worse and worse. I learned in a very short time to just remain quiet and let her do what she was gonna do. Even at a young age, I knew karma was a bitch and she would one day get everything she deserved.

On the way to the cemetery, I sat in the backseat of my daddy's car, fighting off the urge to throw-up from the anguish of watching my momma and Lenzo look so happy. Only a few people showed up to the gravesite to watch my daddy be wheeled into the ground. Amongst those was Aunt Sandy. Watching my daddy, the only man I had ever loved, go down into the earth was the hardest thing I ever had to endure. He was my protector against everything and he was gone. I didn't know how the rest of my life was going to stem out, but I would have to make the best of it. Before leaving the cemetery, Aunt Sandy pulled me to the side and handed me her address and phone number.

"Don't hesitate to call or stop by if you need anything, even if it's just someone to talk to. You're family and I would never abandon you."

She hugged me and told me she loved me. Just then, my momma started honking the horn, telling me to come on. I waived goodbye to my newfound aunt and dreaded to see what was next for me.

By the time the funeral procession was over, there was a long line of traffic behind me waiting to get across. As soon I stepped on the gas, Beyonce's "Drunk in Love" started playing on my phone, which meant Dré was either calling or texting me. I grabbed my phone from in between my legs and saw that it was a text. Dré was just checking in to see if my head was feeling better. That small gesture put a smile on my face, but I didn't have time to answer at the moment. I needed to keep my mind clear so that when I made it to my destination, I would be able to fully, and clearly comprehend the situation I was about to enter into.

I had finally made it to the building where Chance's firm was located. It was a tall, beautiful building right in the heart of New York City. I could just imagine how much the owner of the building charged to rent out a suite. I found a parking space in the huge lot and watched as women and men of the corporate world made their way in to work. The women were dressed in pantsuits, skirt suits, and professional dresses. I suddenly felt underdressed and felt like going back home for a re-do. I had come too far, and I definitely wasn't about to take that ride back home. Whatever was meant to be would be.

After I finished admiring everyone else walking through the parking lot, I took a deep breath, made sure there was no lipstick on my teeth, and got out of the car. On my way to the entrance, I saw a girl that looked to be around my age with a pair of skinny jeans and a halter-top on. God must've known I needed something to help relieve my stress at that moment, because my self-consciousness about what I was wearing immediately left.

When I got inside of the building, there were offices everywhere. I had to pull Chance's card out of my purse to double-check his suite number. As I was searching, a very attractive Caucasian man who looked a lot like the actor, Eddie Cibrian, approached me and said, "Hello ma'am. Do you need help?"

"No, but thank you," I said, grinning at him.

"Ok. You just looked like you were a bit lost. You sure you don't need help finding someone?

As soon as he finished speaking, I pulled Chance's card out of my purse and said, "Nope! Found it," then briskly walked towards the elevator.

As I was walking, I could hear the man say in the distance, "Have a good day, gorgeous!"

Chance's suite was on the tenth floor, which was at the very top of the building. When the elevator doors opened, I stepped out and there was one office door. His office took up the entire tenth floor! *I know for a fact now that he's paying at least a few g's a month to rent out this space!* I thought to myself.

I opened the double doors to the office and there was a circular shaped desk in the middle where three women were sitting. They were all very beautiful. Two of them were Caucasian, and the other one was Black, but looked like she could've been mixed with something else, kind of reminding me of a younger version of Vanessa Williams. Her nametag said "Zahriah". From the time I had walked into the building, all I had seen were beautiful people. I was beginning to believe that being gorgeous was a prerequisite to work in the building.

One of the women at the desk had blonde hair and big beautiful blue eyes. She was the first out of the three to notice me.

"Hello ma'am. How can I help you?" Blondie asked, smiling, showing her bright white teeth that seemed even brighter next to her vivid red lipstick.

"Yes, I'm here to see Chance Robinson."

"Ok. And what time is your appointment?"

"Oh, I don't have an appointment."

As those words came out of my mouth, all three of the ladies looked at each other with a confused look on their faces.

I hesitated before speaking again. Then I said, "He asked me to stop by when I had time, so here I am . . . stopping by when I have time."

"Okaaaaaay . . . It's just that Mr. Robinson normally doesn't see people without an appointment, so I'm just going to have to confirm with him that it's ok that you wait. What's your name?" Blondie, whose nametag said "Heidi" replied.

Before thinking, I said, "Jay." Then I remembered what Chance said the first time we met when I told him my name was Jay. He was insistent on knowing my real name. "Jordyn," I said, correcting myself.

"Ok. I'll be right back," Heidi said.

As I stood at the desk waiting, the two other women seemed to pretend to be busy so they wouldn't have to talk to me. A few minutes later, Heidi came back and said, "Mr. Robinson is on a conference call right now, but he'll be with you as soon as he finishes up. You can have a seat."

"Thank you," I replied and smiled before turning around to find a seat.

The longer I sat there waiting, the more I felt like just leaving. Obviously Chance didn't want to see me bad enough to expedite his meeting with his client. First a half hour went by, and the next thing I knew a whole hour had passed. Dré had texted me a couple more times, so I decided to go ahead and respond. I told him I was feeling a lot better. He then texted me back and asked if I wanted him to bring me anything. I had to double-check to make sure it was Dré who I was conversing with. Never had I ever seen him act so caring and considerate of others. I told him no and that I was out taking care of some business. He had the audacity to ask what I was out doing. I didn't know what had come over Dré, but I hoped he didn't think he bought me for three-thousand dollars! I politely replied by telling Dré I had a meeting with a friend. After that, he didn't text me anymore.

Soon afterwards, the man I had met downstairs walked into the office. All three ladies at the desk looked up, and as soon as they saw that sexy hunk of white chocolate, they smiled from ear to ear.

"Good morning, Mr. Roberts", they said in unison.

He smiled, showing his sexy ass dimples and perfectly straight teeth and said, "Hey ladies. Where's Chance?"

Heidi eagerly replied, "He's in a meeting via conference call right now, but I'll get you in as soon as he's done."

I became infuriated due to the lack of respect for my time. I politely cleared my throat to get Heidi's attention. Everyone looked at me, including Mr. Roberts, who hadn't seen me sitting there.

"Oh, I'm sorry . . . ummm . . ." Heidi said, obviously unable to remember my name.

"Jordyn! My name is Jordyn."

"Yes, Jordyn! I'm sorry, but you may have to wait just a few more minutes once Mr. Robinson is done with his current meeting. Mr. Roberts is . . ."

Mr. Roberts interrupted and while staring at me smiling said, "No, Heidi. Don't worry about it. It can wait. I'm sure whatever Miss Jordyn needs to talk to him about is much more important."

Heidi had the dumbest look on her face I had ever seen. I wanted to ask her if she wanted to pick her face up off the ground, but I didn't want to seem rude. The other two ladies didn't make it any better by snickering amongst each other.

"Oh, ok," Heidi said, and looked down at the desk, pretending to look at something important, probably dying of embarrassment on the inside.

Mr. Roberts walked over to me and stood directly in front of me holding his hand out. "I don't think I got to formally introduce myself downstairs. You were in such a hurry to see Chance. I'm Jacob Roberts. I own Roberts Insurance Agency down on the second floor."

I extended my arm and shook his hand. "I'm Jordyn, as you already know. Jordyn Parker."

"You are an exceptionally beautiful woman, Jordyn. What does Chance owe the pleasure?"

"I blushed and said, "Thank you."

I didn't feel as though I should've answered his question, so I didn't.

"So, are you going to tell me why you're here, or is it personal?"

I didn't know if Jacob was Chance's business partner or what, but what I did know was that he was extremely nosey.

"I'm here on business," I lied.

"Are you looking to rent a space in this building?"

"Rent a space? In this building? Would I talk to Chance about that?"

"I would think so since he does own the building."

I sat there with my mouth wide open realizing I wasn't just a little out of my league. I was way out of my league!

"Oh, I guess you didn't know. You must not know Chance too well."

"No, I don't. I actually just met him the other day and told him I was looking into possibly purchasing a piece of property," I lied again.

"Well, that's good for me. I thought maybe you guys might've had something going on or something; perhaps dating."

"Nooo, not at all."

"Well, I would love if we could maybe get to know each other better."

"Jordyn! What a nice surprise." I heard a familiar voice say.

Jacob turned around and stepped to the side, and there stood the sexy hunk of dark chocolate I had seen in that white Lamborghini. He looked even better than what I had remembered. Maybe it was the suit and tie he was wearing that gave him that extra ounce of sex appeal.

"Hey Chance. I was just getting to know your prospective new client. She told me she was interested in buying some property."

I could tell Jacob was studying the expression on Chance's face to see if I had been honest with him about the reason I was there.

"Is that right?" Chance said. Chance looked at me, and said, "I knew she wanted to talk business. I just didn't know what kind of business." Chance winked at me, confirming that he had my back.

Jacob stuck his hand in his jacket pocket, pulling out a business card, and said, "Well, Jordyn, when you're done doing business here with Chance, you'll probably need to swing by and see me so you can get some insurance on that property you're looking to purchase, so give me a call."

He handed me his business card and told Chance he'd stop by a little later when he wasn't busy.

After Jacob walked out, Chance said, "Jordyn. You can come on back to my office." He looked over at the receptionists and told them to hold all his calls.

As I stood up, he stood there with one hand clasped inside of the other, staring at me from head to toe. He bit his bottom lip and gave me a sneaky grin. The women at the desk tried again to act as if they were working and not paying attention, but I knew they were already making their own assumptions as to who the fuck I was and why in the hell I was able to come in without an appointment. I knew all about bitches and their asinine ways of thinking.

Chance held the door open to his office and I walked in. It was huge. He had exceptionally large windows, and I could probably see the entire city of New York from where his office was located. All of his office furniture was cherry-oak wood with a satin finish, and expensive art hung from the walls.

"This is beautiful, Chance."

"So are you, Jordyn."

I blushed and turned towards the window pretending to look out, but was actually avoiding what felt like an awkward moment.

"I wasn't expecting to see you. What made you stop by?"

I turned back around, not expecting for Chance to be standing directly in front in me. I slightly jumped, then said, "I just thought it was very nice of you to save my life the way you did, and on top of that, made sure I safely made it to the hospital. I felt like I owed it to you to at least thank you in person. You don't find too many people that would do that for a complete stranger. Especially someone like me."

"You didn't have to thank me, but I appreciate you coming by. By the way, I thought it was your pimp's job to make sure you were safe. He didn't seem to want to have anything to do with you the other night. He just left you laying there."

"You're not a part of that life, so you wouldn't understand," I said defensively.

"What is there to understand? What I understand is that as an employer, you should be doing everything possible to protect and keep your employees safe."

"I understand that, but I also understand that Dré also has to protect his business. A lot of what happened was my fault. You don't know the full story. I let my emotions get the best of me, and ended up doing something stupid, jeopardizing everyone's jobs."

Chance looked at me like I was crazy and said, "It seems like no matter what I say, you're gonna protect him and make it seem like what he did was right. I'm not going to agree now, and will never agree with that. But enough about that. I'm sure you didn't come all this way to have a discussion about your pimp's morals, so can I at least have a hug from one of the most exquisite women I've ever seen?"

Chance opened his arms wide and I fell right into them. He tightly wrapped his strong arms around me, and the scent of his SpiceBomb cologne immediately tantalized me. I reciprocated by holding him tight. He put his mouth close to my earlobe and whispered, "You smell so good." He then kissed me on my neck, which turned me on more than he could've ever imagined.

He slowly released his arms from around me and took my hands into his. He looked at me shaking his head. "There's something about you," he said.

I started blushing once again, and pushed one side of my hair behind my ear.

"Can we see each other again outside of here? Or did you just come by to say thank you?" Chance asked.

"Let me ask you something," I said with purpose in my voice.

"Go right ahead," Chance said, putting his hands in his pockets.

"What was your intent when you gave me your card?"

"To be honest, I didn't know what the possibilities were. At the time, I just knew you were intriguing, and I was hoping that I would be able to see you again, and maybe even hang out. I also wanted to help you get off of the streets because that's not where you belong, sweetie."

Chance was doing good until he made that last statement. It made me cringe, but he looked as though he didn't say anything wrong.

"Look, I'm not on the streets. I live under decent living conditions . . ."

Chance put his index finger up to my lips to shush me before I got too carried away. "I didn't say you were living on the streets. I'm talking about your employment. I can tell you're way above what you're doing. I just want you to know I'm here to help. I'm not trying to talk down to you. I just want better for you."

"Why? You don't even know me? Why would you even care?"

"I told you. There's just something about you. With that being said, are you free tonight?"

Chance had shushed me, and spit his little game so fast, he caught me off guard. I stared at his sexy ass for a moment, and before I almost said yes, I had to bring myself back to reality.

"No, I'm not. Sorry."

"Let me guess. You have to work," Chance said sarcastically.

"You're absolutely right! Don't you have to work everyday?" I asked with an attitude.

"Yeah, but I can take time off for things I really want to do."

"Well, you can afford it. I can't!"

"We're getting off on the wrong foot. How about I pay you for a missed night of work. How much do you go for?"

"Now you're trying to buy me?"

"No, I'm just trying to buy some of your time."

I thought to myself, *Jordyn, what are you doing? You know you'll never be able to be involved in a real relationship with your profession and everything else you got going on. Let it go.*

"You know what, Chance? I really don't know why I came here today. I think maybe I was expecting a miracle, but in reality, no man will ever be able to accept me and my profession. This is all I know right now. Dré is all I have and he's gotten me to where I am." I walked over to Chance's desk and grabbed a pen and piece of paper. I wrote down my phone number and handed it to Chance.

"Maybe we can hang out sometimes, but that would be it. Anything more just wouldn't work out." I gave Chance a kiss on the Cheek and ran my hand down his tie before I turned around to walk out of his office.

I could feel Chance following behind me, so I quickly turned towards him, pointed my fingernail directly in the middle of his chest and said, "I can find my own way out." I left him standing there in the middle of his office not knowing what to do or say.

The ride home was pure torture. Chance was everything a girl could ever ask for and more, but I was too afraid to step out of my comfort zone to see what he had to offer, or what could possibly happen. I didn't want to take the chance of being hurt. No one was ever able to accept all of me, and I just didn't think Chance was the one that would break the cycle. I decided that I would avoid any more contact with Chance and stay within my own league.

CHAPTER SEVEN

On my way in to work that night, I had a lot on my mind. I even thought about if I weren't a prostitute, what would I do at night? I had forgotten what a normal lifestyle was even like. Dré was standing outside of his car when I pulled up. Surprisingly he wasn't smoking.

I got out of the car and said, "Hey Dré."

"What's up sexy? Come over here a sec."

Fuck! I am not in the mood for this shit tonight. I thought. Any other night, I would've been ready for Dré.

My life seemed so clear before, and within just a few days, everything had become so foggy. I knew that I was a prostitute, which I had accepted. I knew I wanted Dré, finally got him to go the next step with me, and now I didn't even know if that was what I wanted anymore. I had heard a few times in my life that God gives you what you think you want, just so you can realize that's not really what you want or need. My ultimate goal had been to make Dré my man. My goal before I met Dré was to make good enough grades in college to get accepted into nursing school. I was proud of that goal, but these days, I wasn't sure of my goals, and didn't feel so proud.

I walked over to Dré and he grabbed me by my waist and jerked me, pulling me close.

"Who was you with earlier?" he asked demandingly.

"I told you I was with one of my friends, and since when do you care who I'm hanging out with?"

"Since you gave me some of that good lovin'. Now I gotta make sure you're not out giving it away to anyone outside of work."

"Really? Are you fuckin' kidding me?

"Yeah, really. And I really don't want you givin' it to none of them!"

Dré was making me feel some type of way. Maybe he was really considering taking me off the payroll and having me for himself. Then maybe I would be able to live a somewhat normal life, and even go back to school. I just wanted a man to love me unconditionally. The only man who had ever loved me unconditionally was my daddy, and I lost that when I was thirteen. I had to give it to Dré. He seemed like he was really trying. I was willing to give him a chance to show me how much he really wanted me, and accept everything about me.

I looked at Dré directly in his eyes and asked, "What do you want from me?"

"I don't know. Let's just take it day by day."

Dré grabbed me by the back of my head and pressed his lips up against mine, intertwining his tongue with mine. When our lips parted, I laughed.

"What's so funny?"

"You got all my lipstick on."

"Yeah, and yours is fucked up. Go fix that shit and get to work."

As I walked away to fix my lipstick, Dré smacked me on my ass. After getting myself back in order, I headed towards the strip. As I got closer, Lexi's skinny ass stood there smiling and waving. When I finally got across the street, she ran up to me and hugged me.

"I'm so glad you're ok. I was worried about you girl!"

I wanted to say, *bitch, how in the hell were you worried about me when you and these other hoes left me unconscious, laying in the street?* Instead, I let her have her moment. Besides, Lexi had never done anything to me to make me feel like she was phony towards me in any way. I got along better with her than any of the others. I just learned throughout life to never give a bitch all of your trust. That way you won't be disappointed when they do some foul ass shit.

"Thanks girl, I appreciate that."

All of a sudden, I heard Dena's stank ass voice. "Look who decided to show up."

"Dena, I don't have time for your drama tonight. I just came to do my job and that's it."

Dena flicked me off and continued strutting her wild wildebeest lookin' ass down the street.

"Where's Peaches and Stasia?" I asked Lexi.

Lexi looked as though she really didn't want to answer.

"Well, Stasia already got a client tonight, but Peaches . . . ummm . . . She's no longer with us."

My eyebrows raised and I said, "What? What the fuck happened?"

Lexi lowered her voice and looked around making sure no one else was listening. "Dré got mad at Peaches for calling an ambulance the night you had the accident and he let her go."

I couldn't believe what Lexi had just told me. We were so deep into our conversation, we hadn't noticed the black BMW that had pulled up. It was Rob, who was a regular customer of mine. He was one of those white men who couldn't get enough of black women and he had money up the ass. That's why I was willing to do whatever he wanted because he didn't mind paying at all!

"Lexi, we're gonna have to finish this conversation later."

Lexi nodded her head and I walked towards Rob's car and leaned into his passenger side window. Rob wasn't one of the finest clients that I had, but he was all right. He was kinda thin for my liking, kept his brown hair shaggy, and had a thick brown mustache that completely covered his thin top lip. I'll just say he was bearable and I'd had worse. In my profession, I'd had to learn to tolerate some ugly ass muthafuckas.

"Hey, baby! Where you been? I've been looking for you," Rob said with his nasally voice, and a big goofy smile on his face.

"I took the night off last night. I wasn't feeling too well."

"Well get on in! We can help each other feel better. You know you're my favorite girl."

I hated so much when Rob said some of the lamest shit, but I had to laugh it off and keep it movin'. As soon as I grabbed the door handle to get inside of Rob's ride, I heard a horn blow. Parked behind Rob's BMW was Bronze colored Maserati. I tried to see who was inside, but couldn't tell through the dark tinted windows. As I started to get into Rob's car again, the person driving the Maserati blew the horn again.

"That car has rode down this strip about five times since I've been out here tonight, but this is the first time it stopped!" Lexi said.

Fuck! I thought to myself. "Wait here one minute, baby. I'll be right back."

"You know I'm not going nowhere!"

Before I walked towards the Maserati, I looked across the street to see if I could tell what Dré was doing. I was hoping he was paying attention, just in case this was some lunatic trying to act crazy.

When I started to walk towards the car, Dena's ass was already there, trying to ease her way into the front seat. I could suddenly hear the male's voice inside the car telling her he wanted me, but she wouldn't seem to take no for an answer.

"Jordyn already has a taker, but I'm available. You won't regret it, and trust me . . . After you've had a piece of this, you won't even remember who Jordyn is."

Dena didn't realize I was standing right next to her about to grab the blonde mop up off of her head, even though Chance was looking right at me the entire time. I cleared my throat and Dena jumped, and stood straight up.

"What the fuck you want. Don't you see I'm working? You better gone up there and get you favorite client!" Dena said.

"Bitch, I think I heard this nice man say he don't want you so take your ass on somewhere."

"I'm gon' let you have it this time, but believe me when I say I'm gon' report your greedy ass to Dré. You know he don't like shit like this. He especially don't like us to keep clients waiting!"

"Well, go keep Rob company then!"

Dena walked off, rolling her eyes. I leaned into Chance's window and the first thing I noticed was how good he was looking. He grinned at me, and I looked down trying not to focus on his perfect facial features. That didn't help because my attention was then focused on his gorgeous body. His biceps protruded through his nicely fitted tee, and I could tell he was blessed with a nice piece by the print in his jeans. Trying to hide the fact that I was being distracted by so much temptation, I said, "What the fuck are you doing here?"

"I came to take you with me."

"What? You're trying to pick me up? Are you insane?"

"That's your job isn't it?"

"Yeah, but . . ."

"But nothing. I've been waiting for you all night, and good things come to those who wait, right?"

I sighed, and said, "That's what I hear."

"Were you really about to leave with him?" Chance asked looking straight ahead at the BMW.

"Yes, and I'm still about to leave with him. He's one of my regular, and best clients."

"What if I told you I'll pay you double what he's gonna pay you?"

I felt my eyes get big as quarters, and suddenly I heard my name being called in the distance.

"Jay!"

I looked across the street and saw Dré standing there with his arms folded.

"Why are there cars sitting on my strip for longer than two minutes? Ain't no time for talkin'! If he ain't buying he gotta go."

Dré obviously didn't recognize Chance in the Maserati, and I think that was Chance's reason for driving that particular car instead of his Lamborghini. Dré would've definitely had a problem with Chance showing his face again.

"I got this, Dré!" I said with a smile and wink.

"I ain't playin' wit yo ass! Fix this shit now!"

I waited til he turned around and walked back towards his Impala before I changed the expression on my face so I could really let Chance know how fucked up this was.

"You gotta go, Chance. I gotta get to work. I don't want to upset Dré."

"I'm not leaving without you, so you better do something."

"Shit!" I exclaimed and walked over to Lexi, who was still working on getting picked up. It always took her the longest time to entice someone enough to pick her up. She had a beautiful face, but I think it was probably because she was so skinny. Men who came down our strip liked a little juiciness to come with their purchase. I wasn't the thickest, but I had curves, and something for them to grab on to.

"Lexi, you need to go with Rob. You'll thank me later!"

"What? But that's your client!"

"He's yours tonight."

"But what if he doesn't want me?"

"He will. Trust me!"

I grabbed Lexi by her arm and pulled her to Rob's car.

"Rob, this is Lexi. She's gonna be hanging out with you tonight. She knows how to do things I don't even know how to do! You'll love her."

Lexi was about to say something and I shook my head telling her to be quiet.

"I don't know, Jay. I'm used to being with you."

"Change is always good! I'll catch up with you another night. I'll even do a little extra for a little less next time. Ok?" I said batting my long eyelashes.

At first Rob had a look of disappointment on his face. Then after I made that promise to him, he had an instant smile on his face. He looked at Lexi and said, "Well, ok. She is really pretty."

I whispered in Lexi's ear, "FYI, my clients love to be blindfolded, and the best part of this is, with him, the sky's the limit, baby girl."

Lexi grinned and got in the car. As they pulled off, I looked at Dena, who was the only girl left, and said, "So, am I still greedy?"

"Maybe not, but you're still a bitch, bitch!"

"Whatever," I said, nonchalantly, and jumped in the car with Chance.

I felt Chance staring at me when I got in the car, but I wouldn't look his way. He had just put me in a very difficult situation, and that's exactly what I didn't need in my life.

"Drive now!" I demanded.

Chance hit the gas so hard, all I heard was the shrieking sound of rubber burning. He slowed down as we got off the strip.

I finally turned towards him after a couple of minutes and said, "What is your problem? You could've really gotten me in trouble if Dré would've recognized you!"

"If I have to do this every night to keep you from going to sleep with other men, I will. And I drove my other vehicle to prevent any issues with your boss."

I took a deep breath and said, "Chance, listen to me! I have to do my job! That's why it's best that we don't try to associate in any way. It takes a person with very thick-skin to deal with this."

"Just quit!" Chance said, as if it were that simple.

"Tell me why on earth I would change my lifestyle for someone I've known for five minutes?"

"Because I want to get to know you and take care of you."

"And what if you decide after getting to know me that you're not interested after all? Where does that leave me?"

"You just have to trust me. I know you can do that."

"And how do you know?" I asked curiously.

"Because you do it every night when you jump into the cars of complete strangers."

It took me a minute to respond because Chance actually had a valid point.

"But it's different," I said, not really knowing what I meant, but it was the only thing I could come up with.

I guess Chance was tired of discussing it and decided to change the subject.

"You hungry?"

"Ummm, my clients don't normally take me out to eat."

"Well, I'm not a client, and this is a date. There's a difference. I'm paying you to go out with me, not to sleep with me."

I could see that Chance was adamant about what he wanted, and I saw I wasn't getting anywhere, so I just decided to shut my mouth and let whatever was going to happen, happen.

"So are you hungry or not?" Chance asked again.

"A little bit."

"What do you want to eat? We can go anywhere you want."

"I don't know. Surprise me."

Chance glanced over at me and smiled. I leaned back in my seat, relaxed, and enjoyed the ride.

CHAPTER EIGHT

When Chance and I finally arrived at our destination, he asked, "You ever been here before?"

"I can't say I have," I replied.

"You seem like the type of woman who'll enjoy a place like this."

As Chance reached to open his door to get out of the car, I did the same.

Chance looked back at me and said, "What do you think you're doing?"

"I'm getting out of the car. I am going in with you, right?"

"No lady of mine opens their own door. Sit tight. Get ready to be spoiled."

Chance winked and gave me one of those sexy ass one-sided grins before getting out of the car. I can't even lie. There weren't too many men I would've called gorgeous, but he was definitely one gorgeous man! Chance opened my door and reached his arm out to me to help me out of his beautiful car. This was just the beginning and I could already say no man had ever treated me as well as I had been treated within the past half hour.

As we were walking to the entrance of the exquisite building that was lit up with royal blue lights, I noticed how many cars were parked in its direct vicinity. If they were all customers, this place was jam-packed. It was late, but the nightlife of New York City was always busy. Especially when the weather was nice. I was just hoping not to see any of my clients. I knew most of them hung out at high-class establishments, which is what this seemed to be. The majority of them were married anyway, so I was sure if they happened to be with their wives, they would try to avoid me just as much as I would try to avoid them.

Chance kept me close as we walked in sync with each other. When we entered the building, a beautiful black woman who reminded me of Megan Good, shape and all, greeted us and said, "Welcome to Blue Diamond. My name is Melanie. Have the two of you been here before?"

"Yes, I have." Chance said, then looked at me. "But my lady here hasn't."

"Lucky girl! Trust me, you will enjoy," Melanie said, smiling at me with her full, red lips. "Let me just go and get a table ready for you lovebirds."

As Melanie walked away, I watched Chance's eyes to see if they followed Melanie's big, voluptuous ass, but he didn't even glance at it. His eyes remained glued to me. I looked around the rest of the place. It was sexy, and romantic at the same time. There was a stage where a jazz band was playing. It was full of couples sitting at tables that were lit up in blue, and everyone seemed to be in love. Something that I'd always wanted to be.

After a couple of minutes, Melanie came back to seat us. We walked directly behind her as we followed her to our table. I was so proud of Chance. He looked straight ahead and never once looked down. Out of all the men I had ever been out on dates with, none of them could control themselves when it came to a fat ass!

After Melanie seated us in a cozy little corner, Chance and I sat directly across from each other. While I looked through the menu, Chance sat there with his elbows on the table, and hands clasped. When I looked up from the menu, he was staring directly at me.

"Are you not going to eat?" I asked.

"I already know what I want to eat," he said, and licked his lips.

"I squinted my eyes and said, "I thought this was a date."

"It is."

"Well, why am I starting to feel like you're a client?"

"I thought your clients don't take you out to eat."

"They don't, but right now you're looking at me like a piece of meat!"

Chance was about to respond, but just then my phone rang, and from the ringtone, I knew it was Dré, so I hit the ignore button. Dré never called me while I was working, so that call made me think someone had told him who I'd left with.

Chance continued, and said, "What if I asked you to go home with me tonight?"

I smirked and said, "I'd have to decline."

"Why is that?"

"Because I don't fuck on the first date!" I said, rolling my head from side to side.

"That's fair," Chance said, slowly rubbing his hands together looking like something else was on his mind. Then he continued. "I don't want to fuck you anyway. I want to make love to your mind, if you're willing to let me in. Hopefully we'll get to the point where you'll let me make love to your mind and body simultaneously. I promise you'll never wanna let me go."

I didn't know whether Chance knew it or not, but he was getting me horny as hell. I was ready to bend over the table and let him take it right then and there. My phone rang again, and of course, it was Dré. I hit "ignore" once again.

Chance caught me off guard and asked, "Are you fucking him?"

"What? Who?"

"You know who I'm talking about. I'm not stupid. Your pimp. I know that's who's calling you. How does he expect you to make any money if he's calling while you're on a job?"

"No! Mixing business with pleasure is the worst thing you can do! Absolutely not!" I lied.

"Ok. Sorry for offending you. It just seemed odd he would keep calling you."

"How do you even know that's him?"

"For what other man would you have "Drunk in Love" set as your ringtone?"

I was saved by the bell when our waitress finally came to take our orders, but only for that moment. As soon as the waitress walked away, Chance started up once again.

"How did you get into that line of business?"

"I needed fast money, and Dré showed me how to make that happen."

"Fast money for what?"

"I was working at McDonald's trying to pay my way through school, and pay for some other things that I desired."

"Ok, so you went to school. Why aren't you working in your field because I know prostitution definitely isn't a major at any school I know of."

Chance was the type of man that definitely knew how to press people's buttons and make you wanna slap his ass, but then when you looked at him, you'd forget why you were even mad.

"The money started coming in faster than I thought, and I dropped out of school. I plan on going back one day, but right now, I'm content. Now that's enough about me. I have a question for you."

"Go right ahead, baby," he responded in a voice that made my heart flutter.

"You seem to have everything going for yourself. Why don't you have a woman, and why are you out with me of all people?"

Chance lifted up out of his chair and slid his body halfway across the table. He took his index finger and gestured for me to come close.

"Come here. Let me tell you why."

I then lifted up out of my chair and met him halfway across the table. I gazed into his eyes, waiting for him to answer the question.

He softly spoke and said, "Because I've been waiting for you." He then gently grabbed my chin and pressed his soft lips up against mine. That short, but beautiful kiss must've taken me to another planet, because when it was over, I remained in that same position with my eyes closed. When I finally opened them, Chance was sitting back down, smiling. Embarrassingly, I sat back down and cleared my throat.

After we'd finished our meals and had a few drinks, the ice was officially broken. We talked and laughed about a little bit of everything. I talked a little bit about my family life and started to get emotional, so Chance comforted me, telling me we didn't have to talk about that. He told me he was thirty and lived in the city, not far from the district where his office was located. I imagined that he must've had a very nice home.

When we left Blue Diamond, I looked at the time and I noticed I had been gone three and a half hours, which was long enough for me to have had at least two paying clients. I was a little nervous about going back to the strip because I didn't know how Dré was going to react to me being gone with one person for so long, and not answering his calls.

As Chance cruised through the lit up city, he put his hand on my thigh and caressed it.

"You wanna go anywhere else while I have you out?" he asked.

"No, I better get back."

"Do you really have to go back? You know, I can probably find something for you to do at my office. That way you won't have to do this anymore."

"I would never be able to afford the things I'm used to working as one of your secretaries or some shit like that. I have very expensive taste," I said as I leaned my head back in the seat and closed my eyes.

Mumbling, Chance said, "It was just a suggestion, but I guess you know your worth."

I sat back up in my seat, turned to him, pointed my finger with my long stiletto nail in his face and said, "Don't try that reverse psychology bullshit on me! I know my worth quite well!"

"Ok, ok. Quit being so defensive."

When we finally pulled up to the strip, Chance asked, "How do you get home?"

"I drive!" I said, pointing towards the parking lot where my Jetta was sitting next to Dré's Impala.

"I'll drop you off next to your car then. I don't want you out here by yourself. You are done for the night, right?"

I looked at the clock on the dashboard, which said it was almost three in the morning. That was still early for a girl like me, so I said, "I still have time for one more."

If looks could kill, I would've been dead from the look on Chance's face.

"Are you serious? I asked you if you wanted to go somewhere else, but instead, after I took you out on a nice date with good music and food, you would rather end the night by fucking a stranger?"

"This is exactly why I don't think seeing each other is a good thing. You can't change who I am."

"I can't, but you can."

"I don't want to."

Chance took a deep breath and exhaled. He then rubbed his head. We remained quiet for the next few minutes while Chrisette Michele's "If I Have my Way" played on the radio. Without saying anything, Chance pulled his wallet out of his pant's pocket, and pulled out a stack of bills. After he counted it, he handed me almost half of the stack. I then recounted it and it was fifteen hundred dollars. I knew I wasn't great at math, so I counted it again because I couldn't believe that Chance took me out for a good time, and was still paying me that type of money when I didn't even fuck him.

Chance looked at me confused as I counted the money three times.

"What? Is that not enough for your troubles?"

"More than enough." I paused, and before I knew it, I said, "Are you sure you don't at least want me to give you some head?"

Chance looked at me and shook his head.

"You really have some soul searching to do, Jordyn. I can tell you're really a good person, but your pimp really has your way of thinking fucked up. I wish I would've found you before he did."

I didn't know what to say. All I knew was that I spoiled the entire mood. We had such a great time, and I blew it by asking him if he wanted me to blow him. How ironic.

"I'm still not leaving you out here. I'm gonna drop you off at your car. You should have plenty so you can give your boss his cut."

Before I could say no, Chance pulled off and started driving across the street towards my car. He parked on the other side of my car from where Dré was parked. Dré's tinted windows restricted my view from seeing what he was doing inside the car. As far as I knew, he was looking right back at me.

"Is that his car?" Chance asked.

"Yeah."

"I should've known."

"Well, I guess I'll see you. Thanks. I really had a good time." I leaned over and kissed him on the jaw. He didn't move. That was the first time all night that he didn't open a door for me. The tension was so thick I couldn't wait to get out of the car.

Lo and behold, as soon as I got out and closed the door, Dré stepped out of his car. He started walking towards me and said, "So when are clients allowed to drop you off at your car? Do I need to teach him how business goes around here?" He lifted his shirt above his waist to show his gun holster.

"No, Dré. He's cool. He just didn't want me standing out there by myself."

"Bitch, don't nobody care about yo hoe ass but me. Don't be stupid hoe! How much money you make me tonight? I hope it was worth you not answering my calls."

Chance must've heard the whole conversation between Dré and me because he jumped out the car so fast, and said, "Man, don't talk to her like that!"

"Oh, and it's this nigga from the other night? Why the fuck you still here? I know you ain't caught feelings for no hoe. You look like you're a lot classier than that, but I've been wrong before."

Chance tried his best to defend me, but there was nothing he could say. I tried to put him out of his misery and said, "Chance, just stop. You not about this life, boo. I told you. Just go home. I'll be fine."

Dré started laughing and said, "Are y'all serious right now? Y'all acting like a couple or some shit. What the hell goin' on? Dude, I know you ain't trying to cuff my main hoe. I'm fuckin' this one. She ain't goin' nowhere." Dré put his arm around me, and said, "Ain't that right bitch?"

Chance looked at me with a confused look on his face. I didn't want this to go any further with Chance. I just wanted him to forget about me, so I turned and looked at Dré and said, "That's right, love. I ain't going nowhere." I then tongued him down right in front of Chance.

"That's the way it is huh, Jordyn. I hear you loud and clear."

Chance slowly walked back to his car, got in, and sped off.

Dré pushed me from up off of him and said, "Now why the fuck you didn't answer the phone when I called?"

"I was working! What did you expect me to do? Stop in the middle of making our money?"

"Bitch, you betta not be playing no games with me."

I felt bad about what I had just done to Chance, but we barely even knew each other. It was better to do it now than later. I knew he'd probably forget I ever existed within a couple of days.

"I was craving some of that tonight, but I don't like leftovers. Go home and take your ass a shower. I smell that muthafucka all over you. I gotta stay here and wait for these other hoes to get back," Dré said irritably.

I could sense some jealousy coming from Dré's end. I was eating it up, too. After I gave Dré a thousand of the money

Chance had given me, he gave me my cut, which was a third. That was why I only reported a thousand to him and not the full fifteen hundred. Dré was like the goddamn IRS. As I was about to get in the car to go home, Dré said, "And you better answer the next time I call yo ass. I don't care what the fuck you doin'? Understand?"

"Yes, love," I said, right before I got in the car, drove off, and headed home.

CHAPTER NINE

Before I went to bed, I decided to take a nice, hot bath. To make the atmosphere more relaxing, I poured a glass of wine, lit a few candles, and turned on my Goapele CD. I brushed my hair up into a bun, and as I eased into the hot water, I inhaled, and then slowly exhaled. I loved my water hot, but it was always a struggle getting in.

I had a lot of thoughts roaming through my head that had no idea where to go. I kept hearing Chance telling me to know my worth. Our conversation kept replaying in my head. I kept trying to persuade myself that I knew my worth and he didn't know what he was talking about. I thought about the way Chance treated me just the couple of days we'd known each other versus the way Dré treated me, and we had known each other for a couple of years. You would think that I would've earned more respect by now, but what could I expect? I was his hoe. Truth was, I didn't have any self-worth or self-respect. I could thank my momma for that one, too. Everything negative that had ever happened in my life, my momma was the sole culprit. While soaking in the tub, my memories began to sneak back up on me.

I was sixteen years old. My momma's boyfriend, Lenzo, had been living with us the past few years. As a matter of fact, he had moved in a few days after my daddy's funeral. My momma had calmed down a little bit. As long as I stayed out of her way, she stayed out of mine. I had basically accepted the fact that she did her damage, and there was nothing that was going to change the fact that my daddy was gone forever. Resenting her and calling her out of her name every time she walked past me definitely wasn't helping the situation.

Surprisingly, Lenzo got in her ear too, basically telling her to take it easy on me, and of course she'd listen to her man before she listened to anyone else. What my momma didn't know was that Lenzo had his own ulterior motives. Lenzo and I had become very close over the past couple of years.

Without my daddy bringing home money to support us, we were broke. Obviously, my momma had given up all her men who were helping pay the bills to be with Lenzo. All Lenzo ever did were little handyman jobs that he would get paid fifty dollars here and there for. I didn't know what Lenzo did that was so different from her other men that made her drop everyone else, but whatever it was must've been good. The repercussion of that was that my momma was now working three jobs, so we actually didn't even see each other enough to argue. She was gone from four in the morning til nine most evenings, and she had been doing that for almost two years. I had no pity for her whatsoever.

About two months into Lenzo moving in, one morning, I jumped out of bed to get dressed for school. My momma, of course, was already at her first job of the day. Lenzo was never awake when I got up for school, so I didn't bother putting on clothes when I left my room. I didn't have anything he wasn't familiar with anyway. I walked out into the hall in my panties, and training bra, which I wore religiously, hoping that one day I'd magically wake up with a full set of titties. Evidently, that never happened.

I walked towards the bathroom, and I heard the floor creek like someone was walking around. Before I went into the bathroom, I cracked open my momma's bedroom door, just to find Lenzo's lazy ass knocked out, snoring loud as hell. I closed the door back, went in the bathroom, and the first thing I did was the thing I did every morning. I looked at myself in the mirror to see if my titties had grown any during the night.

My best friend, Asia, had huge titties to be thirteen. One minute her chest was flat as a board, then one Summer passed and she came back to school with "C" cups! She told me she took her mom's prenatal vitamins because they made her momma's titties grow, and they worked for her. She knew how obsessed I was to have titties, so we were experimenting on me, too. Days kept going by and nothing was happening. After another disappointing titty check, I washed my face, brushed my teeth, and took a piss. When I opened the door to leave the bathroom, I almost had a heart attack. Lenzo was standing there holding his erect dick. He pushed me to the side, pulled his dick out, and starting pissing. I stood there staring in amazement of how big it was.

Lenzo turned and looked at me, and said, "You like what you see?"

I rolled my eyes and started to walk out the door when Lenzo said, "I like your little panties."

When I looked back at him, he started laughing.

I walked up closer to him, as he continued to have his long early morning piss and said, "What's so funny, nigga?"

As he shook his dick right in my face, he said, "You funny. You got some issues. You know that? I kinda feel sorry for you, but you gon' be all right. Yo mammy ain't ever here to take care of us, so we gon' have to take care of each other."

He stuck his dick back in his boxers, then gently caressed my arm and said, "Is that cool with you?"

I was feeling something and I didn't know what it was til later on in life. A grown man had turned me on at the age of thirteen, and he happened to be my momma's boyfriend. I nodded my head and quickly walked to my room. That was when I first learned how to satisfy myself and I become very good at it.

By the time I was sixteen, Lenzo had taught me everything I needed to know about pleasing a man. Our relationship was our little secret, and it seemed like Lenzo was the only person in the world who understood me. All my momma would tell me was that I'd never be nothing and I'd never be wanted by anyone. There were so many times I almost threw it in her face and told her, "But your man wants me and can't get enough of me."

One day, I was laying at the bottom of my bed watching TV. Momma was at her second job, and Lenzo had gone out to get us something to eat, like he did most days, unless I cooked. When he got back he cracked my bedroom door open.

I looked back at him and said, "Hey, baby. You get the food?"

He pulled off his T-Shirt and threw it, and said, "Yeah, what you gon' do to pay for it?"

I started to get up and said, "Lenzo, I'm not in the mood for this right now. I'm hungry."

He then jumped on my back, holding me down and said, "What do you mean, you not in the mood? What, you been givin' it away to one of those little boys at your school? They ain't no man like me. You been showing them the tricks I taught you? I helped make you into the real woman you wanna be so badly!"

I tussled with Lenzo and he was just too strong. My body was too frail to fight him off. He pulled off my pants, bent me over, and forced himself inside of me. I remember the pain being so bad I screamed to the top of my lungs, but he kept going and I stopped fighting. I didn't know why he was doing this. He had never forced it before. I felt him grab hold of my ponytail and yanked my head back as he continued to get his pleasure out of my misery.

"What the fuck!!!" my momma yelled. That was the first time in years I was happy to hear my momma's voice.

In that moment, Lenzo stopped, but my momma had to pull him off of me. He quickly pulled his pants up. She then picked me up by my collar and said, "Jordyn! What the fuck do you think you doin'? Do you think you're supposed to have everything I have? It started off with your daddy! He always loved you more than he loved me. He would've done anything for you. I should've turned him in the first time I caught him fondling you when you were only two. I never got over that! I never loved your daddy the same after that! I didn't care how many times he apologized and said it would never happen again. He would always be a pervert in my eyes!"

As my momma was talking and crying at the same time, she shook me every time she tried to stress a point. I couldn't believe my ears. None of what she was saying could've been true. How could I not remember something like that? I would've remembered. She had to have been lying! She hated my daddy and wanted to destroy my memories of him, too.

My momma finally let go of me and continued. "Then when I finally almost came to terms with it happening the first time, I caught him again when you were five. I hated him! He made me feel less of a woman and took your innocence away. Now look at you! You take everything of mine! My clothes, my shoes, my jewelry, and now my man!"

At this point, Lenzo was sitting on the bed with his head down.

"Lenzo," she lowered her voice and said.

Lenzo didn't move.

"Lenzo!" she shouted.

Lenzo jumped.

"Look at me!" she demanded and then grabbed me once more. "Is this what you want? Tell me, is this really what you want, Lenzo? I've given you everything, just like I gave my husband. I give, give, and give, and people take, take, and take, but I never get anything back in return. Can anyone tell me why?"

I snatched away from her and sat on my knees on the floor crying, feeling lost and shameful. Feeling like I had been living a lie my entire life.

"What are you crying for?" my momma said. "You always get what you want. I should be the one crying!"

My momma sat on Lenzo's lap and softly said in a shaky voice, "What do you want?"

Lenzo, looking like the pathetic piece of shit that he was, looked at me, then at her, and said, "I want you. I'm sorry. I made a mistake. Please forgive me." He then kissed her like he hadn't just raped me.

That same day, my momma put me out at the age of sixteen, not caring where I ended up or what happened to me. She let Lenzo stay, and pretended like nothing ever happened. The only good thing that happened out of the entire incident was that I finally found out that my momma resented me because of something my daddy did. That still didn't give her any excuse for the way she treated me all those years. She allowed my daddy to do those things to me, even after she found out. I couldn't understand how any mother could allow their child to endure something like that over and over and not do anything about it. Then she allowed another man to get away with it and took him back.

I had no choice but to figure out how I was gonna survive out on the streets at sixteen years old without a momma or a daddy. I packed two bags of clothes and walked the streets for days. Luckily it was the warmest time of the year and I was able to sleep on the streets with no problem. I didn't have money to eat, so I would wait til after restaurants closed, and dig through their dumpsters and eat whatever half eaten food I could find. I went applying for jobs everyday, and was finally hired at a nearby grocery store called Crockett's Supermarket. I still didn't have a place to live, so in the mornings before the store opened, I would sneak in through the docking area and go in the bathroom to wash up and change clothes. I would also steal enough food for the rest of the day, put it in my bag, and would hide the bag outside where no one would see it until the end of my shift. I did the same thing everyday for a few months and no one ever knew. One day, I guess God just felt like I'd had enough, and while I was bagging groceries for a customer, I heard someone say my name.

"Jordyn? Is that you?"

I turned around to find that it was my Aunt Sandy, who I hadn't seen or talked to since my daddy's funeral. She ran over and gave me a big hug.

"How have you been?"

She looked at me, and I just shook my head with tears in my eyes.

"What's wrong, honey? Do you need something?"

The customer whose groceries I was bagging realized there was something serious going on and began bagging her own groceries.

"I'm homeless," I whispered.

"Homeless?!?!" Aunt Sandy exclaimed. "Didn't I tell you if you needed me to call me?"

"Yes, but I lost your number, and it's been so many years . . ."

"What time do you get off?"

"Nine," I said, trying to hold back more tears that were trying to come down.

"Ok. Well, I'll be back to get you and we're gonna get everything sorted out for you.

The rest of the day, I felt so much better knowing that I would be able to sleep indoors for the first time in over three months. I felt like Christmas was coming early.

I woke up in a panic with my head sinking beneath the water in the tub. I had fallen asleep in the tub while relaxing and trying to sort out my problems in my head. I got out of the tub, dried off, and went straight to my phone subconsciously hoping that I had a missed call from Chance. After reminiscing about everything I had gone through in my life, everything Chance was trying to tell me was confirmed. I was worth a lot more than I was giving myself credit for, and I didn't have a fucked up life because of me. I had a fucked up life because that's what was dealt to me. I just had to find a way to make it better, and with Chance on my side, I knew I would be able to make that happen. Hopefully he was would be willing to forgive me and give me another chance.

CHAPTER TEN

I called Chance the next morning, bright and early, hoping I caught him before he began his busy day. His cell phone rang a few times and went to voicemail.

I took a deep breath before speaking because I really hadn't rehearsed what I was going to say to him next time I spoke to him because I knew what I had done was fucked up.

"Ummm ... Hi ... Good morning, love. This is Jordyn. Of course you probably already knew that. I just wanted to tell you I am so sorry about how things went down last night. That was completely out of character for me. Dré just brings out this bad side in me, and I need someone around that's going to bring out the good. I need to talk to you about having you around more often. Call me soon."

After I hung up, I didn't know how to feel. I didn't want to sound thirsty, but I wanted him to know how I really felt. Chance seemed like a sensible man, so I thought he would give me another chance. He seemed like someone who would one day be able to accept me for me. It would probably take some time, but I believed it could happen.

After I called his cell, I got up enough courage to call his office. The phone rang four times, and as soon as I was about to hang up there was an answer.

A perky voice answered the line and said, "Robinson property investments. Selena speaking. How can I help you?"

Selena was one of the three receptionists sitting at the front desk. She was white, but brunette. She either had one of the best tans I had ever seen, or was blessed with the bronze in her skin tone that many paid a lot of money for. She also had the prettiest set of hazel bedroom eyes I had ever seen.

"Hi Selena. I was hoping to speak with Chance Robinson. Can you please connect me to him?"

"And may I ask who's speaking?"

"Sure. This is Jordyn Parker."

"Just one moment Ms. Parker. I'll see if Mr. Robinson is available."

As I patiently waited on hold, I listened to the company's marketing message, and realized Chance offered a variety of services. He managed, sold, rented, and bought properties. He also managed apartment complexes for owners who didn't have time to do so. From just that, I knew Chance had to have been close to a millionaire, if he wasn't already.

After holding for almost five minutes, Selena finally came back to the phone.

"I'm sorry for the leaving you on hold for so long, but Mr. Robinson is unavailable to talk right now. Can I take your number down and have him to call you back?"

"He already has my number. Just please tell him I called. It's very important that I talk to him."

"Will do!" Selena said, before anxiously hanging up the phone.

When I got to the strip that night, things just weren't the same. Peaches was no longer there. Peaches and I were the two who had been with Dré the longest. There were other girls before us, but they were long gone, so we had more seniority than anyone. There was a really high turnover rate in our line of business. For Dré to have gotten rid of one of us, I knew he wasn't playing. I still needed to get the full story of what happened from Lexi, who hadn't made it to work yet. I stood on one end of the strip, as far away from Dena as I could get, and Stasia walked the area between the two of us. I watched the cars go by, hoping I would spot Chance, but there was no sign of any Lambos or Maseratis. Knowing his stature, he probably owned several other vehicles.

None of us were getting any bites this particular evening, which I wasn't too unhappy about. Yeah, I needed the money, but I had other things on my mind. As soon as I started relaxing and leaned up against the vacant building behind me, a blue Corvette pulled up. There was a brotha inside. He was up in age. I would say he was probably in his mid to late fifties. All three of us looked his way, and of course, he pointed directly at me. I had never seen this man before. I had never even once before seen his car ride down the strip.

I strutted over to his car as if I was really interested, giving him my million-dollar smile. He smiled right back. I leaned into his window, letting my cleavage fully expose itself, so that I could get a better look at my first employer of the night. He had a caramel complexion, with a salt and pepper goatee. He also had short salt and pepper wavy hair that was neatly combed to the back. He was a very attractive older man.

"Hey, love. I'm Jay. What can I do for you tonight?"

"What's your price?"

"Five hundred gets you two hours of the works."

When Pop's eyes got big as saucers, I assumed the price was too steep for him, so I said, "Well, if you want the package right below . . . "

"Wait. What do you mean the package right below? The works is everything you have to offer, right?"

"Certainly is."

"Well that's what I want."

"That's what I like. A man who knows exactly what he wants!"

Pops unlocked the door and I stuck one leg in, then looked around once more to make sure Chance wasn't coming down the street. Disappointedly, I took a seat in the Corvette.

I looked over at the handsome old man, who probably had a wife at home and three grown kids. His wife was probably unable to fulfill his sexual appetite due to her going through the change and having a dry ass pussy that hurt the shit out of his dick each time she attempted to please him. The past couple of years, the only thing he had probably been getting was a blowjob here and there. Instead of waiting for his wife to get through her phase in life, or getting something to at least help keep her moist, he would prefer to go pick up a prostitute who's been with several men, and possibly take something back home to his wife. I had seen and heard it all, so just by looking at a man most of the time, I could tell what their story was. About ninety-nine percent of the time I was right. I guess if men didn't have problems with their sex lives, I wouldn't get paid. I was really starting to despise my job, but until I could come up with something better, I was going to stick with what I knew, and what I knew I was good at.

"What's your name?" I asked

"Eugene. What did you say yours was?"

"Jay."

Eugene glanced over at me as he drove and said, "Jay, huh? Nice to meet you."

I stared at him, waiting for him to say more; something to make me feel good, like when I told Chance my name was Jay, he asked what my real name was because he knew there had to be a beautiful name to go with such a gorgeous woman. I was now comparing everything and everyone to Chance, and there didn't seem to be any comparison.

"Eugene, I think you look like a Pops. Is it ok if I call you that?" I asked as I giggled.

"Eugene smiled and said, "Of course. That's fine. Actually, that's what my three kids call me."

I knew it! I thought to myself.

"And what does your wife call you?"

Pops' expression changed, and in a panicky voice asked, "How did you know I was married?"

"Don't worry. I don't know your wife. I've been doing this for a long time and I just know these things."

Pops wiped the beads of sweat off of his forehead that had suddenly appeared. He then said, "She calls me Gene."

Gene? Ugh! I thought to myself, but out loud I said, "Oh, that's nice."

We finally made it to a motel. I could tell Pops had never done this before, but he certainly had enough sense to go somewhere where we didn't have to go through a lobby, and we could just go directly to the room.

After parking, he told me he'd be right back and got out to go inside to get a key. While he was gone, I looked around. He had a fifty-dollar bill sitting in the center console, which is a definite no-no when you pick up strangers. Next, it was time for the ultimate test. I opened his glove compartment, and bingo. There was his piece. I took it out and opened the chamber. It was fully loaded. Pops had given me everything I needed to rob and kill his old ass. He better had been glad that he picked me up, and not some dishonest, deranged bitch.

Pops came back out, opened my door, and said, "Are you ready?"

I got out of the car, and said, "Yes, but I should ask are you ready?"

He nodded his head and said, "Yep," and led the way towards the room.

"Okaaaay. I'm not gonna take it easy on you either," I replied.

"Please don't. I want my money's worth. By the way, thanks for not taking my money out of the console. At least I know you're not a thief." He then turned back to look at me and winked.

Maybe he wasn't as dumb as I thought. He was testing me, but if he was testing me by leaving that gun in the glove compartment, that was a risky test.

When we finally walked in the room, I said, "Get comfortable."

I took my purse in the bathroom that contained all of my nightly essentials. I undressed, leaving only my royal blue and green lace Victoria's Secret panty and bra set on. When I came out of the bathroom, Pops was laying on his back with a pillow propping up his head. He was wearing leopard briefs, which I found to be cute, and which also told me he was on a mission when he left the house and knew exactly what he was going to do. He was in pretty good shape for his age. He just had a small beer belly, which I could work with. I turned him over on his stomach, and opened my bottle of warming oil. He seemed a little tense so I told him to relax.

"Momma's gonna take good care of you," I said in a soothing tone.

I poured some oil into the palm of my hand, briskly rubbed it in, and put my hand close to my mouth, slowly blowing air into my hand to warm it up. I then started at Pop's shoulder blades with a deep tissue massage. I moved slowly all the way down to his ass, putting more and more oil into my hands, warming it. I scooted my way up his body and straddled his back, and began gently kissing his neck. He moaned . . . A lot! I rubbed a little of my magic oil on his neck, put my lips close, and slowly blew. I turned him over and immediately noticed that Pops had no type of erectile dysfunction whatsoever! Mrs. Pops, whoever she may have been, was a very lucky woman because his dick was one of the fattest, longest dicks I had seen in a very long time! I was asking him was he ready, when I should've been making sure I was.

I rubbed oil all over is chest, teased his dick with the tip of my tongue, and continued down to his feet. I got down on the floor on my knees and massaged his feet. I then quickly got up and went to the bathroom to get my blindfold I had forgotten.

When I returned, I asked, "Pops, do you like being blindfolded?"

"Do whatever you want," he said with a smile on his face.

My clients always liked that. Before I blindfolded him, I unclamped my bra. I climbed on top of him, until I was high enough to get the blindfold on. I then slipped my panties off, and grabbed one of my Magnums for this one! I gently caressed Pop's dick, slid the rubber on, and rolled it down. For a better experience, I lubricated the rubber with a little of my warming sensation KY Jelly. As soon as I sat down on his dick, he reached out and grabbed my voluptuous titties, and we both moaned together. I moved up and down four to five times and that was it for Pops. He came so hard, he squeezed my nipples to the point I thought they were going to fall off in his hands. He shook like an earthquake. It lasted a long time, which told me it had been a long time since he'd had the opportunity.

While he calmed down, I went into the bathroom, freshened up, and dressed. Went I came back out, Pops was still lying there with his blindfold on.

I rubbed my hand across his chest and said, "Pops. Are you ok?"

He then started snoring. "Shit!" I said.

"Pops!" I said as I shook him. "Wake up! We can't stay here all night! You have to go home to your wife."

As soon as I said "wife", Pops jumped and started moving his head all around.

"Wait, let me help you," I said, as I removed the blindfold.

"That was great, Jay."

"I'm glad you enjoyed. I had more in store, but you were a little too quick for me," I said, and giggled.

"I know. I was anxious and it's been a while."

Pops looked like he was fulfilled physically, but not so much mentally. I hated to see when men had regrets. They would never say it, but you could always tell by the look on their face.

"Let me ask you something. Have you ever cheated on your wife?"

Pops looked at me, then stood up, grabbed his clothes, and walked to the bathroom to clean himself up. He shut the door without answering my question. That's when I knew the answer. I felt bad for the poor man. I dealt with men all the time that cheated on their wives, but they did it on a regular basis. I had never had a client where I was their first!

When Pops came back out of the bathroom, he was fully dressed. We both put on our shoes, grabbed out belongings, and left. On the way back to the strip, I asked Pops how long he had been married.

He hesitated, but then said, "Thirty years."

"Wow," I said in amazement.

The rest of the ride was silent. Pops didn't even turn on the radio. I wondered what was going through his mind. When we finally pulled up to the same spot where he had picked me up, he pulled out his wallet, and handed me ten crisp one hundred dollar bills.

I wrinkled up my forehead and said, "I told you it was five hundred, not a thousand."

Pops looked me directly in my eyes and said, "I know, but I'm hoping the extra five hundred will keep you from having to do this at least a couple of days to give you time to think about your life and do something better for yourself."

What Pops had just said was almost the same exact thing Chance said, but when Chance said it, I got defensive. I didn't feel defensive when it came out of Pop's mouth. I listened, and heard it as coming as words of wisdom from a father to a child.

"Well, thank you, and I'm working on a change, but I want you to promise me something."

"What's that?"

"Please never do this again. You went thirty whole years without cheating on your wife. This was so unnecessary!"

"Believe me! It will never happen again! I enjoyed you, but now I feel like a piece of shit. I had sex with someone and I don't even know her real first name. What is your name because I know a pretty girl like you name isn't just Jay."

That brought a smile to my face. He actually wanted to know my name.

"My name is Jordyn," I replied, with a small tear welling up in my eye.

"Thank you, Jordyn. It was nice meeting you."

"Nice meeting you too . . . Eugene."

I smiled as I got out of the car and watched Eugene as he drove off, on his way back to his wife of thirty years.

CHAPTER ELEVEN

I didn't receive a call back from Chance that day, the next day, the next week, or the week after that. I tried calling Chance for weeks after I'd finally realized that I was so much better than the lifestyle I had been living for the past couple of years. Every time I would call his cell, it would go straight voicemail, so I knew that he was either pressing "ignore" or had blocked my calls. Even when I tried calling his office, one of the girls at the desk would pick up, and once I told them who I was, they would tell me he was either in a meeting or out of the office. I figured he had told them to say that, so once I tried to disguise my voice and say I was someone else. I just made up a name, but obviously they were smarter than that and knew it was me. I was once again told Chance wasn't in the office. I left fifty million messages on his voicemail, and finally gave up. I was tired of making myself look and feel desperate. If he wanted to talk to me, he knew where to find me. Then again, when he was ready to talk, maybe I wouldn't want to talk to him anymore.

In the meantime, Dré and I were still fucking. I would say making love, but it was nowhere near that. It was always in the car, and he never tried to come to my place to hang out. He never even wanted to take me out anywhere, but wanted me to give it up any and every time he asked for it. He was obsessed with it, but didn't want anything else that had to do with me. With that being said, all I could call it was pull unadulterated fucking! On Dré's part, there was no love or any other type of emotion except what he felt when he came inside of me each time and he screamed my name. Seeing where this was going, which seemed to be nowhere, I kept my guards up and worked hard not to get myself caught up in my feelings.

Weeks had gone by, and still no one had seen or heard from Lexi. I was a little worried, but I knew she had done this once before when she thought she'd try out a real nine to five at a doctor's office. She did that for about a month, and realized two of those paychecks equaled less than one night on this job and she came running back. Stasia, Dena, who I was now getting along with for the time being, and I had a bet going of when Lexi would come running back. I said it would be a week. The other two said a few days. We joked about where she had probably gone to work this time.

One night, Dena said, "Let's go to McDonald's y'all! Lexi's probably working the drive-thru. Maybe we can get some free fries!"

Stasia and I laughed hysterically. With it only being a few of us girls working the corner, it seemed to be so much more peaceful. It's not like Lexi and Peaches were causing any problems. It was always Dena for the most part, but now she was cool. Maybe she was just the type that couldn't deal with being around too many women at a time.

One long night after having four clients, I didn't get home til almost eight in the morning. I felt so filthy, I soaked in the tub for an hour. Then, after that I stayed in the shower for a half hour. I thought about leaving the business every single day, but where would I go? To McDonald's? Burger King? A doctor's office? Oh, or maybe I could work at a department store! No, no, no, and no! I wouldn't make a quarter of the money I was making now doing any of those jobs no matter how many hours I worked.

After I finished scrubbing til I couldn't scrub anymore, I made some bacon, eggs, and toast, put it on a tray, and went into my room to have breakfast in bed. I turned on my sixty-inch flat screen that I had on my wall directly across from my bed and proceeded to eat my delicious breakfast. My TV was on the Channel 7 news, which I never watched because I really didn't have the desire to keep up with current events, and the news was always so depressing, but I gave it a shot. I knew I was going straight to sleep once I finished my breakfast, so whatever was on the television didn't matter anyway.

"In other news, the body of a young woman was found in a dumpster in an alley outside of a local restaurant late last night. The owner of El Rios Restaurant and grill reported that one of his night employees went out to the dumpster at the close of business to get rid of the trash. To his surprise, when he opened the dumpster, the slain woman's naked body was the first thing he saw," the news reporter stated.

I continued to eat my breakfast, shaking my head, thinking to myself, *This is exactly why I don't watch this bullshit. There's always bad news and never anything positive going on around these parts."*

"There was no identification found on the body, which was brutally mutilated. Detective George Hansel of the NYPD homicide unit has confirmed that the woman looks to be in her early to mid twenties, thin, and has a zodiac sign tattooed over her left shoulder."

As soon as I heard the description of the Jane Doe, my heart dropped, and my mouth almost hit the floor. My entire body went numb as I listened to the rest of what the reporter had to say.

"If anyone has any information about this horrific crime, please contact the NYPD homicide hotline at 1-800-187-NYPD."

I flipped my entire tray onto the floor, food and all, as I jumped up out of the bed to find my phone. I found my purse in the living room, and frantically dug through it, trying to feel for my phone. After having no success, I dumped my entire purse out on the floor. I rummaged through everything on the floor until I recovered my phone within the mess. My hand was shaking so badly, I kept hitting the wrong buttons so I had to keep redialing the number until I got it right. When I finally got it right, I paced the floor while waiting for an answer on the other end.

"Yeah," Dré said when he answered.

"Dré! It's Lexi! Sh-sh-she's gone!"

Dré raised his voice and said, "Calm down girl! What you mean she gone? Gone where?"

I began crying hysterically, unable to hardly speak.

"Jay!"

I kept crying as Dré continued to forcefully say my name.

"Jordyn! You need to stop crying so I can understand what the fuck you're talking about!"

I tried my best to calm down. I stopped crying, but my bottom lip continued to quiver. I took a deep breath before I tried to talk again.

"Now what the fuck you cryin' and shit for? If that hoe left town, that's aight.

She wasn't makin' that much money for me anyway. Her ass didn't even pay me for the last night she was out on my corner, and y'all wasn't all that cool, right?" Dré said, nonchalantly.

"Shut the fuck up, Dré!" I shouted.

There was complete silence in the phone, and when I regained my composure, I calmly said, "Lexi is dead."

"What? How you know?"

"It was just on the news. They found a body in a dumpster behind El Rio."

"Ok? They find dead bodies around here all the time! You calling me crying and shit over an assumption you made?"

"If your ass would shut up and listen, you'd know I wasn't making an assumption! It was a thin woman in her twenties with a zodiac tattoo over her shoulder! It's her, Dré! It's not a coincidence that we haven't seen her in over three weeks!"

Dré continued to be in denial about the entire situation. I didn't know if he just didn't want me to freak out and end up talking to the police, which in turn could've ended up getting him in a lot of trouble, or if he just really didn't believe it was Lexi. Dré had already been locked up a few times. Once for possession of illegal narcotics, once for attempted murder, and another time for rape, which he continues to deny. Each time, his lawyer, who charged an arm and a leg, ended up getting his sentences reduced. After the third time in jail Dré vowed to never go back. That's when he started his little prostitution ring. He always told me this business allowed him to lay low while he still got paid an amount of money he was still comfortable with. He still did other things on the side, like sold weed, but I think he smoked more than he actually sold.

"Jay, that could still be anybody. Do you know how many skinny bitches there are with tattoos?"

Becoming frustrated with Dré's chauvinistic attitude, I exhaled, and said, "You know what? I see I'm not gonna get anywhere with you because I see you don't give a fuck. I would hate to see if it were me they found! Would you even care then?"

Without giving Dré a chance to respond, I continued and said, "Hell naw you wouldn't! Why did I even ask? I'm done with this conversation since you're not gonna do shit!"

Before hanging up, I heard Dré saying, "Jay, you betta not . . ."

After I ended that call, I rushed in my bedroom to throw on some clothes. Dré was blowing up my phone. At first he was calling. After I wouldn't answer, he kept texting me, telling me I better not go to the police, and if I did, I would regret it. I couldn't believe he had resorted to threatening me, but I knew he was worried. He didn't want to get caught up in no drama, but he was only thinking about his damn self, like always.

As soon as I finished getting dressed, I grabbed my purse and keys, and was out the door. As soon as pulled out of my parking space and sped around the apartment building to get out of the parking lot, Dré's Impala swerved in front of me, blocking me in. He looked at me through his driver's side window and shook his head. I looked around, trying to find a way that I could get around him without hitting his car, but there was absolutely no outlet. I sat there and locked my doors.

Dré got out of the car and walked up to my car door with the evilest, grimiest look on his face. He started banging on my window with his fist.

"Where the fuck you think you going bitch? Open this goddamn door!"

"No, Dré! Get the hell away from my car!"

Dré began looking around, then walked away. I saw him walking towards the other side of the building. I didn't know what he was doing, but I needed a way out. I thought about jumping out of the car and trying to make it back to the apartment building entrance on foot. I looked down at my feet, remembering that I had heels on.

All of a sudden, I saw Dré coming back. He had something in his hand, but he was too far away for me to tell what it was. As he got closer, I realized it was a brick, and before I knew it, he threw the brick right through the driver's side window. I ducked, so I avoided getting hit with the brick, but glass shattered all over me, and the inside of the car. As I held my arms over my head, Dré reached in and unlocked the door. He opened it, and grabbed me by my hair.

"Bitch, did you think I was playing with you? No one messes with my livelihood. Y'all know what the possibilities are when you get into this line of business."

Shaking and crying, I said, "I was just going to get something to eat."

"You must really think I'm crazy! You thought you was about to go open your mouth, and try to help somebody, but it's too late. You can't help her now, and now look at you. You're the one all helpless and shit, but you know what? It's kinda sexy. You den made my dick hard looking at your pathetic ass. I would make you suck my dick right now, but I don't want you to cut my shit up with all this glass and shit."

At that moment I feared for my life. That was the first time in my life I had ever felt that way. As many times as I had gotten into a stranger's car, I never felt as unsafe as I felt right then with the person who I felt had been taking care of me the past couple of years.

"Now, what you are gonna do right now is park your car, and go back in your apartment and relax. Everything will take care of itself. And just to make sure you do what I tell you to do, I'm gonna stay here and spend a little time with you. That's what you've been wanting anyway, right?"

I didn't respond, and Dré gripped my hair tighter and said, "I'm talking to you! Answer when I ask you a question."

"Right," I said in a shaky voice.

Dré released my hair, and shut my door. He walked back to his car and got in. He went in reverse to move out of my way so that I was no longer blocked in. I looked towards the exit of the parking lot, and looked at Dré, as he sat there waiting for my car to move. I hesitated because I seriously thought about speeding out of the parking lot, going straight to the police station, but I also thought about the fact that Dré always kept his gun on him, and right now, nothing was stopping him from killing my ass.

I put my car in drive, and slowly drove back to the other side of the building, and parked right back in the parking space I had just left. Dré followed right behind and parked right beside me. I took my time getting out of the car. Dré got out and stood right in front of my car with his arms out, holding a blunt, wondering what the hold up was. To be honest, I was sitting there contemplating about putting my car back in drive and running over his stupid ass, but I knew that would've just landed me in jail, which was the last place I wanted to be.

When I finally decided to get out of the car, Dré looked like he had calmed down a little bit. Before I began walking towards the apartment building, I gently brushed off my clothes and shook out my hair, trying my best not to cut myself from all the glass that had shattered all over me. I slowly, walked towards Dré, not knowing what to expect. He had become Dr. Jekyll and Mr. Hyde all of a sudden.

"Come on girl," he said in one of his more endearing tones, which made me think he was starting to regret what had just happened, and he definitely should have.

After I got close enough, he extended his hand out for me to hold. I looked at him and he winked at me. As crazy as it sounds, I gave him a side grin and grabbed his hand. We walked into the building together without saying a word to each other. As soon as I let us into my apartment, Dré made himself comfortable on my couch, putting one foot up on the coffee table.

"It's been a long time since I been over here. You got it lookin' nice. I guess this life's been good to you."

As I took off my shoes, I listened to Dré, wondering what was going through his mind, and finally got the courage to say, "Are you really gonna sit here and act as if you didn't just throw a goddamn brick through my car window, while I was right on the other side of it? You could've killed me!"

Dré's eyes became dark, and he said, "I know what the fuck I just did! I need your ass to know I'm not playing with you. This ain't no game. You know everything that goes along with this life. Everything is not always roses."

Dré was right about that. Everything wasn't roses, and poor Lexi had learned the hard way.

"Oh, and I wasn't trying to kill you. I knew your ass was smart enough to duck," Dré said, and snickered.

"Whatever," I said, and proceeded to my bedroom to get undressed. I closed and locked the door behind me. Next thing I knew, I could here the doorknob turning. Dré was trying to come in.

"What you doin' in there? You better not be in there doin' no slick shit."

"I'm not! Can a bitch take her clothes off to take a shower?" I asked sarcastically.

"Can a nigga see a bitch's beautiful body?"

I exhaled, and opened the door, wearing only my bra and panties. Dré was leaning on the wall on the other side of the door, smiling, looking high as hell.

"That's what I'm talking about, baby. You gon' give me some of that?"

"Are you serious? I don't have time for this," I said, as I walked past Dré, went into the bathroom, and slammed the door. I locked Dré out and jumped in the shower. I could hear Dré banging on the door, saying my name, but I just tried to tune him out. First, he wanted to hold me hostage, and on top of that, wanted me to be his sex slave? After everything he had done to me, I had no desire to be with him sexually, which was very rare. I can't even say it was rare. I always had some type of sexual desire for Dré, no matter what! I rinsed all the glass off my skin, and washed my hair. I lathered my entire body with my mango scented body wash, and stood right underneath the showerhead with my eyes closed allowing the water to wash away all my impurities.

When I finished, I opened the shower curtain, and to my surprise, Dré was standing there. I didn't know how he managed to get in, but he did. My eyes became so big, it felt like they were gonna pop out of my head. As soon as Dré looked at me from head to toe, before I could even step out of the shower, he attacked me.

"This is some bullshit! Who the fuck you think I am? Some punk ass muthafucka?" he said as he jumped on top of me, pushing me down onto the shower floor. I tried my best to get up and get him off me, but it was so slippery, my naked body just slid all over the place. As Dré punched and slapped me, I was finally able to get one of my legs loose and kick him in his nuts. I jumped up as fast as I could, still sliding, and ran into my room and locked the door. I could hear Dré still moaning from the kick that he endured. I had taken a self-defense and kickboxing class when I first started hooking so that I at least could protect myself if I needed to. Today was the first day I had to actually use my skills.

"Open this door. I ain't done with you!" Dré said from the other side of the door."

"Just leave, Dré!"

"I'm not leaving here until you get what you deserve, and right now you don't even deserve to live. You den committed the worse offense ever and think you gon' get away with it? Trust, you won't live to tell about it!"

Dré began ramming his shoulder into the door, and each time he did it, I could hear the wood of the door cracking, and the hinges loosening. With the last loud boom I heard, my bedroom door came crashing down onto the floor. By that time, I was standing there, still naked, with my nine that I kept underneath my mattress, pointing it directly at Dré.

"Get out Dré!" I shouted.

"You don't know what the fuck to do with that. Put it down!"

"I will shoot your ass dead right now! Just leave!

"Aight, I'm gon' leave, but you owe me some money."

"Money for what? I don't owe you shit!"

"Oh, how soon we forget. Remember the three g's I gave you the other night? Pay up!"

I grabbed my purse, while keeping my eyes and gun on Dré. If giving him the money back was going to keep him away from me and out of my life, then so be it. I found the bundle of money in one of my hidden side pockets and threw it at Dré causing it to fly all over the place.

"Here! Take it. I don't need your money."

Dré gave me another one of his evil looks and bent down to pick the thirty-hundred dollar bills up off the floor. I watched him closely, and as he was picking up the money, he tried to grab his gun from his holster hidden underneath his long t-shirt.

"Don't think about it! I will shoot your ass."

Dré moved his hand, and picked up the rest of the money. When he finished, he stood up and looked up at me, laughing.

"The more I look at you, the more this shit is funny. Jokes on me, huh? I guess I need to be more careful when I recruit hoes."

Dré turned around and walked towards the front door, and I followed close behind. As we walked through the living room, he knocked one of my crystal lamps off of my end table, shattering it.

"You dumb muthafucka. I hope you go to hell!"

"I'll see you there," he said, as he walked out the door.

Before I closed the door, Dré turned around and said, "Don't let me catch your bitch ass on the street, and I bet not hear of my name coming out of your mouth about nothin'."

After I slammed the door in his face, my naked body fell to the floor and I cried. I threw my gun, which didn't have any bullets in it, down on the floor. After that day, I made a promise to myself that I would actually buy bullets for my gun. I was just lucky that I didn't actually have to use it this time. My face throbbed from the multiple times Dré had hit me in it. I didn't have any bruising yet, but I laid in the bed with an icepack the rest of the day, watching the news for any more updates on the body who I just knew was Lexi, and praying that Dré didn't return for retaliation. I knew this was far from being over and I would probably have to watch my back for the rest of my life, or at least until someone killed Dré's ass because it was very likely to happen. If I didn't kill him, someone would.

CHAPTER TWELVE

The next morning, I woke up with a little bruising above one eye, which I easily covered with a little concealer. I had a couple of important errands I needed to run and I needed to make sure I looked good enough to eat. I wore one of my prettiest knee length summer dresses that was beautiful shades of blues and tan. I went against my norm, and instead of wearing pumps, I wore a pair of tan wedges, showing off my French manicure on my perfect toes. I pinned my hair up in a cute updo, with a side swept bang, and wore an earring, necklace, and bracelet set, that set off the entire look that I was going for, which was sophisticated, chic, and sexy.

I grabbed my broom, and before opening the door to my apartment, I looked through the peephole to make sure Dré or anyone else wasn't on the other side waiting to attack. I was so paranoid. I didn't know what Dré had up his sleeve, but I knew he had a plan. I opened the door, and put one foot outside and peeked around the corner, looking both ways. I then stepped completely out, closed the door, and quickly locked the top lock on the door, which I normally didn't do because I felt secure. Now I didn't feel so safe.

I crept down the stairs, and before walking out of the building, I looked both ways again, and briskly walked to my car. As I opened the driver's side door, more glass fell from the window. I took my broom and knocked down the rest of the glass that hadn't fallen, while constantly watching my back. I then swept the glass off of the seat onto the ground. I knew I was going to need to get my window fixed, but that was the last thing on my mind at the moment. For now, I had to save as much money as I could until I decided what was next for my life. Giving Dré that three thousand dollars back really hurt, but I knew it was something I had to do. I had more money, but that extra three thousand made my cushion a little better.

The drive to my first destination was nerve-wracking. At every red light and stop sign, I was looking around, making sure no one was trying to sneak up on me. It was even more unnerving knowing I couldn't even roll up my window to keep someone from grabbing me. Even while I was driving, I was looking through my rearview mirrors every five seconds.

I finally had pulled up at the New York Police Department, and I felt a little safer seeing all the police officers walking around the building. There were two officers standing next to a police car that was parked a few cars down from where I parked. As soon as I got out of my car and shut the door, I could hear their conversation pause, and felt their eyes begin to follow me. As I got closer, I heard one of them say, "Damn!" underneath his breath.

They were both very nice looking black men. They were both tall, but one of them had a caramel complexion, like me, with a goatee, and a muscular build. The other one really caught my eye because he looked like the actor, Brian White, and I was in love with him. His light skin, dark features, beautiful brown eyes, and sexy voice turned me on probably more than any other man I'd only ever seen on TV. I never had a preference between dark, light, white, Hispanic, or even Chinese men. A man was a man, and if he was sexy, he was just sexy, no matter what color or nationality he was.

As I walked past the two officers, I saw the caramel officer nudge Brian White's twin. He then stepped in front of me and said, "Hi. I'm Detective Brian Washington." He held his hand out for me to shake, and continued, "And you are?"

"Jordyn Parker," I said with a sincere smile on my face. I was smiling because it was such a coincidence that this man looked so much like Brian White, and his name was actually Brian. I shook his hand as Brian continued to run his game.

"I couldn't help but notice how beautiful you are. You're stunning."

I put my head down, blushed, and said, "Thank you."

I then heard Brian's friend clear his throat.

Brian said, "Oh, I'm sorry. This is Officer Derek Miles. He's a good friend of mine. We were partners for three years until I became a detective."

Derek extended his hand out and said, "Nice to meet you."

"You as well," I replied.

"Well, we don't want to stop you from doing what you came to do. You're at the police station, so I'm sure whatever you came to do is extremely important," Brian said with a smile.

"Ok. Well, it was really nice meeting the both of you." As I began slowly walking away, I could hear them whispering amongst each other.

Derek said in a louder whisper, "Do it!"

"Um, Jordyn?" Brian said.

I stopped in my tracks and slowly turned around, knowing exactly what he wanted. "Yes?"

"I was just thinking . . . uh . . ."

"Let me interrupt, because this doesn't seem to be going too well for my boy. It's just that he hasn't run into a woman as beautiful as you in a long time. He's not quite sure how to approach you," Derek explained.

Brian seemed to become a little embarrassed and looked at Derek. "I got this bro. I know how to approach a lady. Maybe you've forgotten because you've been in a common law marriage for about a hundred years, but I'm good," he said laughing.

"Derek put his hands up, and said, "Ok bro! Sorry. It just seemed like you needed a little assistance. You know I'm always here to help!"

I stood there laughing at the two who seemed to have a brotherly type of relationship.

Brian then turned to me and said, "Sorry I was so rudely interrupted by that know it all over there who doesn't know much of nothin', but as I was saying, maybe we can go out sometime. Just to hang out."

"Maybe we can," I said in a seductive tone.

Brian gave me his card, which showed he was a homicide detective. I knew he had to have all of the inside scoop about the body they found, but I didn't want to come out and ask him about it. I didn't want him to know what type of life I was involved in, especially since I had just met him. I didn't want to mess this up just in case it could've possibly led to something promising. I gave him my number and headed into the building to take care of some real business.

After I walked into the station, I suddenly felt an uneasiness come over me. I didn't know if I really wanted to do this anymore. I walked straight up to the window and told the heavy-set white woman wearing a police uniform that I needed to speak with someone regarding a crime.

"That's why everyone else is here too," she said sarcastically. She slid a form from underneath the glass and said, "Have a seat, fill this out, and bring it back when you're done." She looked around me and said in a much more comforting tone than she had used with me, "How may I help you today, ma'am?" to the elderly woman that was standing behind me.

I looked at the female officer, rolled my eyes, and went and had a seat as I was told. As I looked over the form, it asked basic information as if this was any other crime. There had to be something that could be done. As I proceeded with filling out the form, I heard the fat officer say, "Hey trouble," from the other side of the window. I looked back to see who she was talking to, and it was Brian. *He sure did seem to brighten up her day.* I thought. I could tell her fat ass liked her some dark meat.

"Hey Bon-Bon. What's up?"

Trouble? Bon-Bon? What? They had nicknames for each other? I thought. I sat there, not saying a word, and continued to attempt to fill out that stupid ass form. I couldn't help myself from continuously glancing up, looking at Brian, whose back was facing me. I couldn't help but notice how nice his ass looked in those uniform pants.

"Busy in here today, huh?" he said to "Bon-Bon".

"Yeah, same ole, same ole. You know how it is."

Brian turned around and said, "Hey, Jordyn, I didn't even notice you sitting there. Is Bonnie taking good care of you?"

Bonnie looked at me sternly, telling me with her eyes that if I said "no", she was gonna jump through that window and attack my ass.

I hesitated, and said, "Yeah, but I really don't see how filling out this form is going to help in any way."

I knew Brian was about to start asking more questions, which I really didn't feel like answering, but with him being a homicide detective, he would find out one way or another.

"So, what are you here for? I just assumed you were here to pay a ticket or something. You don't look like anyone that would be in any more trouble than a speeding ticket or two, however looks can be deceiving," he said, and smiled.

I smiled back at him, and asked, "Can I talk to you in private?"

"Yeah, no problem. We can go back to the interrogation room. No one should be in there right now." Brian looked over at Big Bertha and said, "I'm taking this one back with me." She nodded her head, and continued her job of handing out forms.

Brian took me to a room surrounded by windows. You could see inside of the room from the outside, but couldn't see anything through the windows from the inside. This felt a little too official to me and made me even more nervous. Brian told me to have a seat at the table in the room, and he sat directly across from me. There was a tape recorder in the middle of us.

"Ummm, this isn't being recorded or anything, is it?"

Brian laughed and said, "Noooo. This is all off the record. I would've taken you to my office, but there's not much privacy there; Just a bunch of cubicles. I know you said you wanted to talk in private."

"Yes. I did say that. Didn't I?" I said as I looked around the room, still not feeling very comfortable.

Brian stared at me waiting on me to begin. I stared back at his beautiful smooth skin and intriguing eyes.

"Soooo?" he said, interrupting my moment.

"Right. I'm sorry." I took a deep breath before I started. "You know the Jane Doe you all found the other night in the dumpster?"

Brian sat up in his seat and squinted his eyes, curious as to what information I had. "Yes. That's my case. What do you know about it?"

"What information do you already have?" I asked inquisitively.

"That's confidential, but I can say, not much. No one has even identified the body, but if you know something, you need to tell me everything you do know. This was a brutal crime, and we need to find the person who did this before it happens to someone else."

"I think I know who she is." I stopped talking, looked down at the table and twiddled my thumbs.

"Ok. Who? Do you know her personally?"

"Yes."

"What's her name?"

"Lexi."

"Real name?"

"Alexia."

"Jordyn, this is like pulling teeth. Please just give me the information you have."

"Ok. Ok!" I said.

Brian pulled his notepad and pen out of his jacket pocket, and waited for me to continue.

"Her name is Alexia Caldren. We call . . . Excuse me . . . Called her Lexi." Tears formed in the corners of my eyes.

"Jordyn, don't jump to conclusions so fast. We don't know if the body we have is in fact her. Now who is "we"?"

"Her friends."

"How long has she been missing?"

"We didn't really know she was missing. She was . . . is known to disappear and go on different ventures, then pop up. We never really worried when she did. That's just her.

"What type of ventures, and what makes you think it's her?"

"She would go try different odd jobs here and there. She was still trying to find herself, basically. The zodiac sign on her shoulder that the news said she has. Is it the Capricorn sign?"

Brian looked up from his notepad with a look of confirmation on his face, and continued writing. He didn't even need to answer my question. I knew that it was.

"So, where is she currently working?"

Brian couldn't know the truth, so I said, "I'm not sure. She hadn't mentioned anything lately," I said.

Brian put his pen and notepad away and said, "Jordyn, I need you to come with me."

"What? Why?"

"I need someone to identify this body. You're the first person to step up to the plate. I need you to go down to the morgue with me."

"No, I can't! I gave you her name. Now, can't you check into it? Look at dental records? Check DNA? Something?"

"Look Jordyn, if this is your friend, don't you want to do her this favor? Help us with this case so her soul can be laid to rest. Please?"

Brian made me feel guilty and obligated to do as he asked. I couldn't resist him and tell him no. I didn't have it in me.

I stood up and said, "Ok. Let's go."

As we walked back out into the lobby, there were still a bunch of folks sitting around, filling out paperwork.

"I'll see you later, Bon-Bon!" Brian said, and put up the peace sign.

As we walked out into the parking lot, side by side, I asked, "What's up with her?"

"Who?" Brian asked.

"Bon-Bon, or whatever her name is."

Brian laughed hysterically and said, "You didn't let her intimidate you, did you? She's really a nice lady. She's just a little on the hard side, but she would do anything for almost anyone. She's just been through a lot. She was my first partner, until she witnessed a six-month old baby girl being shot to death by the dad when we were called on the scene of a domestic violence dispute. I was walking the baby's mom to my squad car while Bonnie was supposed to be getting the baby out of the house. The baby was in a walker, and as Bonnie walked towards her, the dad pulled a gun from out of nowhere and emptied the chamber on her. After that, Bonnie was never the same and couldn't handle the job. That's why she has a desk job. Before then, she was a very good cop. She taught me everything I know."

"Wow. You just never know what someone has gone through."

"You got that right." Brian walked over to his squad car that was parked right down from mine. I looked at it and looked at him.

"We're going in this?"

"Yeah. What did you think we were going in?"

"I thought maybe you had a civilian car."

"I do . . . At home. I drove this one in today," he said. "Now get in."

I sat in the passenger's seat. *At least he's not making me sit in the backseat.* I thought.

"This isn't so bad, now is it?" he asked.

"No, but I do kinda feel like a criminal."

"Nah! If you were a criminal, you'd be in handcuffs in the backseat, unless you were my woman, you'd be handcuffed in the backseat for a completely different reason," he said, and winked.

"Funny!" I replied.

The whole drive, Brian had me laughing. He had a great sense of humor. I knew he was just trying to calm me down and prepare me for what was to come, and he was good at his job. However, I had the feeling there would never be enough preparation for what I was about to endure.

We finally pulled up to the city morgue, and got out of the car. I looked around, still paranoid that I was being followed.

Brian began walking towards the building, and I stood there motionless, next to the car. Finally realizing I wasn't behind him, he turned around and said, "You coming?"

"Yeah."

He walked back to where I was, grabbed my hand, and led me to the big, thick steel doors.

When we walked in, the old white-haired man at the desk greeted us and said, "Hi Detective Washington. What can I do you for today?"

"I need to take this nice young lady back to possibly identify our Jane Doe."

"Nice young lady, indeed," the old man said. "But you forget pretty."

"Well, that's obvious, isn't it?" Brian said.

"Yes, it definitely is!" he said, and put a clipboard in front of us. "You know the routine Detective. Sign your life away!"

Brian signed his name, and handed me the pen to sign as well.

"Ok. Go on back," the old man said after I signed on the blank line.

Brian and I walked down a long narrow hallway, until we reached another set of large steel doors. There was a scanner at the door, where Brian swiped his badge. I heard a click, and Brian said, " You ready?"

"As ready as I'm going to be."

He opened the heavy door, and gestured for me to enter. As soon as I walked in, I encountered a dreadful odor that I could describe no other way except for the smell of death. I put my hand over my mouth and nose and looked at Brian.

"Oh, I forgot to warn you about the smell."

"You think?" I said sarcastically, with my hand still up to my face.

A blonde young woman with a white lab coat and gloves greeted us. Brian introduced us.

"Jordyn, this is the morgue technician, Jessica. Jessica, this is Jordyn."

Jessica said, "Hi, Jordyn! Nice to meet you. I would shake your hand, but I'm sure you wouldn't want to right now!" she giggled.

It seemed strange to me that neither Jessica nor Brian had a problem with the smell, but I figured they were just used to it.

"Who would you like to see today, Brian?"

"We need to see the Jane Doe that was found in the dumpster."

"Certainly. She's right over here."

We followed behind Jessica, walking past several other bodies covered with white sheets until we reached the other end of the room. Jessica stood in front of a wall that held several drawers that looked like they could be pulled out.

Jessica said, "Ok. Jordyn, I know you're probably not aware of what these are. These are cooling cells, which is where we put bodies so that they don't decompose as quickly."

I nodded my head.

"You ready?" she asked."

I looked over at Brian, and said, "Let's get this over with."

Jessica pulled out the drawer, and that's when I realized I was further away from ready than I thought.

I took my hands down away from my face and shouted, "Oh my God! Lexi!" I began crying uncontrollably. Brian grabbed me, and nodded his head, telling Jessica she could close the cooler.

As I heard her closing it, I said, "Wait a minute." I had noticed something else before I turned away. I regretfully looked at Lexi's frail body again and saw that in black marker there was a message written on Lexi's stomach. It read, "No one compares to Jay." I turned to Brian, and cried even harder, burying my head in his chest.

"Come on, Jordyn. Let's get out of here," Brian said softly.

"Thanks Jessica. See you soon."

"Anytime, Brian."

As we got back in the car, I continued to cry. I pulled down the visor and looked in the mirror at my bloodshot red eyes. Luckily I had worn waterproof eye makeup.

I could tell Brian felt bad and really didn't know what to do or say.

"Sorry I had to take you through that, but at least we know who she is now."

I fiddled through my purse, until I found tissue to wipe the never-ending tears from my eyes. I kept thinking about how I had forced Lexi to go with Rob that night so that I could leave with Chance. I couldn't believe Rob would do anything like that. He just didn't seem like a person who would murder someone. I was alone with him more times than I could count, and he seemed like he couldn't hurt a fly. I was at fault for all of this and there was no way I could say anything. I was hurting so bad inside, I felt like I was dying.

I was silent the entire way back to the station. Brian turned on some nice old school music to try and soften the atmosphere. He asked me a few questions, but I only answered him by either shaking or nodding my head. This had really opened my eyes to how dangerous my occupation really was. It's sad to say, but sometimes we don't realize things that could be hazardous to us until it's too late. It was too late for Lexi, but not for me. I was ready to change my life. I just had to figure out how to do it. God had been putting a lot of positive, legit people in my life lately. I guess He was using them to try to get his point across. I had never been the type to go to church, but I did indeed know, love, and fear God. First, there was Chance, who tried to tell me I could do better, and that I didn't belong in this life. Then there was Pops, or should I say Eugene, who wanted me to promise him I would quit. Now I meet Brian, who seems to be another nice guy who has my best interest at heart. It was definitely time for me to listen. Being a teenager, I had an excuse for being young and dumb, but now I had no excuses. After I had been through so much with my dysfunctional ass family, I wouldn't listen to anyone. Not even my Aunt Sandy.

After my Aunt Sandy ran into me while I was working at Crockett's Supermarket, I began living with her and her husband, Uncle Ricky. When I first got there, Aunt Sandy and Uncle Ricky accepted me for who I was. I think Aunt Sandy was just happy to have her brother's child around and know that I was safe. My life had never really been normal as a child. Not even when I thought it had been normal. After a while, Aunt Sandy expected way too much out of a child who had endured so much pain and neglect.

My daddy, who I loved so much, had overdosed on heroine and died, leaving me with my deranged mother, who was fucking everything with a dick. Then, I began an affair with Lenzo, my momma's boyfriend, who I thought loved me more than anything. He suddenly decides to rape me, yet and still, my momma chooses him over me, and on top of that I find out that my daddy sexually molested me. How can anyone expect a child to be normal after all of that? I always knew I was different, but I could always think of ways that I could've been worse off.

My Aunt Sandy always tried to drag me to church with her, but wanted me to change the way I dressed and wore my hair, and wanted me to stop wearing makeup. I told her I wasn't changing for anyone. I was who I was. She would then say I was being controlled by a demonic spirit that I needed deliverance from. After none of that would work, she finally let me be me, and if anyone had a problem with it, she did everything in her power to defend me. Uncle Ricky never had much to say about anything. He was laid back and took everything day by day.

Once Aunt Sandy and I got in a comfortable place with each other, I asked her why she was never a part of me and my parent's lives. She told me she was, and that she and my momma were very close at one time. She said they told each other everything and helped each other through a lot of hard times. The one thing that tore them apart was when my momma told Aunt Sandy about the first time my daddy molested me. Aunt Sandy said she couldn't believe it when my momma didn't do anything about it and she criticized her to the point that my momma shut her out. She said she was worried about me, and what was going on in our household, but my momma wouldn't let her see me anymore. She didn't want to go to the police because she didn't want me to end up lost in the system somewhere.

After Aunt Sandy told me the specifics of everything that happened before I was old enough to remember, things made a lot more sense. We got along for a while after that, until I started bringing men to her house, which she felt was unacceptable. I felt at eighteen, I was old enough to do what I wanted. I had started working at McDonald's, making a little more money than I was at the supermarket. I had even bought my own used car to get around in. One day my Aunt Sandy told me she couldn't bear to watch me continue to sin against God, and that I had to find a place of my own. I respected her for her beliefs, and was just glad that she didn't just throw me out on the street. She helped me find an apartment I could afford, and even helped me move. After that, I was basically on my own. Aunt Sandy would still check on me from time to time, and I would do the same. A few years later, the one and only person who really cared about me and my well-being, my beautiful Aunt Sandy, died of a heart attack. I still hadn't heard from my momma since the day she had put me out. I officially had no one.

Brian and I pulled back up to the station. As he put the car in park, he looked over at me as I blankly gazed through the windshield.

"Well, we're back."

I could hear Brian, but I didn't respond. It wasn't that I didn't want to. I just felt numb and couldn't. I continued to gaze.

"Are we gonna get out, or just sit here?" Brian asked. He then snapped his finger in my face and I blinked a couple of times.

"I'm so sorry. I'm just in another world."

"Don't apologize. I can just imagine what you're going through."

Brian was so sincere with his words. I wished I could've been more sincere with mine and told him the whole story about how Lexi and I really knew each other, and about the last time I had seen her.

We got out of the car and as I said goodbye, Brian said, "Call me."

I didn't know if I would for sure, but I said, "I will." As I walked to my car with the missing window, I thanked God it hadn't rained. I didn't know how my next planned errand was gonna pan out, but if I was serious about changing my life, I needed for it to go well.

CHAPTER THIRTEEN

W hen I pulled up in front of the tall building, I looked up towards the tenth floor, where I was hoping to find Chance. I was so eager to talk to Chance and tell him I was through with everything and wanted to see what our possibilities were that I ran through the parking lot in my wedges, all the way to the double glass doors. When I got to the elevator, I repeatedly pressed the button to go up until it finally opened, and I headed to the tenth floor.

I knew the girls at the front desk weren't going to make it easy for me to see Chance, but I had something for them. I wasn't surprised when as soon as I walked into Chance's lobby, Zahriah, the black receptionist, said, "I'm sorry. If you're here to see Mr. Robinson, he's not in the office at the moment."

I could tell she was lying by the insincere smile she gave me after she told that big ass lie. It pissed me off even more when I looked directly in the faces of the other two ladies, and they gave me that same fake smile.

I tapped on the desk and said, "Ok," and turned around, acting as if I was just going to walk away. To their surprise, I turned around and ran towards the back to where Chance's private office was located. The door was closed, but I didn't care. I could hear the three women yelling from behind me, telling me I couldn't go back there. They were getting closer, so I barged into Chance's office and slammed the door. When I turned around, all eyes were on me. Not only Chance, but also a round table full of other men and women were staring at me as if I had fallen from outer space.

The three women came in right after me.

Selena, the brunette, said, "Mr. Robinson, we are so sorry! We tried to stop her."

Chance was at the head of the table looking angrily at me. He stood up and said, "I'm so sorry for the interruption ladies and gentlemen. I'm sure there's a good explanation for these ladies barging into my very important meeting. If you all will please excuse me."

Everyone at the table nodded their heads, as Chance walked towards all four of us. The other three women briskly walked ahead of me, and Chance gripped me tightly by my arm. The other three looked at him fearfully.

"Get back to the front," he demanded of them, as he took me to one of the other offices and slammed the door. I hadn't seen such a serious side of Chance, and it was a little scary. What I can say was that he was a businessman and I guess he took his business and money seriously.

"Jordyn, what the hell do you think you're doing?" he yelled, folding his arms.

"You wouldn't take my calls, and I had to see you, so I thought this was the only way. I'm sorry for interrupting your meeting."

"What's so important that you needed to see me so badly? I haven't been answering your calls for a reason. Didn't you say you were happy with your life, and Dré? You shouldn't have anything to talk to me about."

I looked at Chance shamefully, and said, "I know what I said, and what I did, and I was wrong. I'm sorry. I need you." So much had happened, I just started rambling about everything. "Lexi was murdered and Dré jumped on me. I pulled a gun out on him and now he wants to kill me! I don't know what to do!"

"Whoa! Wait, wait. Slow down!" Chance said as he grabbed me by both shoulders. "Now what's this about Dré jumping on you? Did you go to the police?"

"No. I can't. He knows where I live. I'm already paranoid as hell."

"I have to wrap up this meeting. Stay here, and I'll be back when I'm done. We'll figure something out."

Chance kissed me on my forehead, and left out of the office, closing the door behind him. I felt bad for embarrassing him in front of his clients, or whoever he was having the meeting with. Whoever they were, they looked pretty important. A few minutes after Chance left, there was a knock on the door, then Heidi, the receptionist walked in with a glass of water.

"Hi," she said with a slight smile. "Chance told me you might want some water."

I could tell this was forced upon Heidi. It looked like it hurt her just to talk to me. She couldn't even look me in the eyes.

She looked down at the floor as she handed me the glass, and said, "He told me to tell you he'll be back in no more than ten minutes."

"Thank you," I said. As she turned around to walk back out, I said, "Heidi?"

"Yeah?"

"All those times I called, did Chance tell you ladies to tell me he wasn't available?"

"No comment," she said, without even looking at me, and continued to walk out.

I guess Chance had no intentions on ever seeing or talking to me again. Even though I knew that's what I actually deserved, it still hurt my feelings. It made me want to get up and walk out. I didn't want to impose on his generosity, if he really didn't want me around. I sat the glass of water down. There was no way I was drinking anything that someone who didn't care for me gave me. As soon as I grabbed my purse in an attempt to leave Chance's office without anyone noticing, Chance walked through the door.

"And where do you think you're going? Didn't I tell you to stay put?"

"I-I just didn't want to intrude, putting my problems on you."

"I told you I was going to take care of you, and that's what I'm gonna do. My word is bond."

Chance walked towards the burgundy sofa. "Come sit down," he said as he sat down and patted the seat next to him. I walked over and sat down.

"Now, I heard you say something about Lexi being dead. Who is Lexi?"

Tears welled up in my eyes once again, and I said, "She was one of the girls from the strip. The thin one, who I made go with my client, Rob, the night I left the strip with you. We never saw her again after that night, and now it's my fault that she's dead!"

"No, it's not your fault, sweetie. That could've happened with any car she got into that night. You just don't know, but you can't blame yourself."

At that moment, I had a revelation, which made me snap. I stood up in front of Chance and pointed my finger in his face. "You're absolutely right! It's your fault! If you'd never come down the strip that night, I wouldn't have coerced Lexi to go with Rob just so I could make you happy! Now she's dead because of your stupidity!"

"Wait! Now you're gonna try to blame me because your dangerous occupation lead to one of your co-workers being killed? If not her, it would've been you!"

"No, it wouldn't have! He wrote on her stomach that no one compares to me! He wanted me, and I denied him that! That's why he took it out on her!"

"Look, I'm not going to argue with you about this. All I know is if you're in danger, I want to make sure nothing happens to you. Now, why did Dré feel the need to jump on you?"

"He didn't want me to go to the police to give them any information about Lexi. He came to my place to try and stop me from going and held me hostage. I went and took a shower while he was there, and when he walked in on me as I was getting out of the shower . . . ummm . . . I don't know what made him snap, but he just attacked me in the shower."

"Just for no reason?"

"Yeah! I got away and pulled my gun out on him. That's the only way I got him to leave, but he said he wasn't done with me."

I went on to tell Chance how I went and identified Lexi's body, and how everything I had gone through that day had really opened my eyes to the fact that I needed to leave that life behind and start over new.

"I want to try to start over new with you," I said, and smiled.

Chance rubbed his head and said, "Let's take it one day at a time."

My smile disappeared from my face. Chance just didn't seem as anxious to be with me as he had before. He told me he wanted to take me somewhere and show me something. He went back to his office and grabbed his briefcase. As we walked out together, he told the girls at the desk to cancel the rest of his meetings for the day and that he'd be back tomorrow. I wish I could've taken a picture of the expression on all of their faces so that I could reference back to it and relive the moment whenever I felt like it just for a good laugh.

When we got outside, the sun was shining bright, and I remembered that I had left my sunglasses in my car. Since Chance parked in the parking lot reserved for the VIP's, which included him, he said he would drive me to my car. When we pulled up next to my car, he said, "It looks like you left your window down."

"No. I forgot to tell you. Dré busted out my window with a brick."

Chance shook his head, and I got out of the car to get my sunglasses. On our way to whatever Chance wanted to show me, I could see him continuously glancing over at me out of the corner of my eye.

"Even through everything you've been through, you're still gorgeous," he said.

I smiled and said, "How do you do that?"

"Do what?" he asked curiously.

"Always know the right thing to say to make a girl feel good.

"You're far from a girl," Chance said sarcastically.

"What do you mean by that? I'm all woman!"

"Exactly what I meant. There's nothing about you that says girl. You are a beautiful woman who's about to see what life is really about."

We pulled into the driveway of a stunning, two-story, tan colored brick house.

"Where are we?" I asked

"My house," Chance said, and got out of car and headed over to open my door. He grabbed my hand and lifted me up out of the car. We stood face to face and he gave me a cute little peck on the lips. I felt a warm sensation move through my body. I couldn't help but to show that I was blushing.

I walked behind chance and admired his nice ass as he walked up to the door and unlocked it. He pushed the door open and gestured for me to walk in.

"You have a beautiful home, Chance."

"Thanks, but not nearly as beautiful as you. Let me show you around."

Chance gave me a grand tour of his home. Every room was perfect, from the furniture to the décor. There was nothing out of place. Even though the house was flawless, for some reason, I imagined Chance's home to be like a mansion. I figured he was just a modest guy.

"So, do you love it?" Chance asked after we had visited each room his house.

"I more than love it. You have great taste to be a man."

"Of course I do. Look at you," Chance said and winked.

He wrapped his strong arms around my small waist, and gently forced me up against the living room wall.

"You just don't know what I have in store for you. I'm gonna give you everything you've ever deserved. You're giving up the only life that you know for me, so I'm going to make it worth your while."

Chance held me tighter, and kissed me passionately. I wrapped one leg around his muscular thighs, and pushed my pelvis closer to his abdomen. The heat between us was intense. I wrapped both my arms around his neck and pulled his face even closer to mine to let him know I didn't want him to stop. We ended up in the kitchen with me sitting on the granite countertop. Throughout the entire transition, our lips never parted. I felt Chance's bulge in his pants get harder and harder. I reached down and rubbed my hand up and down against the zipper of his pants, teasing myself with the thought of unzipping them and falling to my knees.

Chance suddenly stopped kissing me and removed my hand from his zipper. I looked at him with a confused expression on my face.

"I have a confession to make," Chance said.

I became worried and jumped down off of the counter. "I knew it was too good to be true."

"I see you have no faith in me," Chance said disappointedly. "Confessions aren't always bad."

"Then what?" I asked.

"I want you to live here."

"Huh? You want me to move in with you?"

"This is one of the properties I own, but I don't live here."

"I want you to have it. It'll still be in my company's name, and I'll pay all the bills. You won't have to worry about a thing."

"What's the catch?"

"What do you mean, what's the catch? Has anyone ever just been nice to you? I see you don't trust or believe in anyone. I'm going to have to work hard to change that."

"You barely know me. Why would you give me a house?"

"You need somewhere to go. You said you want to start over. Here's your start."

I was speechless. I didn't know what else to say. I stood in the middle of the kitchen, looking around in awe. *What on Earth did I do to deserve this?* I thought. Maybe God felt bad about everything I endured growing up, and felt like I needed something to show me there were still good people in the world.

"Well? Are you going to take me up on my offer? No strings attached."

"Oh my God. I don't know what to say, Chance. Honestly, no one has ever even come close to doing something this nice for me. Where have you been all my life?"

"I don't know, baby, but I'm here now."

I was ecstatic, but at the same time, worried. I worried about how long Chance would stick around after he got to really know me, and know everything about me. If he realized later that he wouldn't be able to accept everything about me, there was the chance that everything he's done for me could be pulled from right underneath me. I would just have to put my trust in him and take that chance.

"Thank you so much," I said, and hugged Chance.

"No problem, baby," he said and kissed me on the forehead. "Now we just have to get your belongings from you place."

"I'll work on getting a truck tomorrow. In the meantime, I'll go pack my things," I said, not knowing Chance had an entirely different plan.

"Negative. You're not going back over there. It's not safe. If not Dré, someone will be waiting for you. I'll arrange for my moving company to go by and pack your things up, and put your furniture in storage, since you obviously won't need it in your new fully furnished home," Chance said as he proudly grinned.

I really didn't like other people going through my things, so I said, "I can take care of myself. I'll be fine."

"Not gonna happen."

"Well, what about tonight? I need clothes to sleep in and change into tomorrow."

"We still have time to stop by the mall and pick up something, right?"

Chance's entire demeanor screamed perfect. Everything about him seemed so right, and I tried my best not to be pessimistic and wonder what was wrong with him. Chance handed me a key to my new home and I looked at him with appreciation in my eyes.

CHAPTER FOURTEEN

Late that night around the time I would normally be on the strip, Dré started blowing up my cell phone. I had no idea what he could've possibly been calling me about, until he sent me a text. It read, "Deceiving me was the worst thing you could've done. If you not scared you should be." Dré just wanted to continue to threaten me, but I was over him and the entire situation. What happened, happened, and it was over.

The next morning, I was awakened by the bright sun, beaming through the white curtains in my bedroom. I had almost forgotten where I was until I opened my eyes wide enough to look around the room. Suddenly I realized there was an arm around me. I rolled over to find Chance cuddled up behind me. I instantly sat up and pulled the covers back to give me a better idea of what had happened while I was asleep. I let out a sigh of relief when I saw that I still had my gown and panties on, and Chance had on boxers.

Chance opened his eyes and looked straight up me. "Good morning, baby. You ok?"

"Good morning, love. Yeah, I'm fine. I just thought that we had . . ."

"Nooo! I wouldn't do that to you without your knowledge. I wanna give us time to get to know each other better. Matter of fact, I don't want to be comparably close to any other man you've been with. I want to show you I can love you first. I want to earn your treasure, because that's exactly what it is. It's not meant to be given away to just anyone."

"You wake up spittin' game, huh?" I said, playfully.

Chance laughed and said, "No, I'm serious. I want you to know your worth."

"How long have you been here?"

Chanced looked over at the clock. It was eight o' clock. "I got here around six. I just wanted to cuddle up with you for a little while before I went into the office."

One thing Chance and I hadn't discussed was what I would now do for money. I had a savings stashed away, but I didn't want to have to go into that if I didn't have to. I had been saving up that money for a long time for something that was more important to me than anything else.

I eased into the subject of a job by saying, "I guess I need to start looking for a new career."

"There's no hurry, unless it'll just make you feel better. I got you."

"I have been on my own for a long time, and I appreciate everything you're doing for me, but I don't like depending on others. I've also been saving up for something I've wanted almost my entire life, and I don't want to diminish my savings by living off of it."

"Ok. That's understandable. But just know, anything you want, you can come to me and I'll see what I can do."

"Thanks, Chance."

"Now what type of experience and qualifications do you have?"

"The only legit jobs I've had were at Crockett's Supermarket and McDonald's. I was on my way into nursing school before I met Dré and dropped out of college. I did take a typing class. Not much, huh?"

"Can you cook?" Chance asked.

I looked at Chance thinking, *Are you serious? Does he really expect me to go be a chef somewhere?*

"I'm just asking because I'm pretty hungry, and I brought some groceries in with me this morning. Can a man get some breakfast?" he said humorously.

"I don't think that's too much to ask!" I jumped up out of bed and put on my new pink house shoes. Before I could head to the kitchen, Chance grabbed my arm, pulling me down towards him enough that he could just rise up, and gave me a warm, heartfelt kiss. I didn't know if I was dreaming or not, but I never wanted to wake up. I headed to the kitchen to cook my Chance some breakfast. It was so ironic that his name was Chance, because I truly felt like he was my second chance to make my life right.

As I mixed up my pancake batter, I could see Chance coming down the stairwell. As soon as I saw him I smiled, loving the fact that all that gorgeous body was mine. His chocolate skin had a glow to it, which defined his six pack, biceps, and triceps. His silk boxers allowed me to see his muscular thighs and calves. To make his body even more appealing, he was bow-legged, which was something I had never noticed while he was fully dressed.

He came straight into the kitchen and stood behind me, wrapping his arms around me and pressing his dick against my round ass.

"Don't start nothing you can't finish," I said, as I poured the batter onto the griddle.

"It's just so hard for me to resist you. I've never met a woman quite like you."

I felt his dick getting hard, and he let go of me and said, "Yeah, I better stop."

After breakfast, Chance got dressed for work. I asked him if I could ride with him so I could pick up my car from the parking lot where I had left it the day before. He told me not to worry and he'd take care of it, so I prepared myself to be stuck in the house all day. I figured I shouldn't have been out anyway, especially with the stuff that went down with Dré and me still being so fresh.

After hours of sitting at home bored, doing nothing but watching re-runs of "House of Payne", I felt the need to do something, and my something decided to call.

"Hello," I said, not knowing the number that showed up on my caller ID. I was a little leery of even answering, thinking it may have been Dré calling from a different number, but I took a chance. I knew Chance had several different lines in his office with different numbers, so it could've also been him. I refused to live in fear.

"I thought you were supposed to call me," the male voice on the other end said.

As soon as he said that, I knew it was Brian.

"Hey, hun. I've just been so busy."

"Oh yeah? Busy doing what?"

I knew that I hadn't been busy doing much of anything, but I had to come up with something so he wouldn't think I was trying to avoid him, which I actually was.

"Moving. I've been busy moving."

"I guess I'll forgive you then. Where'd you move to?"

"From the Bronx to the city."

"Oh. Moving on up! Living in the city is expensive. I know all about it!"

"Oh, you live in the city too?"

"I sure do, which makes things with us even better."

Us? I was thinking to myself.

"When am I gonna get to see you again?"

I wasn't prepared for this conversation at all. I didn't really think he would call me if I didn't call him. I had exchanged numbers with several men before and never spoke to them ever again. I was assuming this would be another one of those, but apparently, Brian had other things in mind.

I couldn't think of anything to tell Brian without possibly hurting his feelings, so I told him I don't know, which opened up another can of worms.

"Well, if you're not doing anything, how about right now? I'm off today and I can pick you up."

"Today's really not . . ."

"Wait," Brian interrupted. "Before you answer, please don't tell me no. I would really be disappointed."

Brian was putting pressure on me, and it was working. I looked at the time, and it was almost noon, which meant I had plenty of time before Chance would possibly be stopping by.

"Well . . ."

"Ok!" Brian said excitedly. "What's the address?"

After I gave Brian my address, which felt like a mistake after I did it, he said, "You really did move up! I know that neighborhood. All the ballers live over there."

Brian told me to dress comfortably and bring a bathing suit. I tried to get it out of him where we were going, and he just said he'd be to pick me up in about a half hour, which didn't give me much time to perfect my flaws, but I'd do what I could do. I was nervous, not to see Brian, but about Chance popping up unexpectedly. I felt what I was doing was foul, after everything Chance was doing for me, but I just wasn't in the business of hurting people's feelings. It wasn't like Brian and I were dating. I considered him a friend and no one ever told me I couldn't have friends. Chance and I hadn't made anything official.

After I finished preparing for my outing with Brian, and trying to make myself believe that there was nothing wrong with what I was doing, the doorbell rang. I looked through the peephole to make sure it was Brian. I opened the door, and the first thing I thought was, *When he told me to dress comfortably, he wasn't playing.* He wasn't dressed to impress, but he still looked. He had on a white Nike shirt with ripped off sleeves, which showed off his broad, muscular shoulders that were bronzed from the hot sun, black basketball shorts, showing off his tanned, hairy legs, and a pair of Jordan's.

His eyes were fixated on me through the storm door, and I playfully stuck my tongue out at him from the other side.

He smiled and said, "Are you gonna let me in, or do I have to stand out here and wait for you?"

I opened the storm door and let him in. I quickly stuck my head out the door to make sure there wasn't a police car parked in my driveway. I definitely wasn't going to hang out in the passenger seat of a cop car. Thankfully, I saw a black Cadillac Escalade. Immediately after I stuck my head back in, Brian hugged me tight.

"Girl, you feel so good."

"You smell great," I reciprocated.

After he let me go, he gazed into my eyes as if he was expecting a kiss, but I turned away and started grabbing my purse and other essentials.

"Am I dressed ok?" I asked, as I rubbed my hands down the front of my white shorts. I figured a cute tank, shorts, and my Converse's should've been perfect for wherever we were going from the looks of how he was dressed.

"Yes. You follow instructions very well, but where's your bathing suit?"

"Underneath my clothes."

"Ok. Just making sure."

As I walked around the house, making sure everything was in order before I left, Brian looked around in amazement.

"You really have a nice house. What do you do for a living if you don't mind me asking?"

"I'm in between jobs right now," I said, hoping Brian would just leave that conversation alone. "You ready to go?" I asked.

"Whenever you are."

I turned on the alarm and we headed out. One thing I noticed Brian didn't do, that Chance did every time we went somewhere was open the car door. Not even when I rode with him to the morgue the previous day in the police car, did he ever open the car door. That was already one strike against him, but he earned brownie points when Eric Benet came on the radio singing "Runnin'", and he started singing along with him.

"Wow, a cop who can sing! You have a great voice."

"Thanks. I'm a man of many talents," Brian said, and winked.

"Is that right?"

"Exactly right. I'm gonna make you fall in love with me."

"I'm not looking to fall in love."

"No one is ever looking to fall in love. It just sneaks up on us."

"I guess you may be right about that, but I'm only looking to be friends."

Brian's appearance of contentment became one of disappointment, and he said, "I guess I should stop saying things that may cause for a reply that I don't want to hear."

I didn't know what to say, so I just took a deep breath and exhaled. We pulled up at a park, where I could see the beautiful blue water from the beach in the near distance. He got out of the car, so I followed suit. He went to open the trunk and I thought he was maybe going to pull out a blanket and basket for a nice little picnic, but instead he pulled out a basketball and gym bag.

I had the most dumbfounded look on my face as I stood there holding my purse.

"You want to put that in here before I close it?" he asked, referring to my purse.

"Are you meeting some of your guys up here to get in a game of basketball?"

"No. I thought we'd play a couple of games."

I guess I better then," I said, and threw it in the back.

As I walked ahead of Brian, towards the basketball court, he slapped me on my ass.

I turned around and squinted my eyes at him.

"You know you like it," he said.

I really did, but that was more than he needed to know. As we approached the court, Brian stopped and put his basketball and bag down in the grass. He began stretching as I watched.

"You might wanna stretch with me. I don't wanna wear you out too bad."

I stood in front of Brian and he told me to just follow his lead. When we finished stretching, we started our first game. I gave Brian a run for his money, hitting four three pointers on his ass.

"Why didn't you tell me you knew how to play?" he asked, sounding winded.

I continued to dribble the ball in front of him as he attempted to play defense, and responded by saying, "You didn't ask." I then ran right around him and laid it up.

Brian, looking frustrated, decided to play dirty. He called a timeout and pulled off his torn shirt, exposing his tight abs, that were now glistening with sweat. I started laughing and shaking my head.

"What's so funny?" he asked as he pulled a bottled water from his bag. He opened it and took a sip. I stared as he licked the access water from his lips.

"You want some?" he asked.

I hesitated, and he said, "I don't have nothin'. I promise. I'm disease free."

I grabbed the bottle and took a sip. I then intentionally poured some down my neck and let it trickle down my chest. I handed the bottle back to Brian and pulled my top off, exposing my purple bikini top, which showed off my perky "D" cups. Brian stood there with his mouth open, unable to take his eyes off of me.

"I think that's enough basketball for today."

"Oh, are you forfeiting?" I asked.

"I think it's for the best!"

After basketball, we walked over to the beach and submerged our sweaty bodies into the beautiful water to cool ourselves. We then played like big kids. I was having the most fun that I'd ever had in my life. Once we had worn ourselves out, Brian pulled a beach towel from his bag and laid it in the sand. He laid on his back, and gestured for me to lay right beside him. We talked about everything. Well, I talked about as much as could. He did most of the talking, telling me about his childhood, which was pretty normal. He had a close-knit family. He grew up with both parents in the household. Both of his parents were both living and had just celebrated their thirty-five year wedding anniversary. He had one sister and a brother. Brian was the firstborn.

Brian asked me about my family history. I just told him I was the only child, my dad had died when I was young, and my mom and I didn't get along very well. I guess he could tell I really didn't want to talk about it, so he changed the subject and started asking about my career plans since I had told him I was in between jobs. I told him I had been thinking about going back to school to complete my nursing degree.

"Ok. Nurse Jordyn does have a nice ring to it. It's always good to be in a profession where you help people. It's very rewarding. My profession may not be as financially rewarding as I'd like it to be, but it's rewarding in other ways and I like what I do."

"It's always good to love what you do." I started thinking, I guess I could call what I was doing as helping others in a way, and it was very rewarding, but I never went home feeling good about what I had done.

"Yeah, I love helping victims by bringing people who've committed a criminal act against them to justice. By the way, we still have no leads for Lexi's murderer. I know we're having a good time and you really don't want to talk about this, but is there anything else you can tell me that might give me any type of idea who might've done this?"

I laid there still and quiet, contemplating on whether or not I should give Brian more information, or just leave everything as it was. I tried to think of a way to give him as much information as I could without making it seem like I was a prostitute right along with Lexi and the other girls. I was also worried about the police going down to the strip busting everyone down there. Dré would definitely know it was because of me. I decided to take that Chance. Lexi deserved for her killer to be brought to justice.

"If you don't want to talk about it right now, don't worry about it," Brian said, just as soon as I was about to start talking.

"Lexi was a prostitute," I admitted.

Brian sat up and asked, "Where?"

I hesitantly told him where our corner was located, removing myself from the equation. Brian then asked me if I knew who her pimp was, and I lied, telling him I didn't. I figured telling him where the corner was would be enough. If he was a good cop, he'd be able to figure out who her pimp was. I did, however, tell him that the last time I saw her, I had dropped her off on the strip, and she immediately got into a car with a man she called Rob who drove a black BMW. Brian asked for a description of Rob, and I described him to a tee. I could've also told Brian about Rob's heart-shaped birthmark on his inner-thigh if he wanted to know, too.

"Why didn't you give me this information sooner?" he asked.

"I'm sorry!" I said, as I began to cry. "I was so upset about what had happened, but at the same time, I didn't want to be involved."

"It's ok," Brian said, looking at me sympathetically. He laid back down on his back and said, "Come here."

"I'm right next to you. How much closer can I get?"

"Come here, girl!"

I sat up on my knees and leaned over him, looking him directly in his face, and said, "Yes?"

"You are so beautiful," he said and grabbed me by my arm, pulling me about an inch away from his face. With his eyes, he asked me if he could kiss me. My eyes answered back. I lowered my head as he raised his, and as our lips met, I could've sworn I heard fireworks. He lifted my body, and pulled it on top of his. As he squeezed my ass cheeks with both hands, I heard Chance's voice say, "I told you I was going to take care of you." As soon as I heard that, I jumped up and said, "I can't do this."

Brian sat up and said, "I'm sorry. I don't mean to move so fast, but you are irresistible."

"No, you're fine. It's just so much you don't know about me. I have so much going on in my life right now. I would love to be friends, though. You're a lot of fun."

"It's cool. I'm in no hurry. As long as I can see you, hanging out is enough for me. Ok?"

"Ok," I said.

Brian and I headed back to the car. He put his belongings back in the back of the truck and handed me my purse. When I sat down in the car, I pulled my phone out of my purse, which I had completely forgotten about. I had twenty missed calls and ten text messages. All of them were from Chance.

"Oh shit," I said out loud."

"Brian, pulling out of the parking lot, said, "Everything ok?"

"Yeah, everything's fine."

Everything was not fine. From the texts Chance had left, he was worried about me. All of them were basically asking me where I was and was I all right. The last one, which had only been sent thirty minutes earlier, said that he was at the house waiting for me and hopefully I'd show up soon or he was going to the police. What he didn't know was that I was already with the police. I definitely couldn't have Brian drop me off at home.

"Brian, you know that café around the corner from my house?"

"Yeah, you wanna stop and get something to eat?"

"No. I forgot I was supposed to meet my friend there at ..." I looked at the clock on his dashboard, which said it was four-fifteen, and continued by saying, "four-thirty."

"No problem."

When we finally reached the café, Brian pulled right in front, looking through the glass building.

"Do you see her? Is she here yet?"

"No, I don't see her, but I'm sure she'll be here in a minute."

"You want me to wait with you?"

"No, I'll be fine."

"Ok," Brian said. He reached over to give me a kiss, and I politely turned my head, so he'd kiss my cheek.

"Thanks for everything," I said.

"Talk to you later?"

"We'll see," I replied, teasingly.

Brian watched me as I walked into the café, and didn't pull off until after I had sat down. A waitress came over and asked me what I'd like, and I ordered a BLT to go. I knew I had to hurry and get back home before Chance started blowing things out of proportion, and going to the police.

The waitress finally came over with my bag, and I handed her a ten, which was the smallest bill I had and told her to keep the change. While walking home, I pulled a brush and ponytail holder out of my purse, and brushed my damp hair up into a ponytail. When I finally made it to my street, I saw the

Lamborghini sitting in the driveway, and the front door was wide open. I was surprised as worried as Chance seemed, he wasn't standing out on the porch.

I opened the storm door and walked him. I could hear Chance's dress shoes moving quickly across the hardwood floors. He came walking around the corner and said, "Jordyn! Where you been?"

I sat my purse and bag down and said, "I am so sorry! I stepped out with a girlfriend, and I left my phone in her car. I had no idea you had been calling me until a few minutes ago."

Chance went to the door and looked out. "Where's your friend?" he asked.

"Oh, we went to the café around the corner for some dessert, and I had this big piece of chocolate cake I wanted to walk off, so I told her to go ahead and I'd walk." I held the bag up and said in my cute innocent voice, "I bought you a BLT though, in case you haven't had lunch."

"Thanks, but I'm not hungry. I'm just glad you're ok. You know you shouldn't be walking these streets. Someone might see you."

"Stop being so protective. I can't live in fear, and I've been taking care of myself for a long time. Don't worry so much. I was right around the corner."

Chance gave me a hug and said, "I'm sorry, babe. I just want to keep up my end of the bargain and protect you."

"It's ok. I'm really sorry for not responding. I promise it won't happen again."

CHAPTER FIFTEEN

Chance didn't spend that night with me, but was sure to call me bright and early the next morning.

"Hello?" I said, with my eyes still closed, wondering who was calling me so early in the morning.

"Good morning, babe. You sound like you're still asleep."

"Um, maybe because I am," I said sarcastically, as I sat up in the bed and tried to clear my throat.

"Sorry for waking you, but I need you to take a ride with me real quick."

"Seriously? Right now?"

"Come on. You don't have to get fancy. I'll be there in about ten minutes."

Chance hung up, and I sighed as I stood up and stretched. I took a two-minute shower to wake myself up, and threw on a pair of jeans and a t-shirt. I pulled my hair up in a messy bun, and didn't even care to put on any make-up. As soon as I made it downstairs to make a quick cup of coffee, I heard Chance coming through the front door.

"Jordyn?" I heard him say as he walked through foyer.

"I'm in the kitchen, love."

I heard Chance's voice get closer, as he said, "I hope you're not making coffee."

He came around the corner just as I was about to put a scoop of fresh ground coffee in the coffeemaker.

"Caught you just in time," he said as he held up two Starbuck's cups. "Wow, you are a natural beauty."

I walked over to him, grabbed one of the cups out of his hand, and said, "Thank you, baby. You must've known I needed this. I gave him a hug and a peck on the lips.

"You ready?"

I slipped on a pair of flats I had at the front door, and said, "Where are we going? I hope I don't see anyone important!"

"You'll see when we get there, and why wouldn't you wanna see anyone important? They would just be in awe of how gorgeous you are. I wish I could pound into you head that you look great all the time. You are way better than you think you are."

During our ride, Chance played his new "Black Panties" CD, which was the last thing I needed to hear. I had been so horny the past few weeks, it was pathetic. I wanted Chance to fuck the shit out of me so bad, but at the same time, I didn't think I was prepared for him, and I knew for damn sure he wasn't ready for me.

"So, have you thought about what you want to do yet?" Chance asked as he squeezed my thigh."

I wasn't sure what Chance was referring to, so I asked, "What do you mean?"

"Work? School? Or are you content with doing whatever all day? I know you're a lot more ambitious than that. That's one thing I do know about you. I wish you would tell me more about yourself. You're such a mystery."

You don't even know the half of it. I thought.

"I actually really want to go back to school, but I don't want to live off of you. I need to be able to earn income at the same time." Chance was silent, so I glanced over at him and he looked like his mind was working a mile a minute.

"What are you thinking about?" I asked.

"I was thinking."

"I kinda figured that."

Chance smiled, and said, "Why don't you work for me? I'll make it so your hours will work around your school schedule."

"I'll still be living off of you, which defeats the purpose."

"But you'll be working for it, just as if you were working for someone else, right?"

I shrugged my shoulders, and said, "I just don't know about mixing business with pleasure. I know those kind of situations can sometimes get messy, but I'll definitely consider it."

When I said I knew those situations could get messy, I was referring to Dré and myself, and by the expression on Chance's face, I think he knew that.

"Ok, well just know the offer is out there and you think about it."

As we pulled up to a place called Phil's Auto Body, I said, "Something wrong with your car?"

"Nope. I have to pick something up. I'll be right back," he said as he got out of the car to go inside. While he was inside, I turned off "Black Panties", and turned to something more mellow that wouldn't make me more hot and bothered than I already was. As I was leaning back in my seat, with my eyes closed enjoying the smooth sound of Tweet's voice, singing, "Smoking Cigarettes, someone tapped on my window. I jumped, and opened my eyes, thinking Chance would be on the other side of the glass, but it was a thuggish lookin' dude that I didn't recognize.

I cracked the window just enough so I could hear what he was saying. I thought maybe he worked in the shop and Chance told him to get me.

"Yes?" I said.

"Hey, baby. I seen you sittin' over here and I couldn't help but to come over here and let you know you sexy as hell, but of course I know you probably know that. I know niggas always tryin' to holla at yo ass."

He smiled showing his raggedy ass teeth, and before I could say anything, I heard Chance say, "Hey man. Can I help you?"

Mister thugalicious turned around facing Chance and pointed in my direction saying, "Oh man. This yours?"

Chance looking infuriated, said, "Yes. She belongs to me!"

"Oh. My badd, man! I didn't know, but she fine as fuck though!" the disrespectful ass dude said as he walked away laughing.

Chance got back into the car, shaking his head. You trying to get you another man out here?"

"Are you serious? He just walked over here and started talking shit."

"And you just happened to roll down the window, huh? This is what I have to look forward to being with a woman like you, huh?"

I took offense to that comment. "What do you mean by "a woman like me"?" I asked, folding my arms.

"I don't mean it like you think." Chance licked his lips and put his hand between my thighs. He spoke both slowly and softly looking into my eyes as if he was hypnotizing me, as he said, "I meant a attractive, sexy, strong, intelligent woman like you."

"Ok," I said. "You better be careful with your words."

As we sat there, playfully exchanging words, I saw, what looked like my Jetta come from around the back of the building.

"That looks just like . . ."

"Your car?"

"Yeah. Wait . . . That is my car! Chance, you got my window fixed?"

"Yep, and got it detailed for you."

I appreciated what Chance had done, but I couldn't figure out how he managed to do all of that without my car key. I pulled my keys out of my purse, and noticed my car key wasn't on the ring like it normally was.

"You stole my key without me even noticing? You are so special."

"Now should I take offense to that?" Chance asked.

I laughed, and said, "Of course not!"

The mechanic got out of my car and gestured for one of us to come get it.

"Go ahead. I'm about to head to the office," Chance said.

I leaned over, grabbed Chance's chin, and gave him a kiss, sucking his bottom lip into my mouth."

"Mmmm," he said.

"You took the words right out of my mouth."

Before I got out of the car, Chance said, "Be careful and don't get lost today."

Chance and I went our separate ways. Now that I had my own transportation back, I couldn't think of anywhere to go. I was still paranoid, even though I knew better than to think Dré would be out that early in the morning. I decided to head back home to get some more rest and take some time to seriously think about Chance's offer. On my way home, Brian called me, but I didn't answer. I knew since he didn't call me after we left each other the day before, he would most definitely be calling today. Don't get me wrong, Brian was everything I looked for in a man, but I had to look at the bigger picture. I was with Chance, and he seemed to be willing to do any and everything to make me happy. I could only focus on one thing a time, and at the moment, I needed to put all my focus on Chance so that I could get him in a place where nothing would alter his feelings for me. I needed him to become so in love with me, that he would be blind to everything else. And I mean everything! That's when I would tell him everything about me, and hopefully by then he would have no other choice but accept me.

When I finally made it back home, I checked the message that Brian had left me. When the message began, I heard the wind blowing through the speaker of his phone, which told me, he was somewhere out driving.

"Hey, Jordyn. I have the morning off, so I was just trying to see if we could go to breakfast . . . Or maybe you could be my breakfast this morning before I go to work. I guess maybe you're still asleep. Hopefully you wake up soon. Call me as soon as you get this."

I was so tempted to call Brian after listening to his message. It made me think about us laying on the beach, but my own rendition of it played out with us being on the beach all alone making love in the sand. I would've loved to be his breakfast because Chance was taking this shit about wanting to love me before he made love to me way too serious. I appreciated him trying to be a gentleman, but for a girl who's used to getting it every night, suddenly going through a drought, was not a good feeling. I was starting to wonder if maybe he thought I had some type of STD. I was willing to take any test he wanted me to. All he had to do was ask. Maybe he was waiting on me to offer. Then again, maybe he was just really a gentleman and wanted to wait.

I knew I wouldn't last long just sitting around the house with so much time on my hands. An idle mind was a dangerous mind, so I knew I definitely needed to do something to keep my mind occupied. I got on the Internet and started looking online to see when the next semester of classes began at NYU. I also weighed all the pros and cons of working for Chance, and the only con I could think of was there was the possibility of us getting on each other's nerves from seeing each other too much. After thinking of all the pros, which included, being able to make my own money and continue to put some towards my savings, go to school and finish my prerequisite courses, then go to nursing school, I knew that they definitely outweighed my one con.

Brian continued to call the rest of the morning, but he didn't leave any other messages. He finally stopped during the early afternoon. I figured he must've had gone in to work. I didn't think that I had led Brian on. I told him I was only looking to be friends, but then again, what kind of friend was I being not answering his calls? He was a big boy, so he'd get over it. As fine as he was, he probably had women flocking from everywhere wanting to be with him. Especially with him being a man in uniform. Bitches loved that shit.

Chance called and checked on me a few times during the day. He flirted with me over the phone and me feel like no one had ever made me feel before. He made me feel safe and secure, like my daddy did before I found out about the fucked up shit he did to me. I tried to block it from my mind because every time I thought about it, my skin crawled and I felt like throwing and breaking something.

During one of my phone calls with Chance, I told him that we needed to talk, so he said he'd be over around seven.

"Why can't we go to your house this time? I'd love to see it," I said.

"One day. Not yet. I'm still getting it together. I can't let you outdo me!" he laughed.

I was so anxious to see Chance's house. By the looks of the house he was able to just let me live in, I knew his house had to have been amazing. I dedicated the rest of the day to preparing for my man after his long day at work. I ran down the street to Wal-Mart and grabbed some candles, bubble bath, rose petals, and baby oil. I also picked up some condoms in case Chance had a change of heart. I believed in the saying "The way to a man's heart is through his stomach", so after leaving Wal-Mart, I went to the grocery store and picked up a couple of Filet Mignons, baked potatoes, a bottle of white wine, and few other things to put together a romantic meal for just me and my boo.

When I returned back home, I first made sure the house was spotless, and then I put dinner on. While the steaks were in the oven, I prepared a tossed salad with vinaigrette dressing. I staged everything else perfectly to set the mood, putting two taper candles on the dining room table where we would eat, and vanilla cream scented votive candles around the tub. I ran a nice, hot bubble bath so that it would be the perfect temperature by the time we finished dinner. I sat the baby oil on my nightstand next to the bed, and placed the condoms inside of my top nightstand drawer. I placed the rose petals in a perfect heart shape on top of my purple, satin comforter. Once the house was to my liking, and dinner was almost ready, I freshened up and beautified myself for my soon to be lover. I put on my favorite long, silk, ivory gown that covered my breasts with only see-through lace. I had bought it almost a year ago, but never had anyone that I considered worth wearing it for.

I looked at the clock, and I had about fifteen minutes before Chance would be there. I threw on my robe that matched my sexy ensemble, and tied it to conceal the secret that I would hopefully be able to share later on that evening. I went to take the steaks and baked potatoes out of the oven and prepared our plates. Once the candles were lit, I dimmed the lights, turned on some Anthony Hamilton, and sat at the dining room table, waiting for Chance to arrive.

Just a few minutes later, I heard Chance as he put the key in the door and turned it. I put myself into the sexiest pose I could, as any other woman would. Before even entering the dining room, I heard Chance say, "Something sure does smell good. Where are you, sexy?"

I'm in here . . .waiting on you," I said in my most seductive voice.

Chance came walking around the corner in his lavender dress shirt and black slacks, looking delicious as always.

"Wow. All this for me?"

"Yes, all for you. You definitely deserve it."

Chance came over and lifted me up out of my chair, and whistled, as he looked me up and down. "You are too perfect. There has to be something wrong with you."

"I say the same about you," I said to Chance. "Go get comfortable while I pour us a glass of wine."

"Whatever you say," Chance said with a smile.

While Chance went up the stairs, I took out two wine glasses and poured some of the white wine I had bought earlier, hoping it was to Chance's liking. He was way up there in social class, so I knew he was probably used to the best, most expensive wines. I did what I could do and hopefully my best was good enough for him.

Chance quickly came back down in only a pair of boxers and his robe that he had left, which was open, exposing his beautiful, bare skin.

"You've really been busy today, huh? Rose petals everywhere! I must've really been on your mind today. What else have you done?"

I walked over to him, wrapped my arms around his neck and gave him a sensual kiss on the lips. I wanted to just give him a little taste of what was to come. As soon as I kissed him, I could feel his bulge coming to life beneath his boxers as I held him close, and he said, "Ok, baby. Let's eat before I end up having you for dinner."

"What's wrong with that? You just might enjoy me more than you're gonna enjoy this meal."

I could tell Chance was trying his best to keep his composure, so I decided to leave him alone. It was enough for me just to know I did turn him on, even though I should've known that already.

I pulled out Chance's chair and said, "Have a seat. Tonight is all about you."

Chance looked at me, trying to play it cool and hold back his smile, but I could tell he was enjoying it. He sat down in front of his plate and said, "Everything looks delicious. How did I get so lucky?" As Chance took a sip of his wine, my heart began beating rapidly. Out of everything else I had put together for the night, the wine was what I was most nervous about. I knew he would be able to tell that I only spent fifteen dollars on it, but it should've been the thought that counted.

"Good wine," he said. "You have very good taste."

"You like it? It's not very expensive."

"Jordyn, if you think I'm one of those rich, uptight people who turns my nose up at more reasonably priced things, know that I'm not. I don't let money make me. I'm the same person I was when I was broke, living in a one-bedroom apartment, and barely affording that. Do I now have better cars and homes? Yes, I do, only because I think I do deserve that with all of the hard work I've put in. I'm easy to please, love."

Chance, putting himself out there the way he did made me feel even more comfortable around him. I no longer felt like I needed to try to impress him with expensive things. The more and more I was around Chance, the more he proved to me that he accepted me for me, and the more he would learn about me hopefully wouldn't affect our relationship.

As we enjoyed our meal and the slow, sexy music that played in the backdrop, I decided to go ahead and tell Chance what I had decided.

"Chance, remember the discussion we had earlier and the offer you made me?"

"Yeah," Chance said, after he finished chewing a piece of moist steak he had in his mouth.

"Well, I've decided to accept, as long as you don't think this will negatively affect our relationship. I've already looked into the enrollment period for school. I really want to make something out of myself."

"That's great. I'm proud of you. I already started setting up your office."

I looked at Chance with an expression of bewilderment. "What?"

"I knew you would say yes. I wanted to get a head start on getting everything prepared, so I started today."

"Wow. You're used to never being turned down by women, I see."

"I just feel like you need me in your life just as much as I need you. You need to get back on your feet, and if someone is offering to help you, why not? I need your companionship and someone as beautiful as you on my arm. We complement each other."

"Ok, so when do I start?" I asked, accepting his explanation.

"You can start tomorrow if you want. I understand if you need a few more days to get situated around here, but . . ." Chance looked around the room and continued. "It looks like everything here is in its place."

"Yeah, I'm about done, so tomorrow it is."

Chance finished his meal before I did, and sat back in his chair, watching me as I ate. Once I was done, I led Chance upstairs to the bathroom, where I would get him completely undressed, and see that big bulge in person in person that I've been so curious about. The lights were dimmed, and the candles were still going, and had fragranced the entire bathroom with vanilla.

I walked behind Chance, and pulled his robe from off his shoulders, and slid it down until it was completely off. I kissed him in the center of his back, then placed both of my thumbs inside of his boxers and attempted to pull them down. Chance quickly grabbed my hands and turned towards me.

Before he could say anything, I said, "Relax. I know you
don't want to do anything yet . . ." I looked down at his erect
dick that was unfortunately still beneath his boxers, and said,
"Even though that's not what your body language is telling me
right now." Chance then looked down and gave me a side
smile. "I just wanna pamper you. Can I just do that to show my
appreciation?" I asked sincerely.

Chance took a deep breath and hesitated, then said, "I hope
you don't think I'm not attracted to you. I truly am, as you can
see. I've just had so many relationships go bad once sex was
involved and I always thought it was because I would have sex
prematurely, and if I would've waited until I loved that person,
things would've ended up differently. When you have sex with
a person and don't love them, that's all it is . . . sex. I don't want
it to be that way with you."

After that huge spill that Chance gave, I felt like I was
forcing Chance to do something against his will, so I said, "Ok. I
understand." As I picked up his robe and started to put it back
on him he said, "You give up so easily. I didn't say I wasn't
gonna let you run those soft hands all over my body. I just said
we weren't gonna have sex."

Chance pulled his arms back out of the robe, leaving it
hanging in my hands. He then slowly pulled his boxers down,
lifted each foot, one by one, pulled them off, and threw them to
the other side of the room. I stood there in awe, salivating at
the size of his woman pleaser.

I dropped to my knees, directly in front of Chance, and
stroked his dick slowly, with long strokes that corresponded
with its length. I put the head of his super-sized soldier in my
mouth, and licked it while looking up directly into Chance's
eyes. Looking down at me, he grabbed my hair, and squeezed
his eyes tightly. I then attempted to swallow his dick whole, but
gagged. Chance opened his eyes and smiled, feeling himself
because he knew he was well endowed.

I had to redeem myself, so I sucked fast and hard, using my
triple threat to my advantage. I stroked Chance's dick with my
mouth, taking it in as far as I could. With each stroke, I ran my
tongue along his shaft, each time, suctioning my jaws all the

way back to the tip. He pulled my hair harder and harder, and his legs began to shake. The look on his face told me I was doing my job right. I jacked him with my hand as I sucked and licked his head. I didn't know how much more Chance would be able to take, but I wasn't stopping until my jaws went numb. Before my jaws went numb, Chance began to shake uncontrollably, and I knew what was next. I stayed in position, and kept jacking him. I closed my eyes and opened my mouth. I then stuck out my tongue, and confronted my cum storm like a soldier, enjoying every bit of it.

"Jordyn? You ready?" Chance asked, still standing in front of me with his dick still at attention.

"You know I am," I said, still excited from the fantasy I had just had.

Chance eased into the tub, and I turned on the jets.

"Is the temperature ok?" I asked.

"Perfect," Chance said, as his body sank down into the tub and he closed his eyes."

I grabbed a towel and body wash. As I bathed him from head to toe, "Forever My Lady" by Jodeci played through the intercom system on the wall. I relished in the moment of pleasing my man non-sexually and wished it never had to end. After I bathed Chance, I dried him off, and laid him across the bed full of rose petals. I massaged every bone, joint and muscle of his body, even the largest one that I wished I could've gotten a taste of. By the time I finished, Chance had fallen asleep. I opened my nightstand drawer and hopelessly stared at the package of unopened condoms and shook my head. This whole abstinence thing was a struggle for me, but I was willing to make it work for Chance's sake. I laid down next to Chance's naked body, put my arm around him, and fell asleep.

To no avail, before opening my eyes, I felt around for Chance. I had no idea what time it was, so I managed to force my eyes open, and looked at the clock. I stared at it for about a minute before I was able to focus. It was three in the morning and Chance had left without saying a word. I started to grab my phone and call him, but instead, I grabbed a pillow, and hugged it tight as if it were Chance.

CHAPTER SIXTEEN

The next morning, I was anxious to get to Chance's office, not only to see the new office he set up for me, but also to see his ass and hear what excuse he had for just leaving the way he did. I was hoping he had a good one. I got dressed looking as professional as I possibly could because I knew the bitches at the front desk already didn't care for me. I didn't want to give them anything to talk about, even though I knew they would still find something to say.

When I made it to work, I walked through the lobby and ran into Jacob again.

Before I knew it, he had grabbed and hugged me. "Wow, Jordyn. You look great! I swear I'm gonna have to take you out some time. I love me some chocolate," Jacob said, smiling and exposing his cute dimples."

"I don't think that'll be a good idea," Chance said, coming from out of nowhere." He grabbed my hand and said, "Come on. Let's get to work."

Jacob was left standing there looking dumb.

As soon as we got in the elevator, I looked straight ahead, without saying a word to Chance.

"What's wrong with you?" Chance asked.

"We'll talk about it later." I said, still looking straight ahead.

"There's only the two of us in here. Let's talk about it now. And while we're talking, let's talk about how you were just gonna let Jacob come on to you. Were you gonna let him take you out?"

"Hell no!" I exclaimed. "You came out of nowhere and handled it before I had the chance. And plus, I didn't know if we were supposed to be a . . ." The elevator doors opened and I lowered my voice. "A secret or not."

As we stepped out of the elevator, Chance opened the doors to his personal lobby of his office. The three ladies looked at me rolling their eyes and smacking their lips, but as soon as Chance walked in behind me, they all said, "Good Morning, Mr. Robinson," in unison.

"Good morning, ladies. I'm glad everyone is here. This is the perfect time to tell you all that we will have a new addition to our staff starting today. I was standing behind Chance, and before he finished kicking the girl's while they were already down, he gestured for me to come forward. As I moved up next to him, he affectionately placed the palm of his hand on the small of my back, and said, "Jordyn will be my executive assistant and also the office manager. Once she gets comfortable with these roles, you will go to her with any issues you may have within the office. She will be your superior just as I am, so I expect that you give her the same respect that you give me, including greeting her when she comes into the office everyday.

The girls were so in shock that their mouths were wide open, and they replied by only nodding their heads. I wanted to laugh in their faces, but I knew I had to be a professional role model.

"Let me show you your office," Chance said, as he walked me to the back.

We went into the same office where Chance had sent me after I interrupted his business meeting, which just happened to be right next to his office. He had decorated it beautifully with a few pieces of exotic art, a cherry wood bookcase and desk, and a comfy burgundy suede recliner with brown, tan, and burgundy pillows that matched the burgundy sofa that was already there. It looked like a totally different office from just a few days before, and was completely of my taste as if I had decorated it myself.

As Chance showed me where everything was in the office, my cell phone started ringing. Every time I would hit ignore, it would ring again. Chance was trying to ignore it and continued showing me around, but I guess he got irritated and finally said, "Who is that?"

I wasn't prepared to answer, so I said the first thing that came to mind. "Dré."

"He's still calling? Why didn't you say something? Is he threatening you?"

"He just keeps saying he's not done with me and he will find me."

The first thing you need to do is change your phone number. As a matter of fact, this tour can wait. Let's go back into your office and call the cell phone company right now."

"But I've had this same number for years!"

"Who else that you communicate with needs your number, besides the friend you got lost with who seems to never call you when I'm around?" Chance asked inquisitively. He knew I didn't have any friends or family that I communicated with besides the one I lied about being with when I was actually with Brian. Honestly, the only other person that I might've communicated with in the future was Brian.

After it took so long for me not to answer Chance's question, he said, "Exactly."

While Chance sat right in the office with me, I called Sprint and changed my phone number. After doing that, I snuck off to the bathroom to check the message that Brian had left me during one of the several calls he had made to me.

"Hey, Jordyn. I don't know what's going on with you, but I thought we were good. Well, I just wanted to give you an update on Lexi's case. I'll be planning a stakeout near the corner that Lexi used to work to see what we can find out. We're also still searching our database for people who drive a black BMW and match Rob's description. That's all I wanted. If I don't talk to you anymore, I really had a good time with you. Later."

I felt so bad after listening to Brian's message. He was such a good guy, and I knew it was really gonna hurt his feelings when he would try to call me again and get the recording that the number had been changed. I knew that this was probably for the best so that I could eliminate future unnecessary problems from my life. As long as Brian would keep calling me, I knew I would continue to think about him and the possibilities.

When I came out of the bathroom, Chance was still in my office waiting for me. He continued giving me my tour, and also went over my job description with me. He told me he'd be starting me out at twenty dollars an hour, at least until I got the hang of things. He made me promise not to let that get out to Zahriah, Heidi, and Selena. He was only paying them nine dollars an hour. There was no way in hell I'd be working for that little bit of money, but I guess if they liked it, I loved it. Twenty dollars was on the low side for me. Especially compared to what I was making on a daily basis.

Remembering what Brian had said in the last message he had left me, the next morning, I made sure I woke up early enough to watch the six o' clock news. I knew that if something had gone down on the strip, it would be on the news bright and early, and I was right. As soon as I turned on the TV, the beautiful, black news reporter, Cheryl Burton was standing outside, near the strip, giving her report. She said, "Before this morning, it seemed like the young woman, whose body was found in a dumpster behind El Rios restaurant had been forgotten about, but NYPD has still been working on the case. We have found out that the body now has a name. The young woman was Alexia Caldren, who friends called Lexi. She worked right here on this corner as a prostitute. Andrés Rodriguez, also known as Dré, ran the prostitute ring that she was a part of. Andrés, and others who were caught on the scene this morning were all taken into custody. We have been told that there were also weapons and drug paraphernalia found in the black Chevy Impala owned by Mr. Rodriguez. Andrés, and the others, who have not been identified, are all facing several charges. NYPD also tells us that they do have a lead to a possible suspect in the killing. We will update our viewers as we receive more information. Back to you Linda."

I turned the TV back off and tried to go back to sleep for a little while, but Dré, Dena, Lexi, Stasia, and Peaches kept crossing my mind. Lexi was dead because of me, Peaches had gotten fired because of me, which probably ended up being a blessing in disguise, and Dré, and possibly Dena and Stasia were in jail because of me. I kept wondering where I would be if Lexi was never killed. Would I still be on the strip, or would Chance have still been able to sweep me off my feet without something traumatic happening? I also wondered how long it would take Dré to find me. I knew he had plenty of money to make bail, so he would be on the streets again in less than twenty-four hours, but he would definitely be laying low for a little while. I did so much thinking, I never did go back to sleep. The next thing I knew, my alarm clock was going off for me to get up and get ready for work.

The next few weeks went rather smoothly at the office. Heidi and Selena were getting used to me being around, I didn't think they liked it, but they knew there was nothing they could do about it because they couldn't risk losing their jobs for being a bitch towards me. Zahriah still rolled her eyes at me every chance she got, but she never talked back or got smart with me. I knew deep down, eventually something would happen where we would bump heads and there was going to be a serious altercation between the two of us. That office was big, but wasn't nearly big enough for two beautiful black women with huge egos.

Chance and I were working pretty well together, and seeing each other as often as we did actually seemed to bring us closer. We still hadn't had sex, but I continued to be patient with him. I figured he must've lost someone he really loved and was trying to correct what he felt the issue was by handling him and me as delicately as possible. Chance had me in on all of his meetings and made sure I dressed the part of being his executive assistant. He treated me like I had never been treated before and it was the best feeling in the world, but I was still ready to see what Chance had to offer in other areas. I still didn't understand where he got the power to resist me, but I guessed there was a method to his madness.

One Friday afternoon, Chance and I had decided to go out to dinner later that evening. We went to dinner every Friday, after finishing a long week at work, but this time we were going to a new soul food restaurant that we heard had the best food around town. It was called Black-Eyed Pea. I left work before Chance so that I had time to freshen up and get out of my more conservative clothes and into something more stylish and less boring. He told me he'd call me once he was leaving the office and that it may be a little later than normal because he had some work to catch up on.

On my way home, I listened to Alicia Keys, "Brand New Me", and it made me smile, thinking about how my life had done a complete three-sixty all because of one person. I felt like a new person and like I was moving forward in life and no longer remaining stagnant. My next mission was to find out how many credit hours I had left before I would be able to get into nursing school. I knew I had gotten pretty far, and then let Dré get me off track of the dreams I was trying to pursue. These last two years could've been years that I put towards school, and probably could've been damn near finished. All I could say is we live and we learn. Some of us actually use what we learn and make changes, and some of us go right back to the same ole shit we were doing before. That wasn't gonna be me. I was determined not to be sidetracked by people who weren't on track.

After arriving at home and relaxing a while before my date with Chance, I showered and put on one of the many new outfits I had bought myself with Chance's money. Chance was very generous when it came to spending money on me. Some days, he would just give me his credit card and tell me to go buy myself something nice. He was just that type of man, and I didn't argue with him. When I did try to argue, he would keep insisting anyway until I accepted it.

After getting dressed and making sure my hair and makeup was flawless, I sat around watching TV. While I was watching an old episode of "Scandal", I heard my stomach growl, which made me look at the time. It was after eight, and I was hungry as hell. I hadn't eaten anything since breakfast. The office had been so busy all day, I didn't have time to eat lunch. I knew Chance had said he'd be a little late, so I decided to give him a little more time. In the meantime, I grabbed some celery and ranch dip out of the fridge and snacked on that just to at least get my stomach to shut up.

Another half hour had passed by, and I still hadn't heard anything. This wasn't like Chance, so I grabbed my cell phone and called him. I dialed him about 10 times and it kept going straight to voicemail. I knew Chance wasn't good with keeping a charge on his phone, which I argued with him about on several occasions, but he still didn't get it. I even bought him extra phone chargers to keep with him wherever he was. Another thought was maybe he was on an important business call and couldn't answer at the moment, so I texted him, telling him to call me ASAP.

When another half hour passed and I still hadn't heard anything, I got a little worried. I tried calling once more, and got his voicemail again. I put on my floral print strappy heels that I had put by the door while I waited on Chance, grabbed my purse, and left. I tried not to think the worse of what could've possibly happened, but it was hard, especially due to the fact he had never gone this long without returning my call. I headed to the office because that was the only place I could think of going. When I got halfway there, my phone, which was sitting in my lap just in case Chance had decided to call, started ringing to the tune of Robin Thicke's, "For the Rest of my Life". It wasn't a call though. It was a text. Chance said that he was stuck in a late business meeting and apologized for not being able to answer my calls. He told me to go ahead and have dinner without him because he didn't want me to keep waiting on him, and he'd see me later.

I was a little disappointed, but I understood Chance having to be about his business. He wasn't as accomplished as he was by just sitting around and not doing anything. He worked hard for his money, and I knew that just from working with him the little time that I had. I could just imagine how much work he had to put in to get to where he was now. I texted Chance back and told him not to worry about it.

I then had to decide what I was gonna eat. I had my mouth set for some good soul food, but I didn't want to experience Black-Eyed Pea without Chance. I knew he really wanted to go, so I'd save that for another day. I was dressed to go someplace nice, so I didn't want to go somewhere that was just average. I wanted to go somewhere where I could eat good, have a few drinks, and maybe do a little dancing, so I decided to go to a nice spot called Underground Lounge.

On my way there, I kept looking at my phone, hoping Chance would text or call me to tell me he would be able to make it after all, but it didn't seem like that was going to happen, so I would have to make the best of my night. When I pulled up to the spot, it was packed. I had to drive around the building three or four times before I was able to finally catch a gorgeous black couple walking to their black Lexus. The woman had an hourglass shape that I could tell her man admired by the smile on his face as he looked back at her round, perfect ass. They both looked happy; just as happy as Chance and I looked when we were out together. As I waited for the man to pull his Lexus out of the parking space, I looked at my phone once more to make sure I hadn't missed any calls. I sighed after I looked and saw nothing.

I vowed to myself, even though Chance wasn't with me, I was going to have a good time. I had been working my ass off and I deserved it. I grabbed my Michael Kors bag and switched my ass to the solid oak wood front doors of the establishment. As I went to grab one of the brass handles, someone from behind grabbed it and opened it for me. Without looking back, I said, "Thank you," and walked in.

"Anything for you, baby," the person behind me said.

I turned around to see who the voice belonged to. Expecting someone tall, which is what I normally attracted, I automatically looked up, but saw no one. Then lil man cleared his throat, which made me look down. This sucka couldn't have been any taller than five foot four, trying to get him a tall woman. It was so cute because he looked like a little boy. I made the awful mistake of smiling at him, which gave his little self some hope.

"You here by yourself? If so, we can get a table and hang out. Maybe even go out on the dance floor."

By the uncomfortable looking dance move he did at that moment, I wouldn't have been caught dead on anybody's dance floor with him. He seemed like a nice guy. Just not for me. I had to try to let him off easy.

"I'm going through some things right now. My boyfriend was just thrown in jail for murder, and he has his boys looking after me while he's away, so I don't think that's a good idea."

Lil man wiped the sweat from his forehead as he said, "Uh, yeah. That probably isn't a good idea, but nice meeting you . . ."

"Jordyn. My name is Jordyn."

"Yeah, Jordyn. Nice meeting you. I'm Chauncey," he said as he stuck his hand out for me to shake.

Such a small man with a big name! I thought.

Chauncey and I parted ways. I found a table with nice lighting, small enough for just me, so that no one would think to come by and make himself comfortable like Chauncey thought he was about to do. I first looked through the drink menu. I needed something to give me just the right amount of buzz so I could try to seduce my man tonight. I thought about that, and just a little buzz hadn't been working, so I decided to have something a little stronger than usual.

"Vodka and cranberry on the rocks please," I replied when my waitress came over and asked if I wanted to order a drink.

"My fave! Is there a certain type of Vodka you'd like?"

"Ciroc, thank you," I said with a grin.

"Coming right up!" the bubbly waitress said, and walked off smiling.

As I searched through the food menu, I looked for something that caught my eye, but I was so hungry, I wanted a little bit of everything. All I could hear was the music playing and I was in my own little world, singing to myself. I heard my waitress behind me. It sounded like she was only a few tables away from me, seating someone else. I tried to hurry and find something on the menu as she giggled and carried on a conversation at the other table.

"Ok, I'll give you folks some time to look through the menu. I'll be back in a few minutes."

"How'd you like the movie?" I heard a very familiar voice say as the waitress came from behind and approached my table. She stood there with her pen and pad in her hand ready to take my order as I turned around and looked towards the table she had just come from. I couldn't believe my eyes.

"Are you ready to order?" the waitress asked?

"No, I'm not feeling too good. I'll be leaving."

"Awww! That's a shame!"

"You just don't know how much of a shame it is," I mumbled.

"What was that?" she asked, not hearing what I said."

"Oh nothing. Just thinking out loud."

"I assume you want to cancel that drink too?"

"Definitely. Sorry for your trouble," I apologized.

"Oh, no problem! I do have a break coming up. Maybe I'll have that drink for you!" she said and laughed hysterically. I didn't laugh because I was too focused on trying to hear the conversation going on behind me. I think my waitress may have become offended because she walked away without saying another word. It wasn't personal, but I had some business to take care of.

I got up from my table and walked over to the table where all the talking and laughing was going on. As I got closer, Chance's expression changed completely. He looked like he had seen a ghost. The gorgeous woman he was with glanced up at me showing all thirty-two teeth. She had armpit length Brazilian body-wave hair similar to mine, but of a much more expensive quality. I knew my weave, and I knew that bitch paid top dollar for what she had. She had a light brown complexion and a sexy mole right above her top lip. Her lips were full, but not too full and she wore cherry red lipstick that brought out her perfectly straight teeth.

I smiled back at her, then looked at Chance, wondering what was going through his mind at that moment. "Hey Chance! I thought that was your voice I heard!

"Hi . . ."

"Jordyn," I said, reminding him of what my name was.

"Of course!" he laughed. "I didn't forget your name."

"I would hope not! And who is this lovely lady you're with? Sister, perhaps?"

"Oh, I'm sorry. I'm so rude." Chance looked over at the woman, who began to look just as confused as I was, then looked at me and said, "Let me introduce you first. This is my new Executive Assistant down at the office I've been telling you about."

The woman said, "Oh, Jordyn, right? Nice to finally meet you!"

Every minute that passed I became more and more confused. Then the moment I had been waiting for had come. I was waiting to see how he was gonna introduce her.

"Jordyn . . . This is my wife . . . Sasha."

My heart sank down into the pit of my stomach, but I had to keep it together. I looked at her married finger and noticed the huge rock. I don't know how in the world I had missed that. Then Chance, with his hands clasped together on the table was wearing a wedding band I had never seen him wear before. Chance couldn't even look me in the eyes after he introduced her.

"Oh, this is the famous Sasha I've heard so much about," I said, sarcastically.

Sasha continued to smile, and Chance tried to smile, but he was so uncomfortable, his face was making all types of awkward expressions as if it truly didn't know what to do. I decided to put him out of his misery.

"Sasha, very nice to meet you! See you later Chance. You two have a nice evening."

As I was walking away in my brand new outfit and accessories from the Chance fund, I heard Sasha as she said, "She's very nice. You didn't tell me she was so beautiful."

I snickered to myself as I walked out the doors. Chance was about to find out that I was a force to be reckoned with. He didn't know just how much I had gone through growing up, so he had no idea how strong I really was. This right here was amateur stuff to me, but you better believe he wasn't about to get away with it. Wife? Are you kidding me? As protective as he was of me and didn't want me talking to anyone else, this Negro had the nerve to be married!

I couldn't bring myself to go home after what I had just seen. I just couldn't believe it. I needed to see more. When I left out of the restaurant, I got into my car and drove down the street, where I would still be able to see the entrance of the restaurant, and parked in front of a liquor store. I sat there for almost an hour, listening to the radio, until I finally saw Chance and Sasha walking out of the restaurant. I started up my car, and watched as Chance kissed his wife right before he opened up the car door for her, just like he would always do for me. As soon as he got in and started to pull off, I put my car in drive and slowly followed behind.

I almost lost Chance a few times due to pedestrians crossing the street in front of me, but each time, I managed to catch up to the Lambo. After driving about ten minutes, we drove through an extravagant neighborhood. I tried my best to follow far behind so that Chance wouldn't notice he was being followed. Chance finally pulled into the driveway of one of the largest houses on the block, located in a cul-de-sac. I parked down the street and shut off my lights. I had no idea what I was about to do. I just knew I needed to do something to satisfy my need of confirmation as if Chance's introduction of Sasha as his wife wasn't enough.

I took off my heels and got out the car. I ran in the dark, down the street and hid on the side of the mansion, waiting for Chance's car to pull into the garage. As soon at it opened, and he pulled in, I ran in, kneeled down, and hid behind a large tool shelf in the corner. I heard the garage door coming down, and that's when I realized I was acting crazy, but by then, there was no turning back.

I could hear Chance and Sasha in the car laughing before they got out. Obviously whatever they were laughing at was hilarious because Chance got out of the car still cracking up. It didn't seem as though me seeing him with his wife fazed him at all. I don't think I could've been any further away from his mind. From what I was witnessing, Chance was having a wonderful date night with his wife and it was killing me to watch. My elbow accidently hit the rake that was right next to me, and it fell to the ground. My heart began beating out of my chest as I saw Chance turn around and look over in my direction. I attempted to control my breathing so that he wouldn't hear me.

"Chance, is everything ok?" Sasha said from inside the car."

Looking down at the rake that had fallen, Chance said, "Yeah, babe. The rake fell off of the rack." As he opened the door for her, I moved further behind the shelf, which was just in time. He walked over and picked up the rake, putting it back in its place. Sasha and Chance walked into the house together and it was time for me to make my next move.

I went over to the door that Chance and Sasha had just gone through to get into the house, slowly opened it, and crept through the house. I couldn't hear a thing, which was a good sign, so I continued through the home, admiring the décor. I didn't spot anything that looked liked it was under a thousand dollars. I came across a set of stairs that only had about five steps. It led me up to the huge kitchen that was full of granite counter tops and marble floors. *No wonder it was no big deal for Chance to let me live in his other house. It has nothing on this house!* I thought. I suddenly could hear voices in the distance. I realized they were coming from above, and I noticed the tall staircase.

As I slowly climbed the stairs, the voices got closer and closer. When I got to the top of the staircase I saw that there were four closed doors in front of me, but I heard nothing coming from none of them. I then heard a door open, but it was further down the hall. I heard brisk footsteps and laughter. I darted around the corner right before Chance came charging down the hall. His body was only covered by a pair of black silk boxers with red lips all over them, which coincidentally, I had bought for him as a "just because" gift.

Chance ran down the stairs. I heard Sasha yelling from the room for him to hurry. He came running right back up the steps with a can of whipped cream. I was starting to get nauseous. I thought about just leaving, but I was like an addict, needing more. After a couple of minutes, I convinced myself to continue with my investigation. I tiptoed down the hall and saw the room Chance had entered. The door was open. I peeked around the corner and saw nothing, but heard moans. I slowly entered the room and saw Chance holding Sasha up against the wall, pounding her pussy so hard I could've sworn the entire room was shaking. Their bodies both glistened with sweat they had produced from the love they made. Her eyes were closed and she was taking the big black dick that belonged to me like a soldier. With every thrust, they both moaned in unison. I didn't need to see any more. I watched the man who I thought had deep feelings for me make love to his wife. I wasn't mad at him for that. I was mad because he wasn't honest with me. I let myself out the front door of the house that Chance worked so very hard to keep a secret from me, slowly walked to my car, wishing I had never met Chance Robinson.

I went straight to the hardware store, making it there only five minutes before closing time, and the greeter at the front door made sure to remind me of that as I was walking in. They didn't have to worry about me. I knew exactly what I coming for. I picked up new locks for both the front and back door of my house so Chance would have no way of getting in if he tried. When I got home, I used the skills I had learned from my momma. When she was done using up one man and ready to move on to the other, she would change the locks. She gave every man she began a relationship with a key to our house, which I knew was unsafe, but she didn't seem to think anything was wrong with it.

After I finished changing the locks, I took a shower, and as the water ran all over my body, I began to think about Chance and wonder why he had me around. He had a beautiful wife at home. I couldn't even say he wanted me for the sex because he hadn't experienced that yet. Maybe he needed someone he felt like he had power over. I had never been so confused in my life. This man pursued me like he wanted to spend the rest of his life with me, and he already had a complete life of his own. At least one question was answered. He was obviously able to resist temptation when it came to me because it wasn't like he wasn't getting any, like I initially thought. He was still getting his dick wet with his wife. I was the only one going through a drought like an idiot! I knew I would never be able to forgive Chance.

After I got out of the shower, I saw the green light blinking on my cell phone, which I had thrown on the bed. I grabbed it and saw I had twenty-seven missed calls. All of which were from Chance. He had also texted me several times. He said the same thing in all of them. "Call me please." "I'm sorry." "We need to talk. Call me ASAP."

I had a problem with every text that he sent. I wasn't calling him, because first of all, what in the hell did we have to talk about? The movie that he and his wife went to see, or the great fuck they had just had? Why did we need to talk? There was no logical reason I could possibly think of. Lastly, why was he apologizing for something he knew was wrong from the jump. He wasn't sorry he hurt me! He was sorry he got caught. I was done, and as far as I was concerned, he needed to be done, too.

CHAPTER SEVENTEEN

I spent the rest of the weekend charging up a bunch of shit on Chance's credit card he had left with me. I made sure I left enough on it just in case he stopped paying the bills around the house. I hadn't had to pay any bills as we had agreed. Chance had been taking care of everything. I still had my savings, which I had still been adding to, but I didn't want to have to go into that money unless I just had to. That was my last resort.

Chance had still been blowing up my phone, but I still couldn't bring myself to answer it. I needed to wait til I was mentally stable and I hadn't gotten there yet. If I answered, I might've strangled him through the phone just for trying to make a fool out of me. I knew he had been by the house at least once while I wasn't there because he texted me and asked why I changed the locks. I think that might've been the dumbest question anyone had ever asked me, and I didn't respond.

It was Monday morning, and my alarm clock went off. I shut it off, threw my pillow over my head, and went back to sleep. I definitely was not going in to that office to work for the man

who played me the way he did. My question was, was I the only
dumb ass in the office that didn't know he was married? I slept
for hours and the only thing that woke me up was the sound of
my doorbell a few hours later. I first peeked out my bedroom
window, hoping it wasn't Chance's ass. I saw a van in the
driveway, but couldn't see who it was.

I went down the stairs and looked through the peephole.
There was a white man standing there.

"Who is it?" I shouted through the door.

"Angie's Florist. I have a delivery."

Being extra cautious, I ran to the living room and looked
out of the blinds. I saw that the side of the white van did in fact
say "Angie's Florist". I went back to the door and opened it.

"Sorry about that. You can never be too careful," I said to
the deliveryman.

"That's ok. Sign right here," he said, handing me a
confirmation of receipt and pen. I signed and handed it back to
him.

"I'll be right back," he said.

He walked around to the back of the van, and when he came
back around to the front, he was carrying a vase full of rainbow
colored roses in one arm and an edible arrangement with
balloons in the other.

"Here you go ma'am."

"I didn't know you all did fruit arrangements, too."

"We don't. I just picked this up from Edible Arrangements.
Whoever sent this to you paid us extra to go pick it up so you'd
get that and the flowers all at the same time. Thoughtful,
right?"

I bit my bottom lip and said, "Yeah, real thoughtful."

""Well you have a good day," he said, and went to get back
in his van.

I sat the roses on my dining room table in front of the
window where the sun was shining in beautifully. I sat the
edible arrangement on the kitchen counter and pulled out one
of the daisy shaped pineapples and bit a piece of it. As I ate the
pineapple, I pulled the card out and read it.

Dear Jordyn.

I am deeply sorry and I know I have a lot of explaining to do. I wish you would at least answer my calls. I need to talk to you. I know flowers and fruit won't fix this, but hopefully it's a start. I truly do care for you.

   -Chance

The entire gesture brought tears to my eyes, but I couldn't let Chance off that easily. I let an entire week go by of ignoring Chance's calls, texts, and visits. He had come by the house three times while I was home. He rang the doorbell a million times each time, but I didn't answer. He didn't know whether or not I was home, because each time, my car was in the garage. Then he would start calling me while he was still standing outside. He just wouldn't give up.

One night, after being tired of sitting in the house, I decided to go out to the club, which I rarely ever did. One reason I rarely did it in the past was because I was out on the strip during club hours. The corner was literally my club. Men picked me up, just like women get picked up at the club. To me, it was no different, besides the fact that I got paid for my services.

That night, I put on a top with the lowest neckline I could find in my closet. It showed every part of my titties except my areolas and nipples. I found the smallest pair of shorts I had, and a pair of my tallest heels that strapped all the way up to my nice calves. I pulled my car out of the garage, and before I pulled off, I looked through my purse, making sure I had my phone. I didn't know why, when I wasn't speaking to the only person who called me. Deep down, I kinda got off on him wanting me so badly, even if he had somebody else.

I didn't have my phone, so I left my car running and ran back into the house. When I came back out, I smelled the scent of Prada cologne floating through the air. Chance's fine ass was standing right beside my car. He looked like he had just gotten a fresh haircut, and had grown facial hair, which made him look even sexier. He had on a pair of khaki cargo shorts, showing off his sexy legs, and a wife beater, revealing his strong arms, which reminded me of how it felt when he wrapped them around me.

No matter how good he looked, I had to get my BGWA (Black Girl With an Attitude) act on.

"Don't you look . . . naked," Chance said, standing there with his hands in his pockets. "Not that you probably think it's any of my business, but shouldn't you have on a little more clothing?"

"You're absolutely right. It's none of your business. What the fuck do you want?"

"I told you we need to talk."

"What is there to talk about? You're married and I don't talk to married men."

"But it's ok to just fuck them, huh?"

I looked at Chance with rage in my eyes. He always had to bring up my life as a prostitute. It was like his only way to try to win an argument with me. This was definitely not the time to play those types of games with me. Especially when he was trying to get back in good with me.

Chance must've felt my anger, because he said, "I'm sorry. I didn't mean to say that. Can we just go in and talk. I just want you to better understand my situation."

"I'm about to go out. Maybe I'll try to call you tomorrow."

"No. I've been waiting a week. I paid all your bills for the month. I think I at least deserve for you to at least hear me out."

I stood in front of my front door with my arms folded, looking up to the sky as if God was going to look down and tell me what to do. Everything about this man was perfect, except for the fact that he was married. I was wishing that I 'd continued to walk around naïve to it all. Everything seemed so great, but now it was time to face the truth and talk about it.

Chance looked at my car and said, "Are you going to continue to waste gas or what?"

I began walking towards my car with my arms still folded. The closer I got, the more I smelled him. His scent alone made me feel good, but I had to remain focused on the matter at hand and not be lured in. I opened my car door and took my keys out of the ignition.

"You're not gonna pull it back into the garage?" Chance asked.

"For what? I'm still leaving when we're done here," I said, rolling my eyes as we walked to the front door to go inside. As he walked behind me, I could feel him staring at my ass. Without turning around, I said, "I thought you didn't like what I had on."

"Huh? I don't like what you have on. When did I say anything different?"

"You didn't say anything. Your eyes are doing all the talking."

Chance smiled as we walked into the house and said, "At least you still have a sense of humor."

Chance closed the door behind him.

"You want something to drink?" I asked.

"No thanks. Can we just start this off with a hug?" Chanced asked, and I couldn't resist.

He opened his arms, and I walked right into them. He wrapped his arms around me and held me tight. I felt a strange sensation go through my body. It almost felt like an electrical current.

"I missed you so much, Jordyn. Please don't leave me." Chance released me only enough so he could look me in the eyes to say, "Please say you won't leave me."

"But what about your wi--"

Chance shushed me by gently putting his finger up to my soft lips, not allowing me to finish my sentence.

"Just say it."

"Why should I? You'll never be mine."

"Being away from you this week made me realize a lot of things. One of those things is that I'm in love with you. Not just in love; madly in love. I couldn't stop thinking about you. I can't imagine my world without you in it. You have added so much to my life. I look forward to everyday when I know you're gonna be there. This has been torture for me."

I had shed not one tear for Chance. Not even the night when I ran into him and his wife. I wasn't able cry and couldn't understand why. Maybe it was because I was confused about our feelings for each other because sex wasn't involved and we hadn't told each other that we loved each other. After Chance had just poured his feelings out to me, tears ran down my face without warning. I hugged him tight and said, "I love you, too."

"You won't leave me?" Chance asked.

I hesitated, and said, "No, baby, I won't leave you."

"Jordyn, can I make love to you?"

Chance was throwing all kinds of curveballs out there that I wasn't expecting. I looked at him, with tears still flowing from my eyes, and said, "Are you sure?"

"I don't know why I've been waiting. It's been time."

"Yes, baby."

Chance pulled off his wife beater and threw it to the floor. He grabbed my face with both hands and passionately kissed me. He picked me up and carried me upstairs to my bedroom. The room was dim from the small lamp I had left on on my nightstand. It had gotten late, so there was no light shining into the room through the blinds, which was exactly how I liked it when I made love. Chance laid me down on my back. He untied the straps of my shoes and took them off. He lifted my left leg and brought my foot up to his mouth. He then licked the bottom of my foot with his soft, wet tongue. He made his way up towards my toes, and sucked each of them, one by one, as I breathed heavily, enjoying every moment. He repeated the same with my other foot. He climbed on top of me, straddling me, and then massaged my titties, revealing them from underneath the small piece of cloth that was barely covering them. Pushing them together, he licked, suck and bit my perfectly sized, dark brown nipples. I moaned, pushing his head further into my deep cleavage.

Chance lifted me up and pulled my shirt up over my head. I unbuckled his belt and unbuttoned his pants. He sat up on his knees so that I could pull them down. Before I did, I rubbed the palm of my hand over the large bulge beneath his pants. As I pulled down his shorts, then his boxers, Chance's super-sized treat stared me face to face for the very first time. I looked up at Chance, staring at his beautiful, chocolate, naked body. I licked the tip of the beautiful creature standing at attention right in front of me, and I devoured him. My triple threat had been waiting on him, so I hoped he was prepared. I started off slow and soft, and then I sucked him fast and hard, taking him in as deep as I could, gagging at the same time, just like in my fantasy. I licked his shaft with my long, slender tongue. I looked Chance in his eyes as I pleased him. He closed his eyes and grabbed the back of my hair, bobbing my head up in down, faster and faster. I could hear a faint moan above me, but I wanted it louder. I used my jaws to suction his dick just right, and his moans became louder, and he began to repeatedly say my name. He pushed my head down further until his dick reached the back of my throat with each stroke. Seconds later, Chance was shaking uncontrollably, and I was drinking watermelon from his fountain of love.

Chance took a deep breath and proceeded to unbutton my shorts. He pulled them down, along with my black and white lace panties. I knew Chance and I were sexually compatible when I saw that he was still erect. I reached over and shut off the dim light. I pulled my shorts and panties the rest of the way down over my ankles and feet. I laid Chance back, and straddled him, kissing his lips, and intermingling my tongue with his. I then reached over in my nightstand drawer, feeling around for my warming sensation KY jelly. I squeezed some in my hand and rubbed some on Chance's dick, and then on myself. I lifted up and eased his dick inside of me slowly until I was able to take all of him, as he squeezed my ass. We exhaled together, and as I rode him I screamed his name. Making love to someone when love was involved was so different than fucking random people. I had never had this experience before and it felt so good. It was one that I would never forget. I rode Chance so long and hard, he came again, but this time inside of me and I could feel all of his love exploding throughout my body.

The next morning, I ran my hand across the bed, but felt nothing but empty space. I managed to open my eyes and look around the room. That's when I noticed Chance was gone. I must've fallen asleep before he left. The last thing I remembered from the night before was going in the bathroom to clean myself up after the extraordinary sexual encounter that Chance and I experienced. When I came back into the room, Chance was still butt naked, passed out. I laid on his chest and fondled his package while he slept, until I fell asleep. The night before had been the best night of my life, but I woke up with an indescribable feeling, knowing that Chance had made love to me and went back home to his wife. I had never been the other woman, and I didn't like how it felt at all. I didn't like sharing anything. Especially a man. We still hadn't discussed Sasha at all, and I didn't care how good he had laid it down the night before, he wasn't getting off that easily.

Since Chance and I had obviously made up, I figured I should get my ass up and get ready for work. I assumed Chance hadn't fired me, and if he had, the previous night I had proven in more than one way why I should be rehired. I opened my walk-in closet and revisited the side I hadn't had reason to visit the past week. I had my clothes divided into four categories; Professional, safe, on the verge of ratchet, and ratchet. Professional wear wasn't my favorite, but it would have to suffice for the time being.

When I walked into the office, the girls at the front desk looked at me like they were in a state of confusion.

"Hey ladies!" I said as I smiled, walked past them towards my office. My office was exactly as I'd left it. Nothing had been disturbed. Even the stack of paperwork I was last working on was still sitting on my desk. I guess Chance had really high hopes of my return. I walked over to the picture window and drew back the curtains and opened the blinds to let some of the beautiful, natural sunlight in.

When I turned around, Chance was standing in my doorway.

"Hey you!" I said, excited to see him.

"Hey to you sexy. I'm happy to see you decided to come back." He stepped all the way into my office and closed and locked the door behind him.

"I was hoping I hadn't got fired."

"Well, if it had been anyone else, and under different circumstances, they probably would've been fired for job abandonment, but you know I couldn't do that to your fine self."

We met each other halfway, and held each other.

"You know after last night, you're stuck with me for life," Chance said, with a sly grin.

"Oh, really?"

"Most definitely. I really can't let you go now."

"Oh, but you could've let me go before, huh?"

"No. Quit reading into stuff so much. Just like a woman. That's not what I meant."

"Oh, ok. Just checking," I said, and gave him a sexy wink.

"I'm glad you came in. I was hoping you would. I need for you to ride with me somewhere."

As I started to get comfortable in my leather computer chair, I said, "Ok. Just let me know when."

"I was thinking right now."

"Ohhh!" I said, and got back up out of my seat. I figured we had a business meeting outside of the office, which we had quite often with several large companies. I grabbed my purse and said, "I'm ready when you are."

Chance stopped by the front desk and said, "Ladies, Jordyn and I will be right back. We have a quick run to make."

Heidi nodded and Selena said, "No problem Mr. Robinson!" She grinned at both of us as if she was trying to earn brownie points. She was the smart one out of the group. She knew she better had accepted what she couldn't change.

Zahriah folded her arms, and with a side eye, said, "Mmm hmmm." I felt like telling her, "Bitch, get over it." I didn't know whether Zahriah had a crush on Chance, which is what seemed to be the case, but nevertheless, she had three whole years to pull him while I wasn't in the picture. When you snooze, you lose.

Chance and I walked out to the VIP parking lot. I saw his car sitting in its normal spot that was reserved specifically for him, so I automatically started walking in that direction. Chance grabbed my hand and guided me in a different direction. The next thing I knew, we stood in front of a candy red, sparkling clean Porsche 911.

"Oh wow! This is nice! I didn't know you were getting a new car."

"It wasn't planned."

"Is something wrong with the Lambo or the Maserati?"

"Noooo, not at all. This isn't for me. I thought you'd like it."

My mouth almost hit the ground. "What?!?! Are you serious?"

"Yes. You deserve it. I bought it a few days ago. It's been sitting here while I contemplated on whether giving you this would be the right thing to do, or would it seem like I was just giving you a guilt gift. I didn't want it to seem like that. After last night, it was crystal clear that I just wanted to give a gift to the woman that I love."

I was ecstatic, but there was no way I could accept such an expensive gift. Giving me a place to live was one thing, but buying me a two-hundred thousand-dollar car with something completely different.

"This is very nice of you, but I can't accept this. It's way too pricy."

"Baby, how many times I gotta tell you, I got you? Don't worry about price. I want you to have it."

I opened my mouth to speak, and Chance could tell I was about to say something he didn't want to hear, so he put his magic move on me and put his finger up to my lips to shush me.

"Just say thank you. Nothing else needed," Chance said in a calm tone.

I took a deep breath and said, "Thank you, baby."

"Hold your hands out," Chance demanded.

I cupped my hands out in front of me, and Chance took the keys out of his pocket and placed them in my hands. I had never had a brand new car in my life, and when I finally got one, I didn't even have to pay for it. Chance and I got in the car, and he showed me how everything worked. I was in awe of how happy Chance was to spend that kind of money on me, but I guessed he had it like that to spend on someone he loved.

After he finished introducing me to my new car, I brought up Sasha. We were alone, and it was an issue that needed to be discussed.

"So, how long have you been married?"

"Really, Jordyn? You really wanna talk about this now?"

"Why not? And if not now, when?"

Chance took a deep breath and exhaled. "We've been married five years."

"How long have you been cheating on her?"

"As long as I've been cheating on her with you."

"So you want me to believe that you've never cheated on her before?"

"I want you to believe the truth, and what I'm telling you is the truth. Since we've been married, I've never cheated on her."

"So you're in love with her?"

"I love her. I can't say I've truly ever been in love with her. She's a good person, but she doesn't keep me on my toes the way you do. You're interesting, and fun, and not afraid of who you are and what other people think. She's a "yes" woman. You argue your point. I need a woman that's not gonna always agree with me, because I know I'm not always right. I've always wanted to be with someone like you."

I wanted to tell Chance so badly that I could tell he loved her by the way he had made love to her the night I snuck into their house, but I figured keeping that to myself would probably be the right thing to do.

"You knew all of this before you married her right?"

"True, and I know what your next question is. Why did I marry her?"

"Yes, why did you?"

"Because I felt it was the right thing to do at the time. I got her pregnant, and I didn't want to have a baby out of wedlock. It was against my principles."

"So you have a child too?"

"No. She had a miscarriage at five months. We were married then. I couldn't just divorce her. She was already going through a lot dealing with trying to get past that time in our lives. It was rough. Then by the time she seemed to be coping with the miscarriage, we had been married almost two years."

"So you basically settled."

"If that's what you wanna call it."

"So what are your plans now?" I asked.

"What is this? An interview?"

"I just want to be prepared for what's to come."

"Anything is possible, but I can promise you one thing. I'll be upfront with you from this point on about what's going on. As for right now, all I can tell you is I'm in love with you and I love her, but I care about her too much to see her hurt."

I sat in the driver's seat of my Porsche nodding my head.

"What's all that nodding for?"

"Nothing. Just letting you know I understand all of which you've told me and I can't do anything but respect it. May the best woman win."

Chance laughed and said, "Anything else you wanna know?"

"That's all for now, as long as we have some type of understanding. Oh wait! Since you're married, does that mean I'm free to see other people too?"

Chance frowned up his face and said, "Are you serious right now? Hell no!"

I shrugged my shoulders, and got out of the car.

When we walked back into the office and headed to the back, Zahriah watched us and I watched her until we were no longer visible to one another. When I went towards my office door, Chance snatched me up by my arm and pulled me into his office, then slammed and locked the door. He pushed me up against the wall and began vigorously kissing my neck. He was showing me his rough side, and I liked it. Chance rubbed his hands up and down my ass. Getting hot and bothered, I pulled his face closer to mine, admiring everything that was in front of me. I kissed him, and as soon as our lips met, I felt his dick jump up against my pelvis. Chance then maneuvered his hands underneath my snug fitting black skirt, and he proceeded to pull down both of my thigh highs. He then unzipped my skirt, and knelt down to pull it to the floor. He stared at me as I stood there in my black lace boy shorts, with a million thoughts running through my head. I loved everything that Chance was doing for me, but I felt bad at the same time for being deceitful. Chance had come clean, even though I had to find out on my own, which left him with no choice except to tell me the truth. I didn't want him to find out my secret on his own. I wanted it to be on my own terms and in my timing, and my timing was right at that moment.

Chance put both hands at my waist, preparing to pull down my panties, and I grabbed his wrists and said, "Stop, I can't do this."

Chance stopped and looked at me wondering what was going on. "What's wrong?" he asked nervously.

"I need to tell you something," I said hesitantly, not sure if I was making the right decision.

Chance rubbed his hand over his low cut hair, sat down on the sofa, and said, "I knew you were seeing someone else."

"Nooo! That's not it."

"Then what is it?"

"Maybe it'll be better if I just showed you."

Truth was, I didn't know whether his response would be better if I told him or showed him. I didn't know what to expect, but I was going in.

"Are you ready?" I asked.

Chance looked worried, and said, "I guess."

I stood directly in front of Chance, put my hand on my hip and sighed.

"What is this about to be? Some kind of strip tease? You trying to seduce me?"

"Not hardly," I replied.

I closed my eyes and dropped my panties to my ankles, exposing my mangina, and reached between my legs, untucking the part of my body I was most ashamed of. The thing I considered to be my worst punishment from God. My dick. I never believed I was supposed to be born with one. Growing up, I always believed I was a girl stuck in a boy's body. Everything else about me was feminine, from my slender, yet curvy body, round ass, soft skin, mannerisms, and thinking process. I just never grew titties and was born with a nice sized dick that was only useful when I had to piss. My dick was the only thing that prevented me from being normal twenty-five year old woman.

"What the fuck!" Chance said as he sat further back on the sofa, and held his head down in his hands in a state of shock. It took a lot for Chance to curse, and I guess this was just one of those things. "You've got to be fuckin' kidding me! Please tell me I'm dreaming." Chance looked at me once more as I stood there with my dick and balls hanging in front of my man's eyes. "Jordyn! Tell me I'm dreaming! Please!!!"

"I wish I could, baby," I said with remorse in my voice. I didn't know if I was remorseful for telling him the truth or for keeping the truth from him for so long. I knew he would find out sooner of later, and there was no way around it.

"Don't call me baby! And please put that away!"

Chance was completely distraught, and I couldn't blame him. I put my extra useless accessories away and put my clothes back on as Chance sat on the sofa and stared at the wall. I didn't know what else to say. I wanted to know what Chance was thinking. Now looking back, his secret probably wasn't as bad as mine. I slowly walked over to the sofa and slowly sat down next to Chance, afraid that he might spaz out on me.

He continued to look straight ahead as if he didn't know I was there.

"Chance, I know this is a shock to you, but I'm still Jordyn. The woman you met and fell in love with. Do you . . . have any questions?"

Chance slowly turned and looked at me. "You are not the woman I fell in love with! You deceived me. You're a man! How could you do this to me? How could you let it go this far?"

I angrily stood up and said, "Look at me, Chance! Do I look like a man? I'm not a man! I'm a woman! I can do anything any other woman can do and better! A dick does not define my sexuality! It's what's in here!" I said, and I pounded the palm of my hand on my heart. I love you Chance and I told you I wouldn't leave you and I'm not!"

After I poured my heart out to Chance, the room was completely silent. Chance kept glancing over at me, but couldn't look at me for more than two seconds at a time. He then finally said, "A lot has changed since yesterday. A whole lot. I want you to leave."

"But Chance . . ."

Someone then began pounding on the door and shaking the knob like they were crazy. Chance jumped up and opened the door. As soon as he opened it, Sasha was on the other side of the door shouting, "What the hell is going on in here, and why is the fuckin' door locked?"

Chance grabbed her arms as she looked as if she was about to start swinging on him. "Baby, calm down. What's wrong with you?"

"Don't try to sit here and act like I don't know what's going on! I'm not dumb!" Sasha looked back and forth at Chance and me, trying to read the expressions on our faces, which read "confused as fuck"! "I know exactly what's going on! Is she the reason you spend so many hours away from home?"

"Sasha, to answer your question, no, Jordyn has nothing to do with anything, but this is not the place to have this conversation! What made you come here anyway?"

"Just know that I have eyes everywhere!"

"Obviously, whatever eyes that you have aren't very good ones because they got you acting crazy! This isn't like you. Come on, let me walk you to your car."

As Chance put his arm around his distraught wife, to walk her out, he looked back at me with anger in his eyes. They left the office, and I followed far behind. As they walked past the front desk, I noticed Heidi and Selena looking sympathetic for poor Sasha, while Zahriah had a slick smirk on her face. I stood there in the lobby with my arms folded, trying to piece shit together. I learned two very important things in life. One was, actions always spoke louder than words, and two, what was done in the dark always came to light.

I walked back to my office, sat down, and stared out the window. I didn't know where Chance and I would go from here. He said he wanted me to leave, but I thought he just needed a little time to get past the initial shock and think about what he was saying. Since I had exposed my full self to him, I could tell him more about my childhood and what I had endured growing up. Then maybe he would be able to better understand me, and even accept me.

A few minutes later, I heard footsteps coming around the corner. Chance walked in and said, "And you're still here? Didn't I tell you to leave?"

"Chance, you don't mean that!"

Chance walked over to my desk and looked intensely into my eyes. "I mean it! I could kill you right now. I have so many emotions going through my head right now, but what I feel most is hatred! You've challenged my sexuality as a man, and on top of that, I fucked you raw! You better hope to God you don't have nothin'!"

I felt like someone stabbed me in the heart when Chance said "he fucked me". "Fucked me? Is that what it was? I thought we made love."

"I thought I was making love to my woman with a pussy! Not fucking a man in his . . . I can't even talk about this anymore. Now the KY Jelly makes sense, and why Dré attacked you when he walked in on you while you were in the shower. Hindsight is definitely 20/20."

"Can we please just talk. I'll tell you everything."

"Oh, is there more?" Chance asked sarcastically.

"Yes. Lots more that might help you better understand all of this."

"Look . . . I have a wife that's going crazy over some shit someone has told her. I have to leave here today and go home to deal with that. And to think, you had the nerve to get pissed that I didn't tell you I was married. What did you think was going to happen? We would get married, have kids, and live happily every after? Hell, I'm better off where I am! I don't have time to deal with this, and this better not ever get out to anyone! Get out!" Chance yelled, stormed out, and slammed the door.

I sat there with my face in my hands, crying my heart out. Reality was finally setting in that no man would ever be able to accept me the way I was. It would be years before I would have enough in my savings to have my sex reassignment surgery. Years of passing up hundreds of good men. The surgery would be almost a hundred thousand, and I had only saved up around forty thousand. It had taken me six years to save up that much because I would occasionally have to dibble and dabble into those funds to support myself. It looked like that was about to be the case once again.

Chance entered my office once again. I got my hopes up, thinking maybe he had a change of heart.

"I just came to tell you, you can stay in my house for another month. Long enough for you to find other arrangements, but leave the car where it is."

I stood up and pulled the keys out of my pocket and walked over towards Chance. I stood directly in front of him and dangled the keys in his face as I gazed into his dark eyes, which had a hint of pink as if he had been crying. He snatched the keys from me and walked out.

I grabbed my purse and pulled out my keys to the old Jetta and walked out of my office without looking back. I looked next door, but Chance's office door was closed. I could imagine him on the other side of the door, standing there, staring out of his large picture window. When I walked past the front desk, I didn't tell the girls I wouldn't be back. I left the same way I would leave any other day, telling them to have a good evening. I did, however, cut my eye at Zahriah, letting her know in black girl code that I knew she was up to no good, and whatever it was would soon hit the fan.

CHAPTER EIGHTEEN

A few weeks went by without a word from Chance. I was in a state of depression. The only time I'd leave the house was to get something to eat. Deep down, I didn't want to leave the house, hoping that Chance would stop by, and I didn't want to miss him. I didn't feel the need or even have the desire to date, knowing where it would end up. Exactly where I was now. There were probably more than a hundred instances that I picked up my phone to dial Chance's number, but didn't do it. Why not? Because I didn't know what to say. What was there to say? In his mind, all he thought was that he fucked a man. In my eyes, he made love to a woman that was born with the wrong sex organs.

Everything that seemed to be perfect had backfired on me. I had set real goals and made plans on how I was going to reach those goals. Now, none of that mattered to me. Chance was the only person that made me see myself as more than a prostitute. I had contemplated going back to that life, of course, with a new pimp. Chance said I only had a month to live in his house and that was three weeks ago. I only had a week left and hadn't been on not one job interview. I looked in the classifieds on a daily basis, but nothing interested me. My drive was gone. I was broken.

As I laid across the couch in my favorite Victoria's Secret tank and short pajama set during a beautiful Saturday afternoon, my doorbell rang. I got up and brushed my hair back with my hands, making sure my ponytail was neat. I didn't get any visitors, so I figured it was just someone trying to sell me something, or the kids down the street wanting to make some extra cash by mowing my lawn. When I opened the door, to my surprise it was Brian. My eyes got big as saucers when I saw him standing there.

He smiled as soon as I opened the door and said, "Hey stranger. I see you're trying to avoid me."

"Now why would I do a thing like that?" I asked as I opened the storm door, inviting Brian to come in.

"You tell me. I thought we had something going, and then I stop hearing from you. On top of that, you changed you number. I normally wouldn't stop by unexpectedly, but you forced me to. I had to make sure you were ok, so just consider this to be a "well-being" check by the police, and not a stalker move," Brian laughed.

Brian stared me up and down and said, "You look like you're doing great to me."

"I'm just fabulous," I said dryly.

"So can you tell me why you've been avoiding me? You don't like me anymore?" Brian said as he tickled my side.

That was the first time I had smiled in three weeks.

"You are so sweet," I said. "I really do like you, but like I said before, I just have a lot going on in my life right now. I really don't want to involve or burden anyone else."

"Do you consider me a friend?" Brian asked.

"Of course I do."

"Then don't worry about putting any burden on me. That's what friends are for, and I promise I won't make you do anything you don't want to do."

"Ok," I said, feeling a lot better.

"Now, go put on some clothes so I can take you out to enjoy this beautiful weather. You look like you need some fresh air."

I smiled at Brian and ran upstairs to freshen up and put some clothes on. Brian had really put a smile on my face. Something I definitely needed. When I finished getting dressed and went back downstairs, Brian whistled and said, "Now that's the Jordyn I know! Not that you didn't look good before, but you look sexy as hell now."

"It is ok if I wear my heels isn't it? No basketball today, right?" I asked.

Brian laughed, and said, "Funny! No, I'm not in the mood to whoop on your ass today. I want to take you somewhere nice to celebrate some good news."

I was wondering what good news Brian possibly had to share with me. My first thought was maybe he had gotten a promotion at work. I guessed I would soon find out. When we got outside, Brian surprised me by making sure he walked ahead of me so that he could open my car door. Maybe he had spent some time thinking about where he went wrong and was trying to correct some things with his dating etiquette. Not that I considered it a date.

We rode around the city for about an hour, just enjoying each other's conversation. I looked over at his left hand, and he glanced back at me and said, "What?"

"Are you married?"

"No! Why would you ask that?"

"Apparently, there's a don't ask, don't tell policy in New York City."

"Ohhh. Now the truth comes out. Is that why you threw me away? For some idiot that sold you false hopes and dreams when all along he had a wife?"

"It's a little more complicated than that, but I don't want to talk about it."

"Ok. Cool, but let me know if you need me to lock him up. I'm sure I can find something on him."

Brian had a great personality. He was always able to make a joke out of everything, which is what I liked about him. He was like a breath of fresh air. I knew we wouldn't be a couple due to obvious reasons, but I could see us having a great, long-lasting friendship.

After riding around, we pulled up at a Brazilian Steakhouse called Fogo De Chao.

"So, this is where you're gonna take me to eat, huh?"

"Yeah, why not? You don't like this place?"

"I love this place, but it's kinda on the romantic side for just friends."

"Well, let's pretend to be more than friends just for tonight. Cool?"

"Cool." I said.

Brian got out and opened my door, and we entered the restaurant with interlocking arms. As we sat down to enjoy the delicious assortment of meats, Brian grinned and said, "Now, for that good news I had for you, which is the real reason I stopped by today."

"Oh really? Not just because you missed me and wanted to see me, right?"

"You know I'm just messing with you. But no, I wanted to tell you face to face that we caught Lexi's killer, Rob. It took a while, but we finally got a tip from one of his relatives, which happened to be his sister. I wanted to thank you for helping us get a killer off the streets."

"Glad I was able to help! That is great news. It won't bring Lexi back, but at least he was brought to justice."

I was so glad to hear the news of Brian locking Rob up, but it just reminded me of the fact that it was my fault that Lexi ended up in his car in the first place. I had finally accepted the fact that she was gone, and there was nothing I could do to bring her back. That kinda put a damper on the date, but everything else was perfect.

While we were on the subject, I decided to ask about Dré and the girls, since I hadn't talked to Brian since he had arrested them. He said they all spent the night in jail, but made bail the next day.

"Their court dates are next month. Neither of the girls had records, but him, on the other hand, he's gonna do some time. He has more than a few things on his prison resume. It just makes me mad how these Negros take innocent girls that obviously didn't have anyone at home growing up to teach them to have respect for themselves," Brian said angrily, as his skin turned red.

"Yeah, I know exactly what you mean," I said, as I finished what was on my plate.

I enjoyed myself and was definitely looking forward to spending more time with Brian. On our way back to my place, Brian and I cruised through the city admiring all the beautiful lights of the city's nightlife.

"I wish this night didn't have to end," Brian said.

"Me, too. This is the best I've felt in a while."

"It doesn't have to end."

I looked at the time on Brian's dashboard and said, "It's getting late. I need to get some rest, and I know you have to get up early for work in the morning."

Brian gave me a thumbs down hand gesture, and I said, "We have plenty of time. I promise I won't disappear this time," I said jokingly.

"Ok. I guess I'll let you off the hook this time."

We pulled up in front of my house, and before I got out, Brian leaned over and kissed me with his soft succulent lips. He caught me by surprise and I wasn't even able to close my eyes. When our lips parted, he opened his eyes and we gazed directly into each other's eyes.

"You sure you don't want me to come in just for a few minutes?" Brian said softly as if someone else was listening.

I really did want him to, but I resisted the temptation and said, "No, but thanks for the offer. I'll talk to you tomorrow."

"I would say I'll call you, but you never gave me your new number. You just treat me like a step-child."

"Poor tink-tink. I'm so sorry!" I grabbed my phone and found his number in my contacts. I dialed it and let it ring until I heard his phone vibrate. "There you go!"

"Oh, so I am special enough to be in your contacts, huh?"

"Of course!"

"Ok, baby," Brian said, and licked those sexy lips, attempting to entice me once more.

He walked me to my door, gave me another kiss, and went on his way.

The entire next week, I worked hard trying to find a job. I looked at every newspaper ad in the classifieds, and every job search website there was. My time was winding down, and I was everything but prepared. I still hadn't seen or heard from Chance, but I knew for a fact, when it was time for me to go, he'd show his face. If he didn't, I was gonna ride it out for as long as I could.

Brian was working midnights, so he would call me and we would talk for hours while he drove around, patrolling the city. Every time I talked to him, I tried to seem calm and content. He had no idea of everything I was facing, and I was too embarrassed to tell him. I was always independent, and I didn't want him to think I needed a man for anything. I had allowed Chance to take some of that independence away from me, and it was time for me to get up off my ass and reclaim it.

That week passed, then another. The only time I didn't think about Chance was when Brian was around because he had a way of taking me to a completely different place. A place where I always felt like a giddy schoolgirl with her first crush. I couldn't say I wasn't attracted to Brian because that would've been a complete and utter lie. I don't think any woman would've been able to resist his sexiness that came with a personality that you couldn't help but fall in love with.

It was Tuesday night, and Brian and I had started a weekly ritual of watching our favorite show, "Being Mary Jane". Brian called like he always did when he was on his way to see if I needed him to bring anything. I already had ordered Chinese, and my Strawberrita and his Bud Light were already on the table sitting in front of the TV.

"Babe, you sure you don't need me to bring anything?" Brian asked one more time.

"I told you I got this. You always do everything. Let me take care of it this time."

"Aight! I'll be there in five."

I ran upstairs to put on my pajamas. I enjoyed these nights so much. Even though we were friends, I could still cuddle right up underneath him, while he ran his hands through my hair. We enjoyed each other's company and definitely could be ourselves around each other.

When I opened the door for Brian, he handed me a Snicker bar, which was my favorite.

"You know I had to bring you something. I couldn't come empty-handed."

Brian was always so thoughtful and sweet. I didn't know how he had escaped the paws of so many thirsty women, but I was glad because I truly needed a good friend at this point in my life.

When the show started, we sat up eating our Chinese food and enjoying our drinks. As soon as Omari Hardwick, who played Andre on the show, and who Mary Jane was the mistress to, showed his fine ass on the screen, I grinned from ear to ear. It never failed that Brian would catch me in the act and get to shaking his head. He tried getting me back when they showed Gabby, by saying, "Mmm mmm mm. That don't make no damn sense right there!"

"Ok, don't get slapped!" I playfully said, rolling my eyes.

"You know she don't got nothin' on you. Give me a kiss."

When I looked over to give Brian a kiss, he had his eyes closed, lips puckered, with rice smeared all over them. I couldn't do anything but laugh.

He opened his eyes and said, "What? You not gon' lick it off?"

"Negative!" I said.

As soon as a commercial came on, I ran to use the bathroom. While I was in there, I heard the doorbell ring.

"Jordyn, you want me to get that?"

I couldn't imagine who would've been coming by that time of night. My only friend was already there, and everybody knew I didn't have any family.

"Here I come!" I said as I quickly washed and dried my hands.

I ran through the living room to the front door. As I ran past, I heard Brian say, "I told you I could've gotten it. You know Chinese food only have you full for an hour. You about to be hungry again, running through this house like that."

I turned on the hallway light and looked through the peephole.

"Shit!" I said as I started pacing the floor.

"Open up the door, Jordyn. I saw you turn on the light," Chance said from the other side.

I took a deep breath and slowly opened the door. He quickly opened the storm door and walked in as if he thought I was gonna close the door in his face.

He looked me up and down and said, "Getting ready for bed already?"

"Um, no. Actually I was . . ."

I heard footsteps coming down the hall, and Chance glared in that direction squinting his eyes. Before I could turn around, Brian said, "Hey, I was getting worried about you. Everything ok?"

Brian looked at Chance, extended his hand and said, "Hey man. How you doing? I'm Brian."

Chance looked at Brian and snickered, putting his hands in his pockets. "So, now you got men coming up in my house?"

"He's just a friend, Chance!"

Brian looked at me with a look of confusion. "His house?"

"Look, you don't have anything to do with this," Chance said pointing his finger in Brian's face.

"I'm gon' ask you nicely to get your finger out of my face. I'm a friend of Jordyn's, and as a friend, I feel it's my duty to make sure she's good."

"You must don't know who I am," Chance said, boasting.

"No, you must not know who I am."

"I really don't give a damn," Chance said, and tried to charge him. Brian pulled both of Chance's arms behind his head, and pushed him up against the wall. As he held him there, he pulled out his badge and said, "Let me show you who I am." He flashed the badge in front of Chance's face, and said, "Now do you wanna act like you got some sense?"

"Let him go, Brian. It's ok."

"You're saying it's ok when he just tried to attack me?"

He's just upset. I'm sorry, but can you leave so we can talk?"

The disappointment on Brian's face made me want to cry, but I had to talk to Chance, and I knew we wouldn't be able to have a rational discussion with Brian there.

"Really, Jordyn? If that's how you feel." Brian let go of Chance and walked in the living room to get his phone and keys from off of the table. I stood on one side of the hallway and Chance stood directly across from me. Brian walked directly in between us, holding up the deuces sign, walked out and slammed the door.

"I'm sorry, Chance."

Chance, standing there with his arms folded, shook his head. "I can't believe you! This is the last thing I expected when I finally got up the nerve to come by. It sure didn't take you long."

"It's not even like that! I don't even know why I'm wasting my breath. Never mind."

"So, does he know about you?"

"No! We're just friends. Nothing more!"

"You know, he'll never be able to accept you. You might as well give up."

"Is this what you came over here for? To kick me while I'm down? Or did you come to put me out. I already know my time is up."

Suddenly, I saw a look of sadness come over Chance's face.

"No, I didn't come to do either. I'm sorry. I got thrown off track when I saw another man over here. That wasn't me at all."

I folded my arms and said, "So what did you come for?"

"Can we go sit down?" Chance asked.

I led Chance into the living room and we sat on the couch where Brian and I had just laid. Brian's beer still sat on the table next to his unfinished plate of Chinese food.

Chance looked around in disgust, probably imagining Brian and I doing everything except for what we were actually doing.

"Looks like you two were having a party."

"Nope, just watching TV," I said as I turned the TV off so I wouldn't see what happened at the end of "Being Mary Jane."

"Now to answer your question. I came because I miss you. I was hurt when you told, I mean, showed me your secret, but it was too late. I had already fallen in love with you, and love just doesn't go away like that. You were right when you said you're still the woman I fell in love with. You have no idea how many different scenarios I've gone over in my head this past month of ways this could be resolved or ways I could look past this and make it work."

"So, what'd you come up with?"

"Absolutely nothing. You've put me in a tough spot. Sasha's still riding me about you. She still believes we had something going on, so I definitely can't put you back in the office. I just want to keep the drama down to a minimum. Someone had put something in her ear, but I can't imagine who it could've been. Who knew about us besides us?"

"I know exactly who it is."

"Who?" Chance asked, naively.

"Zahriah."

"Jordyn. Come on now. You two have had it out for each other from day one. My girls don't communicate with Sasha at all, and for what reason would Zahriah do that and risk the job she so badly needs?"

I thought about it and maybe Chance was right. I had no proof that Zahriah had anything to do with Sasha coming to the office out the blue accusing me and Chance of having an affair. I still wouldn't put it past her though.

"Whoever it was, I'll find out sooner or later," Chance said with confidence, and continued. "But let's get back to the matter at hand. I want to know how can I love you? How can I make love to you knowing you have the same thing I do?"

"That's why I was asking you to give me a chance to explain. If you knew more about my background, maybe you would understand. Even as a child, I was never a little boy. I grew up as a little girl. I didn't do things like little boys. I always wore my hair long, my facial features were always of a girl, and I never even peed standing up! My voice . . . this is natural. I've never had to disguise my voice for anyone."

"What about you breasts?"

"Yeah, they're fake. I tried to grow them on my own but was unsuccessful, so I saved enough money to get them done. So, see, nothing differentiates me from any other woman besides what I have between my legs."

I went on to tell Chance how my momma was a hoe and caused my daddy to get addicted to heroine. I also went as far as telling him how my momma waited until after my daddy was dead to tell me how he molested me more than once and she allowed him to stay. Chance listened with a look of pity on his face, and finally spoke.

"Your mom didn't ever address the fact that you were male and looked like a female?"

"No. She just let me do me. When I began wearing girl clothes, she laughed at first, but then acted as if it was normal. My teachers looked at me strange and the other kids made fun of me, but I didn't care. I knew who I was."

"I'm sorry . . . I didn't realize . . ."

"Don't feel sorry for me. I'm fine. Everything I've gone through has just made me stronger. As far as I'm concerned, I was never meant to be a man. Maybe God got distracted while he was creating me and stuck me with the wrong sex parts," I said jokingly. Chance looked like he wanted to laugh, but wasn't sure if that would've been appropriate. "It's ok. Laugh about it. I do all the time, except for when it interferes with me having a real relationship with someone I love."

Chance reached over and hugged me. I inhaled deeply to take in the scent of his cologne that I had missed so much from the collar of his shirt.

"I love you so much Jordan," Chance said as took a deep breath while he still held me. When he let me go, he dug in his pocket and said, "I also came to give this back." Chance handed me the keys to the red Porsche. "I'll take you to go pick it up tomorrow. And don't worry about trying to move. I just better not catch any other men here."

"Don't worry. You won't," I said, wondering what Brian was doing and how many different types of bitches he had called me.

CHAPTER NINETEEN

That evening after Chance left, I decided to take a walk through the crowded city. It didn't matter what time of the day it was, it always seemed like hundreds of pedestrians were walking the streets, with totally different destinations in mind. I didn't have a particular destination. I was just looking to clear my mind. I was happy that Chance had thought about things and found his way back to me. It felt good to talk to him and get some things off my chest and talk to someone about my entire past and not just bits and pieces. That still didn't stop me from thinking about Brian. Even though I had told Brian that I only wanted to be friends with him, and he had been doing a good job of respecting that, truth was, I had begun to develop feelings for him.

With Chance already knowing about all the extra baggage I came with, literally, it would be easier to ease into an almost normal life with him. Brian was an understanding type of man, but I knew he wouldn't understand who I really was. Chance was right when he said that Brian would never accept me the way I was. I knew he was attracted to me, but only the parts of me he knew about; not the reality of me.

I stopped in my tracks within the crowd of people and pulled out my phone. I wanted to send Brian a text, but I had no clue of what to say, or how to apologize to him. I began typing the words "I'm sorry", but I knew that wouldn't be nearly enough and would probably just make him angrier than he probably already was. I deleted those words, and hit the "send" button, sending a blank text. I just wanted him to know I was thinking about him and that I was truly sorry, but didn't want to say the wrong thing. I stuck my phone back in my purse and continued walking.

After walking a few more blocks, I noticed a familiar face in the crowd headed in my direction. I squinted my eyes to make sure I was seeing clearly. I was right. It was Dré headed straight towards me! I turned around, hoping he didn't see me, and increased my walking speed, pushing people out the way.

"Jay!" I heard Dré shout.

I didn't look back. I continued to hear him call my name and it sounded like he was getting closer and closer. I began running as fast as I possibly could in the five-inch wedges I was wearing. Everyone looked at my like I was crazy as I ran, knocking over men, women, kids, and even seniors. I was terrified of what Dré would do to me if he caught me. I cut through an alley, hoping to lose him, and hid behind a dumpster. As I knelt down, I began shaking as I tried to slow down my breathing and heart rate. I felt as if I was going to have a heart attack at any moment.

"Jay! I saw you come this way. You ain't that fast. Didn't I tell you what I was gonna do if I caught you on the street? I guess you didn't believe me," Dré said as he walked down the alley, getting closer and closer to the dumpster.

I felt like getting up running, but I knew I wouldn't make it far without him catching me, so I decided to take my chance and stay where I was, hoping he wouldn't see me. I closed my eyes tight as I heard his footsteps against the torn up gravel. Next thing I knew, I was being lifted up by my hair. After Dré stood me up, he put his hands around my neck and started choking me."

"You a real bitch ass muthafucka! And yo ass really think you a woman. That's what's really funny. I gotta admit though, you tricked the shit outta me."

As Dré tightened his grip around my neck, I closed my eyes and began losing consciousness. He loosened his grip and began shaking me as I gasped for air.

"Hell naw bitch! Wake yo ass up! You not getting off that easy! I'm all man and you tried to take that from me. That's some punk ass shit you did. If you wanted to be a woman, that was yo business, but you went wrong when you tried to drag a straight man into your fiasco. Then sent the punk ass law to my corner fuckin' up my ends!"

Dré punched me in the jaw so hard I went flying up against a brick wall. I hit it so hard it knocked the wind out of me. He picked up a 2x4 he found on the ground, walked over to me and started beating me with it. All I could do was cry. I couldn't move, and felt like I was dying inside.

Dré then straddled me, saying, "You probably like this shit right here. Tell me how much you like this!" he said as he began continuously punching me in my face. The last thing I remembered was Dré dragging me back over behind the dumpster, and kicking me numerous times with his Timberland boots. Suddenly, I couldn't hear or feel a thing, and everything went dark.

I woke up, struggling to open my eyes. They felt glued together, and when I finally forced them open as much as possible, I stared straight up at the ceiling. It was dark in the room. There was a white sheet pulled over me. I lifted it up and saw that I was wearing a hospital gown. I felt like a bus had hit me.

"Ahem." I heard someone sitting in the corner clearing their throat.

I glanced over, and surprisingly saw Brian.

"How do you feel?"

"Horrible. What are you doing here?"

"I am a homicide detective and I was called on the scene to what they thought was a homicide because you were beaten so badly. Did your dude do this to you? You know I'll handle that."

Brian was referring to Chance. I said, "No, it wasn't him."

"Then who was it? He's the first person that comes to mind since he was the last person I saw you with. He was pretty pissed when I left and I should've never left you."

While Brian spoke to me, he stared at my face, making me feel self-conscious, so I wanted to see what he was looking at.

Before we continue, can you please give me a mirror?"

"Why?" Brian asked.

"Because I wanna see myself."

"You're still beautiful."

"Please, Brian! Give me a mirror!"

"Ok." Brian got up and went into the bathroom. He came back with a handheld mirror in his hand. He held it up away from me and asked, "Are you sure?"

"Yes."

Brian handed me the mirror, and as I looked through the mirror at my severely bruised and swollen face, tears began streaming down.

"You said I was still beautiful," I cried.

"You are. It's just a little bruising and swelling."

"But I can even barely open my eyes!"

"Calm down, Jordyn. You'll get through this. It's a miracle you're still alive. Please just tell me who did this to you so we can lock his ass up."

"I don't remember," I said, worried what would happen to me if I sent the police after Dré again and they weren't able to hold him.

"I think you're lying to me. I know we're better than that, Jordyn. Well, maybe not, after last night, but we'll talk about that later. This is business."

"Why do you think I'm lying? I really don't remember!"

"Well, how do you know it wasn't your friend from last night then?"

I laid there, twiddling my fingers, contemplating on whether I should tell him or not. If I did, I would then have to explain to him why Dré' tried to kill me.

"I'm waiting. You can trust me," Brian said.

"It was Dré," I said softly.

"Dré who? Not Rodriguez."

I bit my bottom lip and nodded my head.

"But why would he try to kill you? What's the motive?"

I hesitated before saying, "I used to work for him . . . before I came to you about Lexi. He tried to stop me. He didn't want me to put any unnecessary attention on his operation."

Brian stood up and said, "Wait. What type of work did you do for him?"

"I was one of his girls."

"Jordyn! Why didn't you tell me this?"

"Obviously because I was ashamed."

I told Brian about the night I had to pull my gun out on Dré'. I only left out the part about Dré' walking in on me while I was taking a shower and found out I didn't have a pussy. Brian immediately called the station requesting that someone stayed outside of my hospital room at all times. He told me he'd make sure the hospital officials and news reporters kept the story off the news for now since Dré had left me for dead. He wanted to make sure Dré thought I was dead for as long as possible.

My cell phone started vibrating in the clear bag with all of my possessions in it that was sitting on the table on the other side of the room. Brian went and grabbed it out of the bag, and without even asking my permission, answered it.

"Hello," he answered. "This is Detective Washington. Who is this?"

Brian glanced over at me, as he continued his conversation with the only person it could've possibly been. "I'm answering Jordyn's phone because she's unable to answer the phone right now, let alone do anything else, so I'm here taking care of her. That's what friends are for."

Brian took the phone from his ear and said, "Would you like to speak to Chance?"

I extended my arm so Brian could hand it to me. I could tell the call had upset him, but I didn't know what I was supposed to do. Brian looked out the window the whole time as I stayed on the phone with Chance, telling him what had happened. As we talked, he left his house, and headed to the hospital. I wasn't sure if he was in such a hurry because he was worried about me, or didn't like the fact that Brian was there with me. It was only six in the morning and the sun hadn't even risen yet.

When I hung up from with Chance, I said, "He's on his way."

"Ok?" Brian said.

"I just don't want any drama."

"You still haven't explained to me what your relationship is wit him. I wasn't trying to go there right now because of everything that's going on, but you never once mentioned him to me."

"I did, actually. Remember when I spoke briefly of the guy who didn't tell me he was married?"

"Oh yeah. So he's married, and has you living up in one of his alternate houses, huh? And you're willing to settle for that. You deserve better. You know that right?"

"But he helped me get off the street."

"Ok. He helped you. You're off the street, now thank him and move on. He has a family already."

"It's deeper than that. He loves me."

As soon as Brian was about to respond, Chance walked through the door with flowers, looking debonair as usual.

"Hey, baby," he said. He glared over at Brian who had sat back down in the reclining chair in the corner, and then gave me a peck on my swollen lips. "I'm so sorry this happened to you. What were you doing out there alone? I told you before you didn't need to be roaming the streets alone with him out there."

Brian jumped up out his seat and walked towards Chance. "You knew she was in danger of this maniac and still let her out of your sight?"

"Look, I've been taking care of her, making sure she was ok and we've been doing fine without you, so stay out of this."

"Yeah, you've been taking care of her, but look at her now. Is that what you call taking care of someone?"

"Can you leave me and my girl alone? We need some privacy."

"Your girl, huh?" Brian laughed. I could tell he wanted to say something about Chance being married, but thankfully, he kept quiet. "I'll leave if Jordyn wants me to leave, not because you asked me to."

They both looked at me, and I said, "Brian, thanks for coming."

Brian shook his head and said, "Can you I speak to you alone for a minute before I leave, Jordyn?"

"Chance, can you give us a minute?" I asked.

Chance, not liking the way things were going, said, "I was going to get a cup of coffee anyway. You need anything?"

"No thanks, baby."

Chance walked out the room and I waited for Brian to begin.

"Jordyn, I'm really tired of being dismissed when he comes around. If you want me out of your life, you need to just let me know."

"Brian, he's my man! What do you want me to do? I have to show him the same respect he shows me."

"Listen to yourself! Your man? He's not your man. He has a wife at home! I'm right here, Jordyn! I'm here for you, and single. I would love nothing more than for us to be together . . . At least try it out and see what happens. You see how good we are as friends. That's a start."

"I can't. I'm sorry. I can't offer you anything more than friendship."

"I don't know what he has over you, but hopefully you'll begin to see things for what they really are."

Little did Brian know, I knew exactly what things were. I was far from naïve, but I had to stick with the road I was traveling for now. The room became silent, and soon after, Chance returned. Brian told me he'd be outside until his cop showed up to watch my room. He promised me he would catch Dré and make sure he was locked up for a long time. By the look in Chance's eyes, I could tell the more Brian talked, the more irritated he got. Brian enjoyed knowing that he was getting to Chance. To top it off, before he left the room, he gave me a kiss on the forehead.

I ended up in the hospital for an entire week. I had a few fractured ribs that had a lot of healing to do. Dré' had really done a lot of damage on me. I couldn't believe after everything Dré and I had gone through, he could bring himself to kill me. After that I knew he was one heartless muthafucka.

Both Chance and Brian visited me everyday. Most days, they ended up bumping into each other, and exchanged words each time. By the end of the week, I had a room full of flowers, balloons, and stuffed animals from both of them. On my release date, I was sure that they both would be at the hospital arguing about who would take me home, but surprisingly, Brian didn't show. I was a little disappointed because he had been there for me every day prior, but not on the day I got to go home. At the same time, I was happy because I was tired of all the drama.

All of my swelling had gone down, and most of the bruising was gone, but my ribs were still a little sore. Chance helped me grab my belongings. He made me leave the flowers and balloons from Brian, saying he didn't have room in his car for everything, but I still managed to grab a few of the stuffed animals he had brought me. The nurse wheeled me down to the parking lot in a wheelchair, and Chance took care of me from there. He never asked any questions about Brian, but I guess some things had been on his mind, because that's what our entire conversation was about on the way home.

"So, when did you meet Brian?"

I wasn't expecting that from Chance since he acted nonchalant about Brian, other than the times they were in each other's presence.

"We met at the police station when I went to give them information about Lexi. He took me to go identify her body. We became friends after that."

"So, have you . . ."

"Had sex with him? No. I've only kissed him."

Chance didn't believe what I told him. He didn't say he didn't believe me, but he kept digging deeper to get the gist of what type of relationship Brian and I really had. He asked me what I knew about Brian's family, and if I had ever been to his house. I told Chance what Brian had told me about his family, and that I had never been to his house, which I hadn't. When Chance either got tired of asking questions, or didn't want to hear anything else about me and Brian, he turned up the radio and didn't ask anything else.

When we pulled up to my house, there was a police car sitting out front, and Brian's unmarked car, which was a Black Camaro, was parked in the driveway, and he stood there leaning up against it.

"What the hell is going on here?" Chance said.

"I don't know."

Chance looked at me and said, "Are you sure?"

"Positive! I didn't know he was gonna be here."

Chance pulled up in the driveway, right next to Brian. Before he could get out of the car, Brian had opened my car door, and began helping me out. Chance hurriedly got out, and grabbed me, putting his arm around me and pushing Brian to the side.

"What's you problem, man?" Brian asked.

"I don't appreciate another man sitting in my driveway waiting on my girl. I got this."

"I'm here because we need a cop outside of this house at all times until we have Dré in custody. I came by to let Jordyn know what was going on so that she wouldn't be shocked when she saw the cop car sitting here."

"Thanks, but no thanks. I told you I can take care of her," Chance said, with his arm still around me."

I became frustrated with it all and moved away from Chance. I stood in between Chance and Brian and said, "Look! I can't deal with this anymore! This is not a competition of who has the biggest dick! Chance, Brian is my friend. He was there for me when you weren't around. Brian, Chance is my man, and he was here before you were. You both are looking out for my best interest and I appreciate that. If Brian says I need a cop out here, then so be it. Chance, you can't be here 24/7. You do have to go to work, and home, of course."

Brian had a grin on face that he couldn't disguise if he had even tried. Chance wasn't too happy, but he knew I was right. Until Dré was off the streets, I wasn't gonna feel comfortable being alone, even if he did think I was dead. I knew word spread fast and it would only take one person to go back and tell Dré they saw me somewhere. At the end of the day, Chance and Brian would have to respect each other's roles in my life. If they couldn't do that, then they would have to make the decision on whether or not they wanted to be a part of my life. I was finally starting to realize I had more control of this situation than I thought. I just had to make sure I didn't piss Chance off to the point that he exposed my secret and left me high and dry. I wasn't sure if Brian would be ready to accept me as a roommate, especially if Chance told him everything about me.

CHAPTER TWENTY

Being stuck locked up in the house for weeks was the worst feeling in the world. Don't get me wrong, I could've left the house, but not without a police escort, and I definitely wasn't feeling the fat white man that sat outside my house everyday eating Dunkin' Donuts escorting me around the city. It would've been different if Brian could've been my escort, but I had promised Chance that I wouldn't have Brian around while he wasn't there.

Chance had been trying to be affectionate towards me, but everything not only felt different. It was different. We would still go out on dates, and enjoy each other's company. We would even indulge in a kiss here and there, but it went no further than that. Chance had no desire to be sexual with me. He wouldn't even let me give him head. It was like we had started over from scratch. I had needs and Chance wasn't satisfying them. It really pissed me off when I thought about the fact that he was probably leaving me every evening, then going home bangin' the shit out of Sasha. Chance felt bad about how he reacted towards me and promised it would eventually change. He just needed some time for his mind to absorb everything.

"Jordyn, you have to understand. Before, I thought you were one hundred percent woman, so it was easy to make love to you, or think of making love to you, but now that I know you're not, what's my excuse for being intimate with you?" he asked, as he laid next to me in my bed, easing his way out of making love to me once again.

"Maybe that you love me?"

"I really do, but that's not enough for me to be intimate with you. It would be uncomfortable for me. Just like I waited til I felt I loved you before I was intimate with you before, it's almost the same thing. I don't want to be forced into it. I can't look past this yet, but I have been thinking about some things."

"What kind of things?" I asked Chance.

An excitement suddenly came over Chance as he sat up in the bed. "I've been doing some research on sex reassignment surgery. I know it's expensive, but I want to do that for you as a gift." Chance curiously waited to see how I would respond to his proposition.

"I've already looked into it and know all about the cost and process. I've wanted to have it done for years. That's actually what I've been saving for. Thing is, I didn't want to do it for anyone other than myself. With you putting this on me, it takes my joy away. It makes me feel like the only way you'll want or desire me is if I have this surgery done. What if I don't? Are you going to walk out of my life? This kinda feels like an ultimatum. Is that what this is, Chance?"

"I told you I'm in love with you, Jordyn, and honestly, I don't know what the future holds, but what I do know is that before you threw all this at me, I regularly thought about spending the rest of my life with you. This has thrown a monkey wrench in my plans."

"And please explain to me how you were going to be with me for the rest of your life when you're already married to your supposed life partner?"

"I was looking into a divorce. I had already started talking to my lawyer to make sure she doesn't take all I have. The good thing is, she signed a prenup. I don't want to leave her with nothing, though. I would like her to still live comfortably because like I've told you before, I do love Sasha. She's just not my soulmate."

I wasn't sure if me having surgery would fix Chance and me. The only way we would be able to go back to the way we once were would be for my dick to be erased from his memory for good, and we all knew that was impossible. The only way we would know what the future held for us was to just to do it and wait to see what happened. At least it was something that I wanted to do for me and I would have no regrets because I wouldn't just be doing it for Chance. He would just be financing it.

"Well, I had a consultation a few years ago. The only thing I had to do was schedule the surgery. Unfortunately, I didn't have the funds at that time." I took a deep breath and looked at Chance.

"We're in this together, Jordyn."

The next day, I made my appointment for surgery with Dr. Caldwell, who I had previously had my consultation with. They still had all of my records on file, so I was pretty much set to go. A few days later, I was fasting the night before as the doctor ordered. I was nervous as hell, and Chance tried to comfort me, but I couldn't find much comfort in getting my dick sliced up, but I was sure that I'd be happy when it was all over.

I made a call to Brian, letting him know he could let his officer off duty from watching me for a week because I was having surgery.

"You ok? Do you need me to go with you?"

"No, boo. I'll be ok. There's this female procedure I need to have done. I've just been putting it off for a while."

"Ok. Well hopefully we'll have Dré in custody by the time you get back home. I'll be praying for a successful surgery. Call me and let me know how it goes when you're able."

"Thanks, baby. You're so sweet," I said, before we ended our call.

The big day had finally come, and I found myself sitting next to Chance waiting to be called to the back to get prepared.

A nurse finally came and got us and took us to the pre-op room.
She gave me a cap and gown to put on. I went in the bathroom
and stripped, put on the gown, then took my hair out of its
ponytail and bunched it up into the cap. I came out carrying all
my belongings, and Chance came and quickly grabbed
everything out of my hands.

"Here's a bag to put all of that in," the friendly nurse said.
She opened it up and Chance put everything inside.

The nurse led me to one of the beds and told me to relax. As
soon as I laid down, I saw Dr. Caldwell coming our way.

"Here comes the doctor," I told Chance.

Chance immediately stood up and held out his hand as Dr.
Caldwell approached.

"Good morning. I'm Dr. Caldwell, and you are?"

"I'm Chance . . . Jordyn's friend."

I couldn't believe Chance had just introduced himself as my
friend. That was one of the most hurtful things he had done
thus far, but Dr. Caldwell knew better than that.

"Mmm hmm," Dr. Caldwell said, then turned to me. "Jordyn!
Good to finally see you again. I just always come in before
surgery to let the patient and family, or in your case, friends
know what is about to happen."

Chance and I both nodded.

"The surgery will be approximately six hours. You will then
be taken to the post-op, or recovery room, which at that time,
you'll still be asleep. You'll be there for two hours, and as long
as everything seems to be going ok, you'll be taken to your
permanent room for your week's stay with us."

"Any questions?"

"How much pain will I be in?" I asked.

"Well, this is a pretty serious surgery, in which there will be
a lot of cutting, so you will be in pain, but we will give you more
than enough pain medication to take care of that. Once you get
ready to be released, you shouldn't be in hardly any pain at all."

After the doctor left, his nurse came back to hook up my IV
and other equipment. Chance asked me if I was nervous as he
sat next to me looking more nervous than I did. I wasn't
nervous about having the surgery. I was just nervous about

how I'd feel after the surgery. However I would feel after the surgery might've been a con, but the results of the surgery would be an absolute pro. I would be able to do things I've always wanted to do. Chance told me he was gonna run a few errands since the surgery was so long. When the anesthesiologist came to roll me back to surgery, Chance gave me a peck on the lips and told me he loved me. I told him back. Once I got to the operation room, which was freezing, the last thing I remembered was the anesthesiologist putting the clear mask over my nose and mouth and telling me to count to twenty.

When I struggled to open my eyes, all I could see was a blur. I felt like I had been asleep for at least a week. I finally managed to open my eyes, but still couldn't see very clearly. However, I was able to see Chance standing over me with the appearance that he was looking through my phone. He looked down at me and saw that my eyes were opened and said, "I was just texting Brian back for you."

Disregarding what he said, in a raspy voice I asked, "Where am I?"

"You don't remember? You got out of surgery a couple of hours ago. You're in the recovery room," Chance said as he grinned.

"It's done?" I asked nervously.

"Yes, baby. It's done."

"By the look on your face, I guess everything went ok."

"That's what the doctor said. How do you feel?"

"Numb right now. I can't feel anything down there. You sure they didn't damage a nerve?"

Chance started to look worried. "Let me go see if I can find the doctor."

As Chance walked towards the desk where a bunch of nurses were sitting, I tried to move, but was unsuccessful."

Oh my God. What have I done to myself? I thought.

I looked underneath the sheet, but of course couldn't see a thing because I was wrapped up so tight. Then I notice the catheter, wondering how long I would have to have that. When

I saw Chance walking back over with a nurse, I hurried up and put the sheet back down.

The smiling nurse said, "Welcome back, Jordyn! Your surgery went very well. I hear you have some questions."

"Well, I can't feel anything."

"That's actually a great thing! Trust me, you wouldn't want to feel the pain you would actually be in right now if we hadn't given you the high dosage of pain medication that we've given you. That is absolutely normal. That feeling will subside within the next few days and if necessary, we'll give you a morphine pump."

I felt relieved after talking to the nurse. I was so curious of what I looked liked underneath all of the wraps, but I knew I had at least a few days before I would be able to see my new pussy. Chance looked liked some of his concerns had been relieved, too. I'm sure he felt responsible for me, and if anything bad had happened he would've blamed himself. That was just in his nature.

After the doctor cleared me to be placed in my room where I would be spending the next week, and I finally got all settled in, I asked Chance to hand me my phone.

"You should rest," he said, trying his best to give me reason why he shouldn't give me my phone. Then it dawned on me what he had said earlier,

"So, what did Brian say when he texted me?"

"He just asked how your surgery went. Did you tell him what you were having done?"

"Of course not! He doesn't even know about me! I told you that! What did you tell him?"

"I told him you're fine and that I'm here with you, so you don't need him checking up on you."

I looked at the clock on the wall and realized it was getting late.

"Shouldn't you be heading home to Sasha?" I said, rolling my eyes.

"I'm concerned with you right now. Not Sasha. I know it was wrong of me keeping that part of my life a secret, but I truly hate that you found out about it. I hate that it's going to take forever for you to regain your trust in me. I want you to know how much I love you and want to be with you and only you."

Chance stayed with me another hour. He only left because I kept dozing off on him from all the meds the nurse kept pumping into me. He left my phone on the table next to my bed, so I texted Brian back, thanking him for checking on me, and apologizing for Chance's behavior. The next two days were rough on me. Every time I tried to move, I cried from the pain. Chance wanted to stay with me as much as possible, but I forced him to leave because I didn't like him seeing me like that. Even with the morphine pump, I was still in severe pain. Pain that I wouldn't wish on my worst enemy.

The day had finally come that I would be unwrapped and get to see the new me. Chance knew it was the day, so made sure he made an appearance. I guess he wanted to be the first to see what he had invested in. I burst his bubble when I requested that the doctor and nurse not allow anyone in the room during that moment. When the nurse went out in the hallway to tell Chance I didn't want him to come in, I heard him arguing with her, but she told him they had to respect the wishes of the patient.

As Dr. Caldwell carefully removed all the dressings, I couldn't read the expression on his face. I wanted it to be clear as to whether or not he was proud of his work or not. I looked at the nurse who watched as he removed everything, and her face was also expressionless. When he was done he took a deep breath, and the nurse gave a slight grin. She then said, "Well, Doc, you did it again! Job well done."

She then looked at me and said, "You are going to be a very happy lady!"

"Yes you are. I think this is one of the best I've ever done. Get her cleaned up, please, Kelly," he said to the nurse.

As she cleaned me up, I felt some pain, but nothing comparable to what I had felt during the past days I'd spent there. When she finished, she grabbed a mirror off of her cart and held it in a position so I could see between my legs. At first glance, I was in shock. It was a good shock. Of course I still had some stitches, but other than that, I looked like I'd had a vagina all my life. I smiled from ear to ear, and looked at Dr. Caldwell, who now had a smile on his face.

"Thank you so much for giving me the life I've always wanted!" I said to him as tears poured down my face.

"Is it safe to assume you'd like your friend to come in now?" Nurse Kelly asked.

I had forgotten all about poor Chance who was still standing in the hallway. I was so ecstatic, I felt like I didn't need anyone else in the room to bask in my happiness, besides myself, but I knew that was pretty selfish of me.

"Oh, yes! Please, let him in."

Kelly opened the door, and said, "Sir, you can come in now."

Chance slowly walked in looking not so happy, until he saw the smile on my face. His entire demeanor then changed.

"Well, I know what that smile means," he said, smiling back at me.

"Would you like to take a look, sir?"

"Sure. That is, if the boss doesn't mind," he said jokingly.

Kelly led him to the end of the bed and showed him what I was so very proud of. Chance rubbed his chin, and unless it was my imagination, I could've sworn he teared up.

"Beautiful," he said, and making it back to the other end of the bed, he lifted my chin with one finger and gave me soft, wet kiss that gave me my very first feeling of love within my new gift.

A couple of days later I was discharged to go home. Before Chance came to pick me up from the hospital, I called Brian to let him know I would be home soon and to ask him about their progress with arresting Dré.

"I'm sorry, babe. We still haven't found him, but I promise you we will. Do you want me to send a cop over, or do you feel safe enough to be alone? Or, I can always stay with you," Brian laughed.

"You just had to sneak that one in, didn't you?" I said, laughing with Brian. "I think I might be ok."

"Ok, well if you change your mind, just let me know. I'll send someone right over, and I'll be checking on you from time to time if that's ok ."

"That's fine." I heard someone coming through the door and quickly rushed Brian off of the phone, saying, "Gotta go. Talk to you later."

Luckily I had hung up because it was Chance and the last thing I needed was attitude from him for talking to Brian. Chance looked around the room when he walked in.

"What's wrong?" I asked.

"I thought I heard you talking to someone."

"No. You probably heard the TV. I just shut it off."

Chance looked at me suspiciously and started grabbing my belongings out of the recliner. I had everything bagged up and ready to go. I had been waiting for this moment all morning. It felt so strange to put on panties and not have to tuck anything, but I was sure I would easily and quickly get used to it. That alone would save me ten minutes of time every day.

I stared at Chance in his olive green fitted tee and straight-legged jeans as he walked back and forth throughout the room, making sure I wasn't leaving anything behind. His jeans hugged his ass just right and made me want to walk over and squeeze it. I began imagining us making love the way I always wanted to make love to a man; with all the lights on and without having to hide a thing. Before I knew it, I had walked over to Chance, pushed him back onto the bed, and separated his lips with my tongue. He wrapped his arms around me, and aggressively explored my mouth with his tongue. He began breathing heavily as I felt around for his bulge, and I didn't have to feel too long once I felt its hardness. I was surprised, due to the fact I hadn't gotten that reaction out of Chance since he had learned of my secret. It felt good to know I could turn him on again, but then again, it also made me wonder if Chance just loved me for sex, and not for me.

"Oh, I'm sorry!" a voice from behind said.

Chance and I quickly sat up, looking embarrassed.

"I just came to give you your discharge papers to sign. I can come back!" Nurse Kelly said, red in the face from blushing so hard.

"No, we're sorry. That was very inappropriate of us," Chance said.

"It's absolutely normal! I can just imagine how excited the both of you are."

Kelly handed me the pen and paper to sign the discharge form, and went over some information for me to follow until I was completely healed. I thanked Kelly for everything she had done for me while I was there and told her goodbye. She was one of the best nurses I had ever had and never judged neither my situation or me. When Chance and I got ready to pull out of the hospital parking lot, I looked out the window at the building one last time thinking about the fact that I walked in there as one person, and walked out feeling like a completely different person. I thought I had high self-esteem before the surgery, but now I felt better about myself than I had ever felt before. I felt complete.

CHAPTER TWENTY-ONE

After a week of sitting at home bored, with nothing to do, I asked Chance to bring over some work from the office that he needed help with. I said next time I'd be careful what I asked for because he brought me a stack of folders containing information for a large number of properties that he owned.

"I wanted you to sit here and get some peace and relaxation, but you were determined to do something, so here you go!" he said, putting everything on the dining room table.

"What's all this?" I asked.

"Just busy work. I need you to make sure all these properties have insurance policies. If not, you need to get insurance on them ASAP. The ones that have insurance, make sure everything is up to date."

"Sooo, I guess I'll need to work with Jacob on that."

"Yeah. I'm gonna give him a call and have him to stop by so the two of you can work together in getting everything organized. If he says and does anything out of the way, you make sure you let me know. He thinks he's God's gift to women and I personally don't trust him around you, but I'm trusting you won't let anything happen that shouldn't. I'm gonna head back to the office to get some work done there."

As Chance walked towards the front door to let himself out, he suddenly stopped, and turned around, looking back at me and said, "Damn you sexy!" He then came back towards me, grabbed me by both ass cheeks and kissed me. He made me feel more of a woman than I had ever felt.

When our lips parted, Chance said, "I can't wait."

Chance didn't need to say anything else, because I knew exactly what he meant, and I couldn't wait either.

"See you later, baby. I'm gone for real this time. I'll call you and let you know when Jacob is gonna come by after I talk to him."

"Ok," I said, still smiling from the moment we had just shared. It was just so natural and spontaneous.

After a couple of hours of sorting through the folders separating the properties with policies in their folders from the ones without, and still not hearing anything from Chance about what time Jacob would be coming by, I took a break and grabbed a yogurt out the fridge. I turned on the intercom to the backyard for the music to play, and went and sat outside on the back patio to enjoy the weather before the cool night air set in. When I got out there, I sang along with Jennifer Hudson's, "I'm His Only Woman". I loved that song.

I suddenly heard a noise coming from the side of the house and I quickly grabbed the butcher knife I had hidden under the seat cushion of one of my wicker patio chairs. I stood up straight, trying to control my nervous breathing, when unexpectedly, Brian appeared from around the corner. I held my chest and exhaled.

"Oh my God! You scared the shit out of me!"

"Maybe you do need that officer then," Brian said, laughing.

I didn't see a thing funny, and Brian could tell by the expression on my face.

"Come here girl," he said walking towards me. "Give me that," he said as he grabbed the knife out of my hand and wrapped his arms around me. "Mmmm. You smell so good, like always. I miss you so much," he spoke softly in my ear.

I reluctantly put my arms around him, and we rocked back and forth to the music, not saying a word. After a couple of minutes, Brian said, "I guess you miss me, too."

"Of course I miss you. We're friends, right?"

Brian looked me in my eyes and said, "I wanna be more than friends, and I won't give up until that happens."

"I looked away from Brian because the conversation was making me uncomfortable, and said, "I'm sorry, but it's not gonna happen, Brian."

"Why did you look away from me? You can't even say that to my face. You told me he loves you. I want you to look me in the eyes and tell me you love him. If you can do that, I won't mention us being more than friends ever again. That's unless you change your mind."

I unwrapped my arms from around Brian, stepped back, looked at him, and said, "I'm in love with Chance."

"Ok. Understood," Brian said, and stood close enough to me to give me a kiss on my forehead. "Just know that I'm here and I love you, too."

I was so not expecting Brian to say that he loved me. I didn't know what to say or do, so I said the first thing that came to mind. "You want a beer?"

Brian smiled and said, "Yeah, that's cool. I'm off duty."

I went in the house, and before getting Brian's beer, I went in the bathroom and locked the door. I stared at myself in the mirror, shaking my head because my mind was in shambles. I felt like Brian was complicating things that didn't need to be complicated, but he was a nice guy and I couldn't continue to lie to myself by telling myself I wasn't feeling him like that when I knew I was. That still didn't change my feelings for Chance. In any case, I did feel obligated to Chance.

When I finally returned with Brian's beer, and a margarita for myself, he was sitting at the patio table smiling.

"What are you sitting out here smiling about?"

"Nothing. Just enjoying the atmosphere, and happy I finally get to spend some time with you." Brian popped the top off his beer and gulped down half of it in one sip. "Nice and cold, just like I like it. I'm surprised you still had some beer around here. Oh, wait a minute. For Chance, right?"

"Wrong! He doesn't drink beer. I keep them around for you . . . Just in case."

"Is that right?" Brian said.

I sat there like a groupie, admiring the man sitting in front of me as we talked and finished our drinks.

After a few more drinks, we were both a little tipsy; me a little more than he was. He could at least still walk straight. I, on the other hand, was feeling real good. I told Brian he better leave before he had too much to drink. I grabbed my cup that had been filled a few too many times, and he grabbed his four beer bottles. We sat everything down on the dining room table and he laughed as I wobbled my way to the door to let him out. He caught me when I almost fell trying to get there. When I landed in his strong arms, I rubbed the back of my hand along his defined jawline. I already knew Brian was sexy, but every man seemed to have a little more sex appeal or attractiveness when I was tipsy. At that moment I started thinking to myself, *What the fuck am I thinking? This man is fine as fuck! Why am I wasting my time on a married man when this one is single and loves my dirty draws?* I leaned up to kiss Brian and he moved his head away from me.

I became offended and pushed Brian away from me. "Now you wanna reject me after you did all that talking about how you wanted me?"

"And you know I was telling you the truth, but I'm not about to let you do nothin' that you might wake up regretting tomorrow. I don't get down like that. If anything does happen between us, it'll be while we're both sober."

The more Brian spoke, the more he turned me on. I quickly grabbed his face before he could stop me and kissed him passionately. Brian didn't stop me this time. He wrapped one arm around me, then took his other arm and reached down pulling my leg up around him. From that one motion, I remembered that I was in no condition to be doing what this was about to lead to.

I parted lips with Brian and said, "You're right. We're both tipsy, and this isn't right."

"Now look what you did," Brian said as he looked down at his dick, which was so erect, it looked like it was about to poke a hole straight through his grey Nike sweatpants.

I began laughing, trying to apologize at the same time.

"You laugh, but I wanna know what you think I should do with that." Brian looked like he was serious as a heart-attach, but still had some laughter in his voice.

"Well, you have hands, and there's the bathroom!" I said, giggling.

"Really? That's what it is, huh?"

Brian and I laughed all the way to the front door. Some of that adrenaline rushing through my body must've taken my high down because suddenly I felt like I could function. As soon as I opened the front door, Jacob was standing there looking as shocked as Brian and I did. Brian quickly put his hands in front of his erection and straightened his face.

"Jacob! Heyyyy!" I said, trying to act innocent, but not doing a very good job at it.

"Hey to you," Jacob said, waiting on me to welcome him in, and looking at Brian, trying to figure out who he was.

"Ok, Jordyn. I'll see you later," Brian said, as he walked around Jacob.

"All right, Brian. Thanks for checking that out for me," I said, not knowing what in the world I was saying. "Come on in, Jacob. Chance told me he was gonna call me to let me know when you were gonna stop by."

"Yeah, I briefly talked to him, but I was in the middle of a few things and told him I wasn't sure what time I'd be available and that I'd call him when I was, but since I made it to this side of town, I figured I'd just stop. I guess I should've called first. Chance didn't tell me you were having company over."

As Jacob and I sat at the dining room table, I said, "Well, I wouldn't consider that company. He's one of my cop friends. I thought I heard something in the backyard and I called him to come check it out."

Jacob looked in front of him at all the beer bottles and said, looks like you two had a good time. Do you make it a habit of calling him over when you think you hear something, then have drinks with him?"

"No, it's not like that."

"Would it matter to Chance anyway? You two are just friends, right? Although, I did realize that this house is one of the properties he has insured with me."

Jacob was catching me off guard and confusing the shit out of me. The fact that I had alcohol in my system wasn't making things any better. I couldn't tell whether or not he knew about me and Chance, so I just thought I'd play it safe and pretend nothing was going on.

"Yes, we are just friends, so if Brian and I were more than friends, that would be fine, but we aren't. And yes, this house is insured with you, but I pay rent and the other bills. Chance is my landlord."

"Well, that's good to know, because I told you how I felt about you before. I love me a beautiful black woman and I haven't seen one as beautiful as you in a long time. When are you gonna let me take you out?"

"I don't know if that'll be a good idea."

"Why not?"

"I'm seeing someone."

"You're not married, are you?"

"No, but . . ."

"But nothing. No ring means you're single, and personally, I don't believe you. I think Chance is letting you stay here for something in return, and by that, I don't mean helping him manage his properties. If I was in his position, I know I wouldn't want no other man in my house drinking with my investment."

"You don't know what you're talking about. Quit assuming shit you know nothing about!"

"You're right. Let's get to work, and we'll see how much I really assumed when . . . what's his name? Brian, right? accidentally comes up in a conversation with Chance."

I tried to remain calm, but I knew worry was showing up all across my face. I cleared my throat and said, "Ok. Lets get to work."

Jacob and I worked for a couple of hours, and surprisingly ended up getting a lot of work done. I began yawning and Jacob asked if I wanted to call it quits for the night and resume the next afternoon. I told him that would probably be a good idea because my brain couldn't process anything else. Brian stood up and packed up his briefcase as I sat there and watched. Once he was done, I stood up and walked him towards the door, wondering if he would call Chance as soon as he got in his car to tell him what he walked in on.

When we got to the front door, I turned around in front of Jacob and asked him to please not mention anything to Chance.

"Although nothing's going on with me and Brian, you were right when you said Chance wouldn't like for another man to be here having drinks with me."

Jacob sat his briefcase on the floor and put his hands in his pockets. "Now you want to negotiate?"

"No. I'm just asking that you keep the peace. What you walked in on was innocent."

"Well, then you should have nothing to worry about, right?"

"Can you please promise me you'll keep quiet about it?"

"And what are you gonna do for me?"

I hesitantly asked, "What do you want me to do for you?"

Jacob began unbuckling his belt, grinning at me. "Come on, baby."

"I'm not gonna fuck you!"

"You don't gotta fuck me. Just blow me."

I began thinking to myself if it was that important for Chance not to know Brian was at the house spending time with me after I had promised Chance it wouldn't happen again. I also thought about what if Jacob didn't keep his side of the deal and still told Chance. It was a gamble I would have to take. I took Jacob by the hand and walked him to the living room. I then unbuttoned his pants and let them drop to the floor. He was already on hard, anticipating the talent I was about to impose on him.

I pushed him down on the couch and spread his legs just enough so I could kneel in between them. I got on my knees and began jacking his dick. I already knew that the popular myth about white men's dicks was untrue from the line of business I was once a part of, but I still had not seen a white one as big as the one that was right in front of me at that moment.

I spit on his dick and spread my saliva all over his head and shaft, and massaged his balls with it. I did that until everything was evenly moistened to the point that his dick easily slid into my mouth. As I polished it, Jacob grabbed my hair and tensed up his thighs. When I looked up and saw the expression on his face, I knew I was doing a good job. Hopefully good enough that he'd forget all about what he had seen tonight.

"I'm about to cum," Jacob said.

I lifted my head and started jacking him again. He grabbed my head, pushing it down and said, "Keep sucking. I want you to taste this cum."

Reluctantly, I slid his dick back into my mouth, and he bobbed my head up and down, until I could feel the cum pulsating through his dick, and exiting into my mouth. Jacob opened his eyes and watched as I let it run out of my mouth, down my chin.

Jacob took a deep breath and exhaled. "Damn girl! You're better than I thought you would be. You made me want some of that pussy. Maybe next time, huh?" Jacob laughed. "I was wondering why Chance would cheat on his beautiful wife, but if he's getting it like that on the regular, I can see why!"

I got up off the floor and went into the bathroom to clean myself up. As I dried my face, I looked in the mirror at someone I wasn't proud of. I had just regressed into my old ways, which I was trying to stay away from, but I didn't know what else to do. When I came out of the bathroom, Jacob was already put back together. He looked ecstatic while I tried to keep from crying. Jacob followed me to the door once more. He picked up his briefcase from where he had left it and said, "Your secret is safe with me, Jordyn. Thanks for a good time." Jacob winked at me and walked out the door. I slammed it behind him and immediately ran upstairs to take a shower.

CHAPTER TWENTY-TWO

Chance stopped by later on that evening. I was already in bed trying to forget what I had done. When I heard Chance coming up the steps, I closed my eyes, trying to pretend I was asleep. When he walked in the room he said my name. Then he sat on the bed and nudged me on the shoulder. I turned over and looked act him, trying to act like I had been in a deep sleep.

"Hey, baby. You feeling ok? It's kinda early for you to already be in the bed," he said, sounding very concerned.

"Yeah, I'm good." I said in a sleepy, raspy voice.

"What'd you do today?"

I sat up and said, "What do you mean? I did what you asked me to do. Jacob and I worked on getting the properties together."

"Jacob came by?" Chance said, looking at me like he was bothered when in fact, he was the one that sent that asshole over here.

"Ummm, yeah! Remember, you did tell him to come by."

"Yeah, but he never called to confirm, or never even called me when he left here to let me know he had come."

What Chance didn't know was he came all right; all in his woman's mouth.

"What happened? Did he try anything?"

I tried to keep a straight face when I said, "Nothing happened. We just worked on what you asked us to work on and he said he'd be back tomorrow so we can finish up."

"Are you sure?"

"Positive. Stop being so overprotective!" I exclaimed.

Chance said, "I'm sorry. I just wanna make sure you're ok."

I could feel that there was some type of tension between Chance and Jacob, but I just couldn't figure out what it was. I needed to know so I could know exactly what kind of man I was dealing with when it came to Jacob, so I asked.

"What's up with you and Jacob?"

"What do you mean?" Chance asked curiously.

Every time he's around, you act different. Are you and Jacob friends, or is it strictly business?"

"We actually lived down the street from each other growing up. Our parents we're really good friends and we were best friends, but . . ."

Chance stopped and wiped the beads of sweat from his forehead. That only happened when he was in an uncomfortable situation, so I knew he didn't want to continue our conversation.

"But what?" I asked, curiously.

"It's getting late. I better go. I'll tell you all about it another day.

"No! I need to know. What happened?"

"Why is it so important to you all of a sudden?"

"I just feel like you hold so much back from me. You know so much about me, and I feel like I don't know enough about you."

Chance took a deep breath and reluctantly said, "Ok. We fell out in high school about a girl. Ever since then, I don't trust him around any woman that I love."

That told me enough right there. Obviously, Jacob had come between Chance and a woman that was apparently very special to Chance. I knew that it takes a lot to come between boys. They were so different from women. They could get into an argument one minute, and an hour later, be best buddies again. Women held grudges forever, and that's what it seemed had happened between Chance and Jacob. I just wondered what ever happened to the special woman. It was apparent that Jacob didn't end up with her either.

After hounding Chance for information, he laid me flat on my back and straddled me. He then grabbed both of my wrists and held them down. He looked at me with a smirk, then lowered his head, licking me from my cleavage, all the way to my top lip. I opened my mouth allowing his soft, warm tongue to slide in, and proceeded with giving him his good night kiss. Every time Chance left me at night, it was a sad occasion for me. I didn't know how much longer I would be able to knowingly share my man with another woman. I knew he told me he needed some time, but I had decided if he didn't try to give me any information regarding his intentions and plans for him and me within the next couple of weeks, I would be forced to bring it up and give him an ultimatum.

"Hey, baby. I really enjoyed our time together yesterday. Hopefully we can do it again real soon, and I hope I didn't get you in trouble. Call me when you get time. Love you girl," Brian said in the voicemail he had left me while I was in the shower the next morning. I didn't feel comfortable with Brian telling me he loved me when I couldn't reciprocate because I knew I didn't feel the same way. Even though I had told Brian how I felt about Chance, and how that wasn't going to change, I still felt like I was somehow leading Brian on.

I didn't call Brian back. I didn't feel like talking to anyone. I was lost in my emotions and was losing patience on waiting for something to happen. I could imagine Chance telling Sasha that he wanted a divorce, putting her out, and putting me up in that beautiful, extravagant house of his. It seemed so easy in my mind, but Chance made it seem so difficult. She had signed a prenup, which I understood meant that whatever she came into the marriage with, she would walk away with. Nothing more and nothing less.

To keep my mind off of things, I used the rest of the morning and afternoon to get some housework done. I threw on some sweats and a t-shirt, and tied my hair up with a scarf. I cleaned every room in the house from top to bottom, rearranged my bedroom, and even did some gardening in the backyard. Chance called a few times throughout the day, checking on me like he always did. His last call he made to me, he told me that he called Jacob and told him it wasn't cool for him to stop by without getting back with him to let him know. He said that Jacob apologized and said he'd be by that evening.

I had begun to feel pretty good until I received that news. I was hoping that with Chance being so concerned about what happened between me and Jacob the night before that he wouldn't want Jacob to come back over without him being around. I guess I was wrong. Obviously he wasn't too concerned, which he just didn't know, he should've been.

As the afternoon winded down and evening was setting in, I became apprehensive. I was hoping Jacob would be a no-show because I really didn't have time for his shenanigans. I had cleared my mind so much that I was at the point that I felt like if he told Chance, so what! Maybe that would push Chance to make some major decisions in his life.

When I heard my doorbell ring I sighed. I pouted all the way to the front door and before I looked through the peephole, I said a short prayer, asking God to please not let it be Jacob on the other side of the door. Obviously I hadn't given God enough time to answer that prayer, because when I looked out, there stood Jacob with that sneaky grin on his face. His dimples were so adorable. If he hadn't been such an asshole, I probably would've let him get it without him needing to blackmail me! Not really, but his dimples were definitely a turn on.

I opened the door without saying a word to Jacob, and walked straight to the dining room table and sat down, ready to get to work. The faster we could get done, the faster I could kick him out of my house.

"What? No kiss, baby?" Jacob said.

"Ha. Very funny," I responded.

"Chance didn't seem very happy that I came by without telling him yesterday," Jacob said, and laughed. "I wonder how he would've felt if he knew I wasn't the only one that decided to stop by yesterday."

"Jacob, please don't start with this bullshit today. Let's just get this done."

"Oh, so you must think you finished paying up yesterday. You still owe me a little more. I dreamed about your sexy ass last night. I might have to steal you. I know that landlord shit is some bullshit. You wouldn't have gone to the extent that you did last night just to keep your little friend a secret if you were only Chance's tenant. You might as well admit that you're the side chick and that's all you'll ever be."

Already irritated, I stood up and walked towards the kitchen. "Would you like something to drink?" I politely asked.

Jacob came up behind me as I reached in the cabinet to get a glass. He wrapped his arms around me from behind, and pushed up against me so I could feel his bulge up against my ass.

"I got all I need right here," he said directly in my ear.

We heard footsteps coming around the corner and I quickly grabbed two glasses as Jacob released me. Chance came from around the corner and I put on a phony smile.

"Chance! I didn't even hear you come in."

"The front door was unlocked," Chance said, winking at me, letting me know to play along.

I knew I never left doors unlocked. I was a little OCD when it came to locking doors. Chance just didn't want Jacob to know he had just come in with his key.

"Hey man," Jacob said with a dumb, uncomfortable look on his face. "I didn't know you were gonna stop by."

"Yeah, I thought since the two of you would be finishing up everything tonight, I'd look over everything so that this wouldn't have to be extended into another day. I know you have better things to do than come over here and do more work once you leave your office every evening."

"You know it's no problem. Anything for my boy. You'd do the same for me."

"Yeah. You're right about that," Chance replied.

The tension in the air was thick, and everyone could feel it. "Jacob, what was that you wanted to drink?"

"I'll just take some water. Thanks beautiful," Jacob said, knowing exactly what he was doing.

Chanced grabbed a paper towel and wiped his forehead.

"Did you want anything, bae . . . Chance?" I asked, almost forgetting that we weren't supposed to be a couple in front of Jacob.

"Nah, I'm good. Thanks love," Chance replied.

"Love, huh?" Jacob said. "When do they get that title, Chance?"

"When they get the "beautiful" title from you. But you know that's in my character. I call all the ladies "love"."

I tried my best to calm things down. I wasn't in the mood to be breaking up any fights. I'd had enough of that shit. I thought that kind of shit only happened in the hood, but apparently not. Professional businessmen did the same dumb shit.

"Look, we really need to get to work you two. I don't know what's going on between the two of you, but I'm tired and would like to get started if you don't mind."

After I got Jacob and Chance back on track, I experienced the longest two hours of my life. I just knew another argument was going to break out in the midst of it all, but they remained calm and respectful towards each other. I realized not only that night, but also the night Chance had popped up on me and Brian, that a beautiful woman could really bring the ugly out of two fine ass men. I was hoping that I would never have to be in the presence of Jacob ever again.

Once that night was over, I think Chance kicked himself for ever allowing Jacob to come by my place in the first place, because after that, he would still bring me work to do, but nothing that involved having to see Jacob. He would've kicked himself even harder and then kicked me to the curb if he had known what I had done for Jacob. I regretted it and wished I would've just let whatever was gonna happen, happen.

The next few weeks, I spoiled Chance like never before. Not only because I felt guilty about what happened between me and Jacob, but also because it was getting close to time that I would be able to use my new tool with Chance, and for some reason, deep down in my heart I felt like however that first encounter went would be the deciding factor of whether or not Chance would be able to commit to me. It sucked, but that's the way it seemed. Anytime I brought up Sasha's name, or asked him how things were going at home, he would quickly change the subject. The last time I asked, Chance snapped, saying, "I have you in my life and spend so much time with you as an outlet from what I have to go home to. It becomes not so much of an outlet when that's all you want to talk about! I'm here with you, so obviously this is where I want to be."

"So if this is where you want to be, then why won't you stay with me and not go home to her? Don't you think about how that makes me feel? You're having your cake and eating it, too. What about me?"

"Oh, is that what this is about? Because I'm married, you think that's an excuse for you to go out and be with someone else?"

"No, I'm just sayin' . . ."

"Look around you, baby. Look at everything I've given you. Don't I deserve just a little time to get things in order on my end? Divorces don't happen overnight."

A smile came upon my face and I said, "So, you're divorcing her?"

"That's my plan. Always has been."

I ran and jumped up on Chance, wrapping my legs around him.

Before kissing me and carrying me over to the bed laying me down, Chance said, "You don't have to worry about anything. Let me handle this and you just sit back and enjoy."

He leaned over me and unbuttoned my jeans, then slid my heels of my feet through the tiny openings of the skinniest part of my jeans. I was looking confused. I definitely wanted Chance, but I didn't want to do anything too soon.

"What are you doing?" I asked.

"I want to show my woman how her man is supposed to make love to her."

"But it hasn't been six weeks."

"Close enough, now shhhh," Chance said. He pulled my pants off and threw them on the floor all in one motion, exposing nothing, but my red, lace thong. He then grabbed both of my arms to sit me up, and raised my arms to the ceiling. I closed my eyes, anxious about what was about to happen, as he raised my tank over my full bare breasts. Before pulling it completely off, he knelt down and spent equal time with each of my girls until my nipples throbbed and stood at full attention. He stood back up, staring at me and said, "You are the most beautiful and intriguing woman I've ever seen."

I blushed and then watched as Chance pulled his white V-neck t-shirt up over his head, revealing more of the only chocolate I had an acquired taste for. Every muscle in his chest and stomach were perfectly defined. He grabbed both sides of my thong and took a deep breath before he pulled them down to the floor. I was sure Chance was probably nervous about what he'd see because he hadn't seen that part of me since before I had left the hospital. He hadn't even asked about it.

Chance lifted my legs, spreading them apart, and smiled, admiring my new, freshly shaven pussy. He immediately pushed my legs further over my head and took his long, soft tongue and ran it from my ass all the way to the front of my pussy and the sensation was wonderful. I sighed as he explored all of the ins and outs of my pussy and sucked and tickled my clit all at the same time. He spread me open and stuck his tongue as far as it could go as if he wanted to get to know every part of his new best friend. I was feeling so good, I pulled my legs back even further and held them. Chance grabbed one of my titties and squeezed my hard nipple, which caused even more of an unforgettable feeling. I moaned and breathed heavily. From my response, Chance sucked my clit, harder and faster. My legs began to shake, and suddenly, I had this uncontrollable feeling come over me. I grabbed the back of Chance's head with both hands and arched my back. My body shook the entire bed as I released all the power, love, and passion I had within my mind, body, and soul.

"Hold that pose," Chance told me as I continued to hold my legs, unable to move anyway. He stripped the rest of the way down showing me how pleased he was to see me. He rubbed his rock hard dick up against my pussy. It brushed up against my clit, which was still sensitive from the major orgasm I had just experienced, and caused an aftershock. He then slowly, and gently offered his blessing and I cordially accepted. I held my breath with the first thrust.

"You ok?" Chance whispered.

"Yeah." I whispered back.

"You want me to keep going?"

I wanted Chance to shut his ass up and work the shit out of me. That's what I wanted.

"Yes, baby."

Chance slid his monster in and out, slowly at first, and the more comfortable he got and more of a positive response he got from me, he became more aggressive and sped it up to be just right. He securely wrapped his arms around my lower back, lifting up my body and thrusting harder. His breathing quickened and I felt his body begin to spasm, right along with mine. We moaned together until both of our juices started flowing between our warm, damp bodies.

After the main event, I remained on my back, feeling comatose, and Chance laid on my chest like a baby that had just been given a pacifier. There was an uncomfortable silence in the room. I didn't know what to say, whether it had been, "So, does it work well?" or "Do we need to return it?" Chance finally broke the silence and said, "I know I don't normally talk like this, and I'm apologizing before I say this in case I offend you . . ."

Uh oh. And here it comes . . . Drum Roll! I thought to myself.

I waited for Chance to say what he wanted to say, but he said nothing.

"What is it, baby?" I asked.

"That was the best goddamn pussy I've ever had in my life! I'll tell you one thing. It was well worth the hundred grand! You better take good care of that cuz that's a blessing right there."

I smiled as I stroked my hand across the top of Chance's head in the direction of his hair.

He looked up at me and asked, "So how do you feel? How was it?"

"It was awesome. The best feeling I've ever had in my life, and I only want to share that feeling with you."

Chance scooted up and gave me a kiss. "I love you, baby," he said.

I reciprocated.

CHAPTER TWENTY-THREE

After Chance and I unwrapped our new gift, we used it at least every other day. We were definitely sexually compatible, but things still weren't going completely as I wanted them to. After Chance had told me he was getting a divorce, which was what led up to us having sex with my new vajayjay, he hadn't mentioned it again. I was beginning to think he only told me that to keep me hanging around, waiting on something that wasn't gonna happen. With the new me, I felt like I could have any man I wanted, so I was definitely feeling myself. I knew damn well I didn't have to settle for a married man. I didn't want it to be like that because I didn't want to seem like a gold-digger who got want I needed and wanted, and moved on.

Brian made it part of his daily regimen to at least text or call just to tell me he loved me. No matter how many times I told him to stop telling me that because he didn't mean it, he continued to do it. One time he even got very defensive and told me not to tell him how he felt. I tried to keep our phone conversations at a minimum because the longer we talked, the more we seemed to get lost in our feelings. The feelings that I did have for Brian were never unmasked until we had a conversation that was way too long, or we were in each other's presence for too long. We also still managed to sneak in our weekly get together for "Mary Jane" night. We learned our lesson from the last time Chance had snuck up on us, so Brian started parking his car around the corner, so if Chance decided to drop by, he could just sneak out the patio door. Nothing sexual had happened between me and Brian. I didn't have the desire, but he did. I just enjoyed our intimate kisses that made me feel warm inside, and his company, period.

After so long of just kissing and hugging, I started to feel like Brian was becoming distant. Our "Mary Jane" nights became almost non-existent and the texts became scarce. His "I love you" texts became "How are you?" texts. I never questioned Brian because I couldn't expect him to wait around for me forever. I got to the point where I had gotten tired of lying to Chance about not talking to Brian anyway. It was a chore cleaning up after our nights together to make sure there was no trace of Brian anywhere. I decided to just let everything flow and allow things to happen in the manner they were meant to happen. I can't lie. Life wasn't as exciting and spontaneous without Brian around as much. Chance and I did things together, but everything was always so planned.

I remembered the time Chance told me what he loved about me was that I was so interesting and fun, and Sasha was nothing like that. I didn't feel like that person when I was around Chance anymore. I kinda felt like he was turning me into Sasha. I was a totally different person when I was around Brian. I felt like I could let loose, get tipsy, and act a fool if I wanted to, but it would all be in fun. I felt like if I did that with Chance, he would look at me like I was crazy, but that was the real me. I liked to have a good time, which involved embarrassing myself at times.

Chance had just purchased a huge property that he'd had his eye on for a while. He had finally gotten it for a reasonable price and asked me to go out so we could celebrate. I was surprised because I thought he would've wanted to go out with his wife to celebrate something so big. This definitely made me feel like I was moving up to where I needed to be to steal his heart completely. Chance told me he wanted to go to the Blue Diamond to celebrate. That was the first place he ever took me when he picked me up off the strip. I would never forget that night because that was the last night I saw Lexi. Chance said he wanted to celebrate us and the purchase of the property.

While I got ready for my night out that evening, I sat at my vanity, putting on my makeup, never seeing myself as beautiful as I saw myself that night. I was feeling myself, and it definitely showed all over my face. I loved Chance, but tonight was the night I would make it clear that he would need to make a decision. No more telling me one thing and never bringing it up again. I was tired of him coming to my house, kissing me all in my mouth while I wondered if he had just got done eating Sasha's pussy. I felt I had given him plenty of time to get his shit together. If he needed longer than the time I had given him to figure out if he wanted to commit to me and only me, then obviously this wasn't what he wanted. People know what they want when they want it, and it usually doesn't take months to realize that.

I put my hair up in a high classy bun, added some lashes, which I hadn't done in a while, and made myself up with my new pink sparkly eye shadow and lip gloss that I had bought from Love and Hip Hop's, Rasheeda's Poiz Cosmetics line. I wanted to look classy, beautiful, and serious when I had my much-needed conversation with Chance. I wore my long, fitted, strapless, pink and black Maxi dress with my pink rhinestone, open toe shoes. I promised myself I would be no one but myself tonight. That's the person Chance had fallen in love with and I needed her to come back.

When Chance got home, I was sitting at the dining room table waiting for him. He looked at me and whistled.

"You look gorgeous," Chance said.

I looked him up and down, and sucked my teeth. "Damn, baby. You are fine," I said in my ratchet girl voice.

Chance laughed and said, "Thanks, Jordyniqua!"

Maybe Chance was just following suit, and needed for me to be myself in order for him to relax and let his sense of humor come out. I knew he had one. I had seen it quite a few times.

Chance grabbed my hand and helped me up out of the chair, staring at me, shaking his head. "Who are you trying to impress? You trying to make me have to fight someone tonight?"

"This is all for you," I assured Chance.

Before we exited the house, Chance gave me a sensual kiss on my shoulder that made my heart flutter.

When we walked into Blue Diamond, it seemed liked everyone focused their attention on us, as if we were the Obamas. This particular night, everyone was able to seat themselves, so we took it upon ourselves to look for the same table we sat at the last time we were there. As soon as we spotted it, we saw a couple sit down.

"Shit!" I said.

"Stay right here," Chance said, as he walked towards the couple sitting at our table.

I stood there watching Chance as he talked to the couple, pulling out that magic charm that he used to pull me. They looked at him smiling and nodding. Chance pointed in my direction and they looked at me. The next thing I knew, they were getting up out of our seats. Chanced gestured for me to come over.

When I got to the table the other couple was still standing there, waiting for Chance to introduce us.

"Jordyn, this is Maxine and Vince Kindred. They were nice enough to let us sit here since it means so much to us."

I shook both of their hands and told them thank you.

"No problem!" Maxine said, grinning from ear to ear. She seemed way to happy to be giving up her table to some people they had never seen in their lives. "And congratulations on your engagement!" Vince added.

I glared over at Chance, who was nodding at me, then back at Vince and said, "Thank you! We appreciate that."

After they walked off to find another table, I said, "What was that all about?"

"Well, I had to give them a good reason to give up this table. What did you want me to say? Well, this is the table we sat at right after I picked her up off the corner she used to work. As a matter of fact, Vince, you probably picked up her once or twice," Chance laughed.

I became so hot at that moment I wanted to scream. "Are you serious right now?!?!" I said, trying my best not to be so loud to draw any unwanted attention our way.

"It was a joke. Sorry!"

"Whenever you joke, it's about that the majority of the time! That tells me that it still really bothers you, but you try to make light of it by making jokes of it. You knew what you were doing when you pursued me. You're the one that wanted to be a part of the "help a hooker" foundation!"

"Ok. I get it. I'm sorry. We're not gonna start the night like this. It's supposed to be special. I promise I won't bring it up again."

"Thanks! I appreciate it," I said sarcastically.

During our meal, I ordered a few drinks just so that I would mellow out. Chance had completely changed my mood with the dumb ass joke he made, even though he had apologized. When I ordered my third Vodka and cranberry, Chance said, "You sure you haven't had too much?"

"No, I'm haven't a great time. Aren't you?"

"I'm with you, so of course I am."

"Ok. Well, maybe you should have a couple more drinks, too. I know two shots of Patron hasn't done much for you."

"You're right. I better try to catch up with you before I get left behind."

I felt like I had enough alcohol in me at that moment to get my point across, so I decided to put everything on the table.

"Chance, there's something I want to talk to you about."

"Yeah, I feel we need to talk, too."

I was shocked by Chance's response. "Ok, well, you wanna go first?" Deep inside, I was hoping that whatever Chance wanted to talk about was the answer to what I wanted to talk about, so it would alleviate the need to repeat everything a second time.

"No, you go ahead," he said.

That wasn't the answer I was looking for, but I proceeded anyway. "Well, Chance, you know I love you . . ."

"Uh oh. Sounds like you're breaking up with me."

"You wanted me to go first, so hear me out. And for starters, I don't think I can break up with a married man. I need clarity in this relationship. I need to know where it's going, and an approximate time frame of when this is supposed to happen. If you can't tell me that much, I can't see myself waiting around for you to leave Sasha and be with me. I feel like you're stringing me along until you decide you want to make a move. How do I know that won't be forever? I just can't do it. I appreciate everything you've done for me, but this shit just ain't right and I refuse to let you make all the rules and I follow them like a flunky any longer." I looked at Chance waiting for him to respond.

"Are you finished? I don't want to interrupt."

"Yes. Go ahead."

"Ok, so sounds like you're giving me an ultimatum. If I understood correctly, if I don't tell you tonight that I'm divorcing Sasha and give you an approximate date of when this is to happen, you're leaving me. My question is, what if I give you a date and you don't approve of it? Do you still leave?"

"Yes," I said with confidence and power in my voice.

"Truth is, Jordyn, I've been thinking about some things. Yes, I love you too, but I need someone who can bear my children, and unfortunately, you can't do that for me. That's about the only reason I can't tell you right here, right now that I'll leave Sasha tomorrow."

"Chance! Are you fuckin' kidding me? So you're gonna sit here and tell me you can't be with me and only me because I can't have babies? It's one excuse after another with you! I'll never be good enough! What's wrong with adoption? We can adopt a baby."

"I want a baby with my blood. And don't ever say you're not good enough. You're great. I wouldn't still be around if you weren't."

"Lie, lie, lie! You don't think Sasha is great, but you're still hanging around. Or do you? Maybe that was a lie."

"I still plan on eventually being with only you, but I want to have a baby first. Sasha and I have been working on that, so it shouldn't be long. Then, once she has the baby, I'll file for divorce."

I felt like I was in another world; like I was a volcano getting ready to erupt. "What was I? A science project for you?"

"Come on, Jordyn. Just think about it. You know I'm crazy in love with you. This will work. I promise."

I had no words for what I was feeling, so I sat there, still looking beautiful for the man I felt would take the ultimatum I presented to him and do what I imagined him to do, which was to give me a date and stick with it. He did the complete opposite.

"Look who the wind blew in," Chance said.

I looked in the same direction Chance was looking, and saw Brian walking in with some heifa he was interlocking arms with. I felt my eyes grow in disbelief. As they walked in our direction, the high-yellow bitch with the beautiful golden honey-blonde bob leaned her head on Brian's shoulder, with a huge smile on her face. The waitress brought my drink just in time and sat it in front of me. As I kept my eye on Brian and his date, I lifted my glass and drank the whole thing in one gulp.

"Jordyn!"

I heard Chance calling my name, but it was irritating me more than anything, so I tried to block it out.

"Jordyn! What is wrong with you?"

I finally looked over at Chance, smiling, and said, "Nothing. What's wrong with you?"

Chance shook his head. I wasn't sure if Brian didn't see Chance and I sitting at the table when they walked past, or if he was trying to ignore me, but I wasn't having it.

"Brian!"

Brian's date's name must've been Brian too, because she looked back just as fast as he did.

"'I know you're not just gonna walk by and not say nothing. I know we're better than that."

Brian's frail date looked at me and I could tell by the look in her eyes that she immediately became intimidated by me. She was skinny as hell. Her titties were so non-existent that I was waiting for her strapless top to fall at any given moment, exposing nothing but nipples.

I stood up out of my chair so that both Brian and his little friend could see the rest of me. I walked over to Brian and gave him a hug, wishing I could see the look on Chance's face.

As I hugged Brian, he whispered in my ear, "I can smell the Vodka. Please don't show your ass."

Brian knew how I could act once I had alcohol in my system and he obviously didn't want a scene. I let go of Brian and saw the smile on his face, which let me know he loved what he saw.

"Now who is this beautiful lady?" I asked.

Brian's friend smiled, as he introduced her. "Jordyn, this is my lady, Noelle. Noelle, this is a good friend of mine, Jordyn.

"Nice to meet you!" Noelle said as she shook my hand.

"You too," I said.

Chance was sitting there looking left out, so even though I really wasn't feeling him enough to introduce him, I did anyway.

"Nice seeing you, Jordyn . . . And Chance. We're gonna go find a table," Brian said as he snuck in a wink.

"Ok! Have fun! Talk to you later!"

When they had disappeared in the distance, I sarcastically said, "Well, they made a nice couple, didn't they?"

"So, is that where we are now, Jordyn? That's what we do?"

"What are you talking about?"

"You're gonna sit right here and disrespect me right in front of my face?"

"How did I disrespect you? By hugging a friend, and being introduced to his new girlfriend?"

"You know how I feel about him. Don't act naïve."

"Well, did that turn you on? Seeing me hug another man? Do you want to go over there in the bathroom right now and fuck the shit out of me? Let me show you just how spontaneous and fun I can be. I'll tell you one thing! I'm way more spontaneous than Sasha's boring ass!"

"Jordyn, you're drunk."

"No, I'm not drunk! I'm pissed! Pissed because you can't love me as much as I love you . . . unconditionally!"

The waitress walked over and asked was there anything else she could get us. Chance told her we would be leaving soon, and to just bring the check. He stared across the table at me until the waitress returned, leaving the check in front of him, and telling us to have a good night.

"You look so beautiful tonight, but have acted so ugly. I'm gonna take you home and hope you sleep this shit off, because I refuse to talk to you any longer while you're under the influence."

I looked at Chance and rolled my eyes. He just didn't know how many other nasty, ugly words I had for him, but it took everything in me to just sit there and keep my mouth closed. The car was completely silent for the entire ride home. Chance didn't even turn on the radio. As soon as he pulled up in the driveway, he unbuckled his seatbelt to get out so he could let me out. Before he had the Chance, I opened my own door, briskly walked to my front door, went in and slammed it before he had a chance to follow behind. I felt like shit and prayed to God that tomorrow would be a better day.

CHAPTER TWENTY-FOUR

The next morning, I woke up to a text message from Brian. He was apologizing for letting me see what I saw the night before. I replied by telling him there was no reason for him to apologize and I completely understood. I did get upset seeing Brian with Noelle, but what could I have possibly said? It didn't make it any better that I was already pissed with Chance. Honestly, I would've probably felt better if the chick had been of some competition to me, but unfortunately she wasn't.

"Can I come by to see you a second?" Brian texted back.

I told him I had just woke up with a hangover, but he was welcome to stop by. I went in the bathroom and washed my face and brushed my teeth. It was the least I could do before he got there.

Only a few minutes later, Brian was at my door. He must've been on duty because he was driving his Black Camaro. He was also wearing slacks and a button down.

"Mmmm. Don't you look nice," I said to Brian as I let him in.

"You, too."

I rolled my eyes and said, "Yeah right! You've never seen me look like this."

"You're even more beautiful natural than you are all made up, but I have to say, you looked good as fuck last night! I could've thrown you right across that table!"

"Thank you," I said as I grabbed the orange juice out of the fridge and fixed us both a glass. "You want Vodka with yours?" I asked, slightly grinning.

"No thanks! Too early for that," Brian laughed. "I hope you don't mind that I didn't park down the street. I didn't think Chance would stop by this early, and I don't plan on being here long. I just needed to give you an update in person and make sure we're ok."

Brian and I both sat down at the table and drank our orange juice as we continued our discussion.

"Yeah, we're cool. Why wouldn't we be?"

"I know all this just happened so fast, with me and Noelle. And I know I hadn't mentioned any of it to you."

"You're not obligated to tell me everything."

"Yes, something like that, I am. I feel we're better than that and I owed that much to you and I apologize."

"Thanks for that. I appreciate you being considerate of my feelings," I said. "Now what news do you have for me?"

"We finally got him!"

"Dré?"

"Yeah, late last night, or I should probably say early this morning. We got a tip from a so-called friend he was staying with. He must've done something to piss her off for her to turn him in."

That was the best news I had heard in a long time. I jumped up out of my chair and sat in Brian's lap, giving him a long, well-deserved kiss.

"What was that for?"

"For working so hard to make sure you put him away."

"That's my job. If everybody came up to me kissing me after I caught their bad guy, I'd be walking around here with all kinds of heebie jeebies," Brian laughed.

"I'll take it from you though. Can I have another one?"

I got up, straddled Brian in his chair, and pressed my lips up against his once more. I felt his dick jump beneath his slacks. Our noses touched and we looked at each other in the eye and smiled. Brian stood up, picking me up with my legs wrapped around him. He kissed me all over my neck and lips until I couldn't control my emotions.

"I love you," I whispered.

Brian stopped and said, "What?"

I looked him in the eyes and repeated it.

"Why are you telling me this now, after I have someone?"

"I'm not asking you to leave her. I'm just telling you I love you. Now don't spoil the moment."

I wrapped my arms around Brian and kissed and sucked his neck as he carried me upstairs to my bedroom. He put me down, and as I stood there in front of him, we stared at each other like we wanted to tear each other apart, and that's exactly what I wanted to do. I jumped it off by ripping open Brian's shirt, popping off every last button. We then quickly, and uncontrollably started ripping each other's clothes off until we both stood there naked. Brian's dick wasn't only long, but was also thick as hell. I knew he was packing by the bulge he always had in his pants, but I really had no idea. Brian picked me up and sat me on top of the dresser, and spread my legs as far as they would go. He then ate my pussy like it was his last supper, like a man that just had gotten out of prison and hadn't had a good home cooked meal in years. I leaned my head back up against the mirror, massaging the back of Brian's head as he pleasured my pussy better than Chance had. As I shook and moaned, like a pro, Brian rolled my clit between his teeth and tongue causing my body to go into convulsions. I screamed his name so loud, I was sure the whole block probably heard me.

After Brian gave me the most memorable orgasm thus far, he lifted me up off the dresser and wiped my juices from around his mouth. I pushed him onto the bed and got on my knees as I straddled him. I let out a deep sigh as I eased his dick into my pussy that was eager to welcome him in. Brian grabbed my ass as I gyrated and thrust my hips forward until I felt his dick in my stomach.

"You feel so Goddamn good, Jordyn."

As I continued to ride him, he moaned and sucked my titties so hard, I just knew I was gonna have hickeys all over them, but I didn't have anyone to answer to, so I wasn't concerned. At that moment, I wanted Brian to do whatever he wanted to do with my body. When Brian began to moan louder, I rode him faster. When he began to shake and he closed his eyes tight, I just knew I was about to accomplish my mission. Brian had other plans. Brian got up and threw me down on my back, pushed my legs over my head, and began giving me long, hard thrusts with his magic stick. I was just glad I was completely healed, because if not, he would've tore something up!

Sweat ran down his face as he gave me his all. He suddenly stopped, letting out one last deep breath as I felt his dick pulsating inside of me. Without pulling out, Brian exhaled and laid on top of me.

"Baby, baby, baby!" he said, trying to catch his breath.

"I know exactly what you mean."

After laying in the mess we made for a few minutes, I slid from underneath Brian and went into the bathroom. I looked in the mirror and my hair looked like I had got caught in rain. Not even a minute later, Brian was walking in with his dick hanging to almost the middle of his thigh. He stood behind me and palmed both of my titties. He looked in the mirror and said, "Now that's a beautiful couple right there."

"Brian. You can't tell me you've forgotten about Noelle so quickly."

"What do you expect me to do after you put all that on me? I can't let you go now."

I hadn't told Brian about Chance and I not speaking and didn't plan to because I didn't want that to affect any decisions he made, or cause him to make any rash decisions regarding his relationship with Noelle.

"So, you just forgot about Chance too?" I asked.

"Now you know Chance don't know what to do with you. It seemed like you've never had it put on you the way I just put it on you."

"I know you probably don't wanna hear this, but Chance is good. You two just have two different approaches."

"Which approach do you prefer?" Brian asked.

I almost answered, but decided against it and said, "I plead the fifth."

"Exactly!"

I turned around and started running the shower.

"You want me to take a shower with you?"

"If you'd like. You know what, yeah, so we can continue this conversation."

We stepped into the shower together and I stood in front of Brian, letting the warm water run down my face as Brian washed my back.

"So, am I better than Noelle?"

"I'm not about to beat around the bush. Hell yeah!"

I laughed hysterically. That's what I liked about Brian. He was always straightforward. Whatever he felt at that moment, that's what he said. I didn't have to guess about anything with him.

After Brian and I finished our shower, we cuddled up in the bed and talked some more while we watched TV.

"Are you gonna get in trouble for being on duty, and not being on duty?" I asked Brian.

"Nah. They'll call if they need me. They know I'm out in the streets taking care of business."

"Yeah. You ain't lyin'!"

Since we had nothing but time and opportunity, I used the opportunity to ask Brian as many questions as I could think of. I knew he would be real and have no problem answering them.

"I've never asked you if you had any kids."

"Nah. I don't think kids are for me. It might sound selfish, but I'm enjoying my life, and I like to come and go as I please. What about you? You want kids?"

Good answer. I thought to myself.

"No. I feel the same way you do."

"So, when are you gonna tell Chance about us?"

I sat up and said, "What? Who said anything about telling Chance?"

"I just assumed since you started talking about kids, you're looking for something long term with me. Women don't ask men about kids unless they're considering being with them for a long time, or were you missing that page in your handbook?"

"We'll have to first see what happens with me and Chance. He was in my life before you. If things don't work out and if you're still around, you never know." As hard as it was for me to say, I said, "Give Noelle a chance, though. She seems like a nice girl."

Brian looked at me with his big, pretty brown eyes, and said, "Yeah, she is, but I still hope you change your mind. I've been meaning to say this. Chance really doesn't seem like your type."

We both laughed, and I didn't even ask Brian to state his reasoning because I knew he would say something crazy. Brian's phone started ringing, so he grabbed it out of his pants pocket. He looked at the number and said that it was the captain and he had to go.

"He looked down at his buttonless shirt he had put back on and said, "I'm glad I have extra clothes in the car, just for times like this!"

"Oh, so you have bootie calls often in the middle of your work day, huh?"

"Well, I wouldn't say often, but probably three to four times a week," Brian said, laughing.

I threw a pillow at his silly ass. He always had to be mister funny man.

"You can tell me if it's Noelle on the phone, though. You won't hurt my feelings."

Brian showed me his call log, and said, "I don't have any reason to lie to you, baby. You know I'd drop everything for you in a heartbeat. I'm just waiting for you to say the word. Just don't wait til I get in too deep. When I fall in love, it's hard for me to fall out of love."

In other words, Brian was telling me if he happened to fall in love with Noelle that would be it for me. I kinda took that as a threat, but I guess he was just giving me a forewarning so I couldn't say he didn't give me the opportunity to be a part of his life. I walked Brian to the door and told him I'd see him later.

Chance hadn't called me yet, and I wasn't sure that he would. The reason he gave me for not leaving Sasha, plus my over-consumption of alcohol caused me to act crazy, but I still wouldn't have apologized for the way I acted. Everything I said, I meant. He was either going to be with me, or stay with her.

CHAPTER TWENTY-FIVE

A few days went by, and Chance finally decided to call. I started to not answer the phone, but I took a deep breath and said, "Whoosah" before I did.

"Hey, Jordyn."

I decided to kill him with kindness.

"Hey, love. How are you?"

With confusion in his voice, Chance said, "I'm not good. Not without you."

"Well, I've already told you what you need to do if you want me to continue to stick around."

"These few days have been hell for me. I've driven past your house a few times, wanting to stop by, but just couldn't. I know what I said was messed up. I shouldn't hold not being able to have kids against you, but that doesn't change the fact that I do want kids that have my blood."

Before I replied, I wondered when Chance had rode past my house. I was hoping it wasn't the day that Brian had spent the morning with me, but knowing Chance, I'm sure he would've come in and caused a scene if he would've seen Brian's car in the driveway.

"Ok. That's all fine and dandy. If you didn't know, Sasha isn't the only woman in the world that can have babies."

I then threw a low blow, which I didn't mean to throw, but it just slipped out from the anger I was holding in.

"As a matter of fact, there are probably a lot of other women who would be able to carry a baby for its full nine months. You'll probably be better off trying them out."

"Wow, Jordyn. I didn't know you could be so cold."

I felt bad for what I said and didn't have a problem apologizing on the spot, unlike Chance. "I'm sorry. I'm just angry. I just meant to say, you can get a surrogate to carry a baby for you, and it'll still have your blood. There are way more options than the one you're looking at."

"Yeah, I know. Is it ok if I stop by tonight?"

"That's fine."

Later that evening, Chance stopped by, and I let myself down once again. He knew exactly what he was doing. He came over smelling all good, wearing his Prada cologne, and looking good as hell. I couldn't resist him, so I made love to him again, without having any indication of what would happen with us in the future. Chance and I were like each other's drug and we both needed a fix. There was just something about Chance that wouldn't allow me to leave him alone and just move on.

Everything with Chance and I went back to normal, although I kept having dreams of making love to Brian. What was crazy about the dreams was that while we made love, Noelle and Chance each sat in a corner of the room in a wicker chair and watched. It was very weird, yet sexy. I craved his sexy, yellow ass at least five out of the seven days of the week. Chance worked me on a regular basis, but to answer Brian's question about whose approach did I prefer, his or Chance's, the answer was his. I liked it aggressive and rough. Chance was a little too gentle for me, and when I'd try to get him to be forceful with me, he would pull back, so I quit trying.

Brian didn't make things any better by texting me and leaving me messages, telling me how bad he wanted me, and all the things he wanted to do to me. I already knew what I was missing. There was no need for any reminders. I envied Noelle for being able to get that whenever she wanted it, but I couldn't even imagine her little ass being able to take all of him because there was a whole lot of him!

Weeks went by of me walking around, trying to pretend like Sasha didn't exist while I fucked her husband religiously. One night after Chance got off work and made his nightly pit stop to see me, I fucked his brains out, like always, he got up, washed up, put his clothes on, and got ready to go home to his "real" life.

As he sat on the edge of the bed, putting his shoes on, and I laid on top of the covers, butt naked watching him, I started feeling some type of way. I felt like a prostitute, and last I had checked, Chance had taken me out of that line of business. He actually hadn't. He just took me off the market to the public and made me his own personal prostitute. Something like Julia Roberts in the movie "Pretty Woman." The big difference was that Richard Gere wasn't an asshole who thought it was ok to have a wife and a prostitute on the side. He fell in love and did what he needed to do. Where was my happy ending? The way things were going, it looked like I wasn't gonna have one. At least not with Chance, so it was time to put some fire under his ass and see what type of response I got.

"I'm gonna tell her."

Chance stopped what he was doing and turned around and said, "Tell who what?"

I sucked my teeth and said, "I think it's time that Sasha knew what we mean to each other."

"And you think you're the person that should share that with her?"

"Apparently you don't want to do it, so I'll do it for you."

"Chill out, Jordyn. There's a method to my madness! It's gonna happen, very soon."

"Ok. I'll give you a few more days."

"Days? Here you go with your ultimatums and threats."

"And here you go with your game playing! I'm tired of being your sex toy who you sometimes flaunt around town."

"Ok. I got this, Jordyn. I promise. Just don't make any sudden moves."

I looked at Chance and smiled. Not because I was happy that he promised he was going to tell Sasha. Shit, his promises didn't mean much to me these days. I was smiling because of how nervous he got just from those four words. I was curious to see what he was gonna come up with next.

Chance finished putting on his shoes, gave me a kiss, and said, "Remember, I got you. I'm gonna take care of you."

I was beginning to feel like that was Chance's favorite line and wondered how many times he had used it on how many people just to get his way.

After Chance left, I rolled over, grabbed my phone, and texted Brian, "What are you doing?"

I sat there waiting for him to respond, and got nothing, so I figured he was busy. As soon as I got up and left my phone laying on the bed, he responded, "At the movies. What's up?"

I really just needed someone to talk to. I wanted to vent to Brian about all the shit Chance had been taking me through, but I didn't want to interrupt his date with all my drama. These were those times when I felt like I needed a momma to talk to. I didn't know where mine was, and didn't care to know. It was probably best that I kept it all to myself anyway. All Brian was gonna do was badmouth Chance, and try to get me to leave him alone.

I replied, "Nothing. I was just thinking about you. Carry on."

I just knew Brian would reply again, but he didn't. It was late, but I decided to put on clothes and ride through the city in my sparkling clean Porsche. I drove through parts of New York that I hadn't seen in forever. I drove through the strip, which was empty. I looked over towards the parking lot, reminiscing about the good times Dré and I had before all the drama. I even took a trip to the Bronx and checked out my old neighborhood.

When I slowly drove down my old street, I felt a feeling of sadness coming over me. I hadn't been there since my momma put me out on the street without anywhere to go, and didn't care what happened to me. I stopped in front of the house I had once shared with my momma and daddy, and put the car in park. I stood in front of the house and stared at it, remembering the good times, and trying to block out the bad. I saw the porch light come on and heard the front door opening. I tried to walk back to my car before anyone saw me, but it was too late. An older black woman came to the door with a head full of long, silver, gorgeous hair. She reminded me of Della Reese.

"Can I help you?" she said with a strong voice that would overpower any man's.

"No, I'm sorry. I used to live here. I hadn't seen it in years, and decided to stop by."

"You ain't that woman that got beat up so badly by her boyfriend, she was in the hospital for months, are you?"

"Noooo, I said," wondering if she was talking about my momma. The woman and I walked closer towards each other, as we continued our conversation.

"I didn't think you was her. You way too pretty for that. And tall. I hear she was a petite lil thang. A redbone is what they called her. They said she'll never be the same again. That sorry excuse for a man messed her up."

The woman described my momma to a tee. She valued her looks more than anything in the world, so I knew if whatever man she had around after I left messed her up as badly as the woman made it sound, I knew it was detrimental to my momma.

"The woman extended her hand and said, "I'm Evangeline Miller. What's your name, honey?"

"I'm Jordyn."

"Jordyn? What kind of name is that for a beautiful young lady like yourself?"

I just loved old people because they said what was on their mind at all times. I laughed and said, "I don't know, Ms. Miller."

"You can call me Ms. Eva. Do you want to come in and look around?"

"Sure."

I followed behind Ms. Eva, and she turned around before we walked into the house and said, "You're not some crazy person, are you?"

"Fine time to ask that, isn't it, Ms. Eva?" I said, and laughed.

"It don't matter no way cause I ain't neva been sane!" Ms. Eva joked.

I looked around in astonishment of how things had not changed much in all these years.

"Did you decorate yourself?" I asked.

"I did a little decorating, but I'm not trying to impress anyone. The woman who lived here was in a hurry to leave, so she left most of the furniture. It was better than what I had, so I kept it."

Tears streamed down my face as I stared at my daddy's favorite chair. It was the one he died in. I walked over and ran my hand across the back of it.

"That chair right there is my favorite! You ok, sweetheart?" Ms. Eva asked.

"Yes, I'm fine. The woman who lived here was my momma. This was my daddy's favorite chair, but he died when I was thirteen."

"I'm so sorry! How is your momma?"

"I don't know. I haven't seen her since I was sixteen. Right before she put me out."

Ms. Eva made us some lemonade, and I sat and talked to her for hours about my life in that house. She truly listened, and for that to have been the first time we ever met, it felt good to talk to her. That was exactly what I needed at that moment; someone to vent to, and God put me in exactly the right place at the right time. After talking with Ms. Eva, I felt cleansed. I left her house feeling brand new, and like I was ready to take on whatever. I almost even felt like I wanted to look for my momma and check on her. I said almost. Not this particular day, but maybe one day.

I also began thinking about how living off of Chance had truly gotten me off track and made me lose focus of what I wanted to do in life. It was time to refocus and think about what would happen to me if Chance wasn't around and I ran out of savings. I couldn't depend on him to be there for me no matter how much he promised that he would. I was giving

Chance this one last Chance to prove to me that I would be his number one, and soon, so I hoped he had a plan.

After I finished riding around, I headed back home. As soon as I pulled up, I saw Brian's car sitting in front of my house. I opened the garage but didn't pull in. Instead I turned my car off and walked over to Brian's car. Before I could make it there, he opened his door and stepped out.

"Where the hell you been?"

"What?" I said, wondering who had given him the authority to question me.

"I've been sitting here for hours. I kept trying to call and text you after I left the movies cuz I felt like something wasn't right."

I pulled my phone out of my purse and saw that it somehow ended up on silent. I had several missed calls and messages and they were all from Brian.

"I'm sorry. I don't know how my phone got on silent."

"Woman, you had me worried about you. I was about to put an APB out on your ass."

Brian walked over to me and hugged me. "You ok, baby?"

As Brian held me, I didn't smell his cologne like I always did. Instead, I smelled Noelle's sweet smelling perfume. "Yeah, I'm good," I said.

"Why don't I believe you?"

"I don't know, because everything is fine." I wiped the side of his mouth with the pad of my thumb.

"Something on my face?" he asked.

"You just had a little lipstick there, that's all. I'll talk to you later," I said, as I left Brian standing there, went and jumped in my car and pulled it into the garage. It began to hurt more and more when I saw any evidence of Brian being with Noelle. I didn't feel like I wanted to be with Brian on a serious level, but it was like I didn't want him to be with her either, even though I pretended to be good with it when I talked to him. That night, I didn't hide very well, the fact that the shit bothered the fuck out of me.

I didn't know if Chance had a revelation, but whatever happened, the next couple of days he came correct, with flowers, smiles, no bad jokes, and an overall good attitude, making me feel like things were definitely looking up for us. However, I wouldn't know for a fact until day three was over. I told him he had a few days to make something happen, and that's exactly what I meant.

At the end of day two, Chance came by my house with a folder in his hand. I figured he was bringing me some work that he wanted me to do for him. He sat the folder down on the dining room table and said, "This is for you."

I sat down and opened the folder, reading what was in front of me. They were Chance's divorce petition papers.

"She'll be served with those tomorrow," Chance said.

I was happy, but I had heard this a couple of times before, just without the papers being in front of me, so I couldn't be ecstatic. I wouldn't get my hopes up until she was served and gone.

"Ok," I said.

"Ok? I imagined your reaction to be different."

"It will be when I see it happen. So, after tomorrow, you'll probably need a place to stay."

"No, I'm not leaving my home that I paid for. We'll just be in different bedrooms until everything is resolved."

I didn't agree with that, but I was done arguing with Chance about things I had no control over, so I didn't open my mouth.

After Sasha was served the divorce papers, much didn't change. Chance and I continued to see each other the same amount of time that we had before. He told me it would be just a month or so before the divorce would be final and that Sasha was looking for a place. He said since there was a prenup in place and no children in the picture, the divorce was gonna be quick and painless. I could only go by what Chance told me, so that was the information that I relied on at that moment. I could've easily driven to Chance's house and spoke to Sasha myself, but I was trying to trust my man, and I believed everything done in the dark would come to light. Sasha would eventually find out the truth about us.

I spent the next few weeks helping Chance run his office from home, and when I wasn't doing that, I was secretly getting everything squared away with me starting school the next semester which would be in the next couple of months. I actually felt like I had finally begun accomplishing things on my own that I could one day be proud of.

One day, out of the blue, Chance called me a little while before he was to leave the office for the evening and told me to be ready when he came by because Jacob wanted us to stop by his place to go over some things he had taken home to look over.

"Did I do something wrong?" I asked Chance.

"I don't think so. Jake wasn't very specific. He was just working on some stuff at home, trying to catch up and ran across some things."

I was hoping that Jacob wasn't doing some slick type shit, trying to get Chance and me over his place so he could put me on the spot. When Chance picked me up, he didn't even come in. He just blew his horn for me to come out. When we pulled up to Jacob's house, I noticed it was just a couple of streets over from Chance's house. It was beautiful, just like all of the other homes in the neighborhood.

Chance's house was on a hill and we walked up a dozen steps until finally reaching Jacob's front door. Before Chance could ring the doorbell, Jacob opened the door, with a smile on his face, like always. I knew there was a reason I didn't trust people who smiled all the time. No one was happy all the Goddamn time.

"Come on in guys."

When we walked in, the first thing I noticed was the elegant dual cherry-wood staircase.

"You guys can make yourselves comfortable right here on the sofa while I go get the stuff we need to go over."

Jacob disappeared around the corner, and I began to feel strange. Something didn't seem right at all.

"Baby, I think we should do this another day. I just want to go home," I said to Chance.

"I'm sure it won't take long. We'll be quick."

Suddenly, I saw someone coming down the staircase. As first, I couldn't focus due to the lighting from the beautiful chandelier that hung directly above the staircase. Once I was able to focus in on who it was, I said, "What the fuck is going on?"

Chance, not paying attention looked at me and said, "What's wrong?" He then followed my eyes and saw the same thing that I saw. It was Sasha coming down the staircase looking like America's Next Top Model in lingerie. She had on a black see-through bustier with a black lace thong, thigh highs held up by a garter belt, and black red bottom heels. Jacob came back from around the corner with a large envelope in his hand and said, "Oh, I see we've already begun."

Chance stood up angrily, and said, "What the hell is this? What is she doing here?"

Sasha finally made it down the staircase and walked towards us. She rolled her eyes at me, and said, "Baby . . ."

"What?" Chance and Jacob both said in unison.

Sasha pointed her long fingernail into Chance's chest and said, "No, you are not my baby." She then stood right next to Jacob and said, "This is my baby. While you were out having fun, I was having fun, too."

"Remember bro, what goes around comes around," Jacob said to Chance.

I was still sitting on the sofa in awe of what was going on. I didn't know if I was dreaming, but if not, this was the craziest shit I had ever seen in real life.

Jacob continued, "Remember when we were supposed to be boys and you fucked Sasha, and convinced her that black dick was better and made her leave me to be with you?"

Chance took a deep breath, trying to control his anger.

"Yeah, I know you do. How could you possibly forget that? Well evidently Sasha missed me. She made her way over here one night while you were probably with that bitch over there, and I gave her this white dick one good time, and she kept coming back for more. I guess there's no truth to the saying "When you go black, you never go back."

Chance charged towards Jacob and I quickly jumped up to pull him back.

"What you trying to fight for? You obviously didn't want this beautiful black queen."

"Don't let this get to you. She's just doing this out of spite because of the divorce papers," I said to Chance, trying to calm him down.

"Divorce papers?" Sasha said. "Who got divorce papers?"

Chance looked at me and said, "Jordyn, just leave it alone."

Chance should have known better than to think I was going to leave that topic alone. I was waiting on the moment Sasha and I had the opportunity to talk.

"Didn't he serve you with divorce papers a few weeks ago?" I asked Sasha.

Sasha and Jacob looked at each other and both started laughing. "Girl, sit down! Chance would never serve me with divorce papers. He would never leave me. You know why? Because everything belongs to me. Without me, he has nothing. Yeah, the business is his, but guess who funded the money to start that business. He would be nothing without me. Ain't that right, Chance?"

Chance stood there looking dumber than I'd ever seen him look.

"So, Jordyn . . . That is your name, right? If you want this sorry excuse for a man, you can have him. I was young and dumb at one time. So dumb I didn't even make him sign a prenup, but I don't have to even worry about that. He gets nothing if I can prove he cheated on me, and guess what. I can prove just that."

Sasha snatched the envelope out of Jacob's hand. By this time, Chance was sweating profusely. She dumped everything out of the folder onto the table. There were dozens of pictures of Chance and me. There were pictures of us hanging out together, having sex in my house, and even pictures of us interacting with each other in the office.

"You both can thank Zahriah for tipping us off as to what was going on, even though Jacob had figured it out on his own anyway. You know us women, though. We have to have our own proof, especially for the lawyers. You know how that is, right, Jordyn?"

I was still staring at the pictures scattered across the table when I noticed pictures of me and Brian having sex. Jacob noticed when I slowly picked one of them up off the table, and he stood beside me.

"Oh yeah, those were just for fun . . . just to show Chance what he gave up a great woman and life for, which was basically for a hoe."

Chance turned around and punched Jacob so hard, he fell to the floor. Jacob couldn't get up quick enough before Chance jumped down on top of him. Sasha stood there screaming for Chance to get off of Jacob. Chance was in another frame of mind, continuously punching Jacob in the face like he was a human punching bag. It brought back memories of when my daddy jumped on my momma's boyfriend, Marcus, outside in front of the house. He was so angry, there was no stopping him. I didn't see any need in me getting in between that. After I heard everything I had heard, I knew exactly where I stood. Chance never had any intentions on leaving Sasha. I believed Chance did love me, but he was more in love with Sasha and her money.

What I didn't understand was why Chance still felt the need to stay. Even though she helped him start the business with her money, he had made it successful and made a lot of money in it. The business would've still been his, but I guess he still had too much love for Sasha to leave.

Before grabbing my things, including my pictures of me and Brian, I looked at Chance once more, acting like an animal, before walking out the door. I politely stepped out onto the porch and called NYPD. I continued to hear all kinds of ruckus in the house. Glass was shattering, objects were being thrown, and I still heard Sasha's annoying ass voice in the mix of everything. I had no more respect for Chance. He had put on a huge façade, and deceived me no less than anyone else in my life that had hurt me. It seemed like almost everyone I had come across in my life had pretended to have my best interest at heart, but ended up having totally different intentions, and I always ended up getting hurt one way or another. The only person who hadn't been deceitful was Brian, and I had fucked that up. I let him get away, and would regret it until I found someone who was just as fine, sexy, funny, honest, and loving as he was. Men like that were hard to come by.

I heard the police sirens in the distance. I knew it wouldn't take long for them to get to the rich, white section of New York City. I made it down all the steps, and leaned on Chance's Lamborghini waiting on the squad to arrive. Five police cars arrived, and the men jumped out of their vehicles with guns drawn.

"Put your hands up!" they shouted at me.

I put my hands up and said, "I'm the one who called! Someone is about to be killed inside!"

The cops ran up the stairs to go inside the house, except one that stayed behind to pat me down for weapons. As he was patting me down, I saw a black Camaro pull up with police lights flashing in the window. I saw Brian jump out the car and he immediately ran towards me.

He looked at the cop who was patting me down and said, "Whoa! Wait a minute. What are you doing?"

"I'm doing what I was trained to do on a crime scene, Sir."

"Ok, well forget about all that right now and get in there! She's good."

The cop ran up the stairs to follow after the others.

"What is going on? You ok?"

"It's a long story, and yes, I'm fine. Why are you here? There's no one dead yet," I laughed. I was surprised that I was still able to laugh after all that had happened.

"I like to be a part of the excitement. Let's just say looking at dead people all day can get boring sometimes," Brian laughed and smiled. "I'm starting to believe you're a trouble-maker."

"Why would you say that?" I said, flirtatiously batting my eyelashes at Brian."

"You're always a witness to a crime scene. That's not good. That means you attract trouble."

"Nah. Trouble just seems to follow me everywhere I go."

A couple of officers came out of the house, and the others came out with Chance in handcuffs."

Chance wickedly looked at me and Brian. He then shouted, "You've been fuckin' a man!"

"I cleared my throat and didn't say a word.

"What is he talking about?" Brian asked.

"Who knows?" I said. "He lost it in there."

"What happened?"

"Let's just say it was an ugly domestic dispute."

"So the wife found out, huh?"

"Yep. And he just found out she's been fuckin' a white man."

"Whoa! And to think, you told me he was puttin' it down."

"Well, maybe the white man put it down a little better," I said, grinning.

"I think you need me to be around a little more to keep you out of trouble." Brian looked over at Chance being put into the back of the police car. "It doesn't look like homeboy's gonna be around."

An ambulance pulled up and the EMTs pulled a gurney out the back and ran into Jacob's home.

"And they needed an ambulance? Yeah, homeboy is in trouble. Let me go in here and make sure nobody's dead."

I stayed put while Brian went to do his job. Next thing I know, Jacob was being wheeled out on the gurney with a bloodied up face and blood-shot eyes.

Brian came back out and said, "Nope, no one's dead, but Chance beat the shit out that man! That don't count though. He was a white man. If it had been me and Chance one on one, he would've got it!"

"Shut your ass up!" I said, playfully hitting him in his arm.

"Oh yeah. His wife is . . ."

"Please don't get slapped, Brian."

"No, I was gonna say she's just ok. Not hot like you. I would've left her in a heartbeat to be with you."

"Really . . ." I said sarcastically. "You don't have to try and flatter me."

Brian and I walked towards his car so he could take me home. We got in and he just sat there, without starting the car.

"What?" I asked.

"I was just thinking. I guess he was still in love with his wife to beat that man up so badly over her."

"Yeah, I guess so."

"And I'm in love with you."

I blushed and tried to hold in my smile.

"You mind if I keep you company since it looks like you're gonna be alone?

"I don't want to keep you from your woman."

"Noelle?"

"Yeah. Who else?"

"Oh, we broke up."

"Seriously? Why?" I asked trying to sound sympathetic.

"Don't try to sound like you care. No matter how much you try to say it didn't bother you, you know you weren't feeling that situation. But anyway, I kinda called out your name while we were . . ."

I stopped Brian right there and said, "Brian, please tell me you are lying."

"Nope, but everything happens for a reason, right?"

I knew it wasn't funny to Noelle, but it was funny as hell to me, and flattered the hell out of me. I felt bad for her just a little bit.

"Let me get you home," Brian said as he squeezed my thigh. He leaned over and gave me a kiss, then said, "Remember, everything happens for a reason."

Brian started the car and we headed to the home that would soon no longer be mine, so that I could begin starting my life all over once again.

The End

www.ingramcontent.com/pod-product-compliance
Lightning Source LLC
Chambersburg PA
CBHW021954170626
46808CB00001B/146